The *Lone* RICE BALL

Camy's Books
Sushi series
Sushi for One?
"The Sushi Toss" (short story)
Only Uni
Single Sashimi
Weddings and Wasabi (novella)
"White Soup" (short story)
The Lone Rice Ball

Protection for Hire Series
Protection for Hire
A Dangerous Stage

Sonoma Series
Deadly Intent
Formula for Danger
Stalker in the Shadows
Narrow Escape
Necessary Proof (novella)
Unshakeable Pursuit
Treacherous Intent
Gone Missing

Mahina Security series
Bento and Betrayal (novella)
The Lone Rice Ball
Sushi and Suspicions
Year of the Dog

Warubozu Spa Chronicles
The Wedding Kimono (novella)

Devotional
Who I Want to Be

The Lone RICE BALL

A Witty Christian Romantic Suspense

Sushi series, Book 5

Mahina Security series, Book 1

CAMY TANG

USA Today Bestselling Author

If we confess our sins, he is faithful and just and will forgive us our sins and purify us from all unrighteousness.

— 1 JOHN 1:9

Not that I have already obtained this or am already perfect, but I press on to make it my own, because Christ Jesus has made me his own. Brothers, I do not consider that I have made it my own. But one thing I do: forgetting what lies behind and straining forward to what lies ahead, I press on toward the goal for the prize of the upward call of God in Christ Jesus.

— PHILIPPIANS 3:12-14

PROLOGUE

A pologize and leave. That's all she had to do.

Assuming her apology wasn't coming too late.

Mimi turned into the driveway to the Molokai Red Restaurant, narrowly avoiding stalling out. She hated driving her cousin's ancient stick shift pickup truck, but while she was staying in Hawaii, this was the only vehicle she could borrow if she didn't want to spend the money on a rental car.

The truck lumbered down an aisle as she looked for parking. The lot was small, as was most parking lots for stores and restaurants here in Haleiwa, and was packed full since it was eight o'clock at night.

Mimi groaned when she realized she would have to back the truck into the parking stall she found because the aisle was too narrow for her to turn into it. Gritting her teeth, she went excruciatingly slow, because she wasn't very good at parking.

She might have been a tad too close to the car next to her passenger-side door. Well, she didn't intend to be here that long.

Mimi squeezed herself out of the driver's seat since her door could only open a scant few inches, but it was probably a bit easier for her than it would've been for someone taller. Since she was less than five feet in height, people often mistook her for a middle school child. It used to bother her a lot, but these days, she was just glad that she looked much younger than her actual age.

The humid air crawled down her blouse and clung to her skin. It wouldn't have been quite so bad if she hadn't been wearing pantyhose, but that was a requirement of her uniform for her aunt's cosmetics store. Mimi's legs felt like they were wrapped in wool as she walked to the front door of the restaurant.

There were rows of hibiscus bushes lining the path up to the front door. The blooms were a dark, velvety crimson, the rare Molokai Red variant from which the restaurant took its name. Mimi wished she could have seen the flowers in daylight. Especially because it was unlikely she would be here again.

This restaurant had not been here the last time she had been to Haleiwa, which had been several years ago. Most of her family lived near Honolulu, and she had only rarely gone to the North Shore whenever she came to visit. When she looked the restaurant up online, she saw that it had quickly grown popular and was known for its excellent food as well as the extensive bar lounge attached.

She paused in front of the door, which was made of some heavy, dark-colored wood, and took a deep breath. Then she grasped the handle and pulled it open.

Air conditioning blasted into her, making her feel less like she was melting. She expected to hear the din of voices from the diners, but it was only a soft murmur.

She had entered at the end of a short hallway, with a reception desk facing her several yards ahead. A closed set of wooden double doors stood to the left of the reception desk, while an open archway led out on the right.

As Mimi approached the desk, she glanced into the archway and saw that it led to the large, dimly lit bar lounge, which looked almost as large as a restaurant itself.

The young woman at the reception desk gave a polite smile. "How may I help you?"

"I came to speak to an employee, Toshiro."

"He's working in the lounge tonight." The girl gestured toward the open archway. "It isn't very busy at the moment, so he should have a few minutes to speak to you."

Mimi thanked the girl and headed through the archway. The long bar counter ran along the left side of the large room and boasted a dizzying array of alcohol stacked on shelves behind it. A few people sat on stools at the counter, but the majority of people reclined in chairs and sofas scattered around the room, with small tables set up between them within easy-reaching distance. The lighting was not too dim, in varying shades of gold and rose. Servers wove their way around the various groupings of chairs, taking orders and delivering food and drinks.

Mimi glanced at the servers closest to the door but didn't recognize any of them. She then realized that she might not recognize Tosh at all. After all, it had been more than twenty years.

She decided to make her way to the bar. Surely the bartender could point out Tosh to her.

There were three bartenders, one woman and two men. The woman was about Mimi's age, not quite as short as Mimi. She was at the right height for men's protective instincts to kick in and want to protect her, and she had the sweet features and delicate figure that brought to mind a geisha. The bartenders wore uniforms, but the top buttons of her blouse were opened, revealing a shadow of cleavage cut off by her dark red vest.

Of the remaining two bartenders, one looked to be in his mid-twenties. He was lean and slender as if he had only just shed the coltish awkwardness of his teenage years and was starting to fill out. His prominent Adam's apple bobbed as he spoke to a patron, and his nose was much larger than she remembered Tosh's nose had been. The patron said something, and the man gave a wide, toothy smile while tossing back his long, dark hair. No, that smile was not Tosh's.

The third bartender had his back to her, but he had wide shoulders, and she could see the curve of muscle under the long sleeves of his white dress shirt. His short-cut hair was dark, but as she looked at it, she recalled that Tosh's hair had been a lighter brown color. But then again, he had spent a lot of time at the beach in those days, so it could have been bleached by the sun.

Then the bartender turned around and she got a good look at his face.

Mimi froze. Was that Tosh? Now that she was looking closely at him, scrutinizing his features, her recognition kicked in and she saw the familiar features of the boy she had once known. He was smiling at a patron, and she saw his sweeping black eyebrows, his eyes crinkled in mirth with laugh lines at the corners, the gentle smile with the dimple that only appeared on one side, and only when his smile was wide enough, as it was now.

But recognizing Tosh wasn't what caused her to feel as if a bucket of ice water had been poured over her head.

She had seen this man just yesterday.

He had come into her aunt's cosmetics store. But at that time, he had colored hair swept far forward over his forehead, a prominent overbite, and rounded cheeks.

And very pale skin. It had been the skin that piqued her interest because when she came up close to him, she'd seen that he was wearing makeup. It lightened his skin dramatically, but he'd forgotten to apply makeup to his ears, which were slightly tanned.

It wasn't just the fact he wore makeup—it was the fact that it seemed to have been applied to disguise his features.

She had quickly chided herself as being ridiculous. She'd probably been watching too many Korean suspense dramas.

But now, standing only a few feet away from him, Mimi was almost certain that this bartender was the same man. It might have been difficult to tell because of the man's possibly false teeth and thick makeup, and his nose might have been a slightly different shape from the bartender's, too.

But she remembered the man's figure. This bartender stood with his shoulders back, projecting a confident, affable air while the man had been slightly hunched as he looked over the cosmetics on the display table.

However, the proportions of the two men were the same, as was their height and the width of their shoulders. The bartender's skin was darker than the man's had been—in fact, the same tanned color of his ears.

It was as if this bartender had come into her aunt's store as a secret undercover agent. But why would he do that?

And if this bartender was indeed Tosh, did that have anything to do with it?

What in the world was going on?

1

A few weeks earlier

At least the food was good.

Mimi tried not to look as though she were suffering quite so much as she clapped with the rest of the wedding guests. On the dance floor at the front of the Chinese restaurant, the bride and groom cut the wedding cake.

For once, her family didn't dominate the guest list since the groom had nearly as many relatives on his side. They had reserved the entire restaurant for the wedding, but the round tables were still packed closely together, making it difficult for waiters to maneuver around and deliver the food.

The next course, a platter of steamed seabass, was finally delivered to the table with a *thunk* as the waiter rushed away with another plate for another table.

"Yay!" Lex cheered as she served herself some of the fish. Her seat was nearest to the narrow aisle, so most of the food was placed in front of her.

Lex's ginormous appetite had tapered in her mid-forties, so she didn't take half the platter as she would have a few years ago. She moved the Lazy Susan toward Mimi on her left. Mimi took a small serving and moved it toward Venus on her left.

"The seafood has been really good so far." Venus served herself some fish.

"This restaurant is known for good seafood," her husband Drake said.

On Drake's left, Jenn's eyes practically had stars in them as she stared at the fish, impatient for it to move the few inches to bring it in front of her. "I was reading that out of all the Chinese restaurants in Milpitas, this ranked number one for fish and crustacean dishes," she said. "I've been waiting for the fish dish."

"You said that about the shrimp dish," her husband Edward said.

"And the clams," Trish added, seated on Edward's left. "And clams aren't crustaceans."

Spencer jabbed his wife with an elbow. "Cut your cousin some slack. Especially because I distinctly remember you saying a few weeks ago that you might actually look forward to this wedding because the reception was being held in this restaurant."

Mimi hadn't been looking forward to the wedding, but she also hadn't been dreading it like a triple root canal—she had begged the bride's mother, her Auntie Noriko, to seat her with her cousins rather than trying to shove her at a table filled with other singles.

After Jenn married, Mimi was the Oldest Single Female Cousin in the Sakai clan, and she had held the title for many years now. She had gone to more weddings as the OSFC than the other four cousins combined.

Mimi had been mostly ignoring the MC, partly because the acoustics in the restaurant were terrible, with the wedding guests' conversations drowning out the speakers. But naturally, she would pick up the two words she hated most in all the world, "bouquet toss."

Mimi's hands clenched the side of her padded seat. For the last three weddings, she'd aimed straight for the restaurant bathroom like a rocket, conveniently missing the bouquet toss. But her mother had called her last night specifically to tell her that under no circumstances was she allowed to miss another bouquet toss.

Mimi told herself that she no longer lived with her mother, she was thirty-eight years old and had no obligation to obey a parental order that was obviously cruel and unusual punishment.

On the flip side, the last time she had annoyed her mom, she'd been given the silent treatment for two solid months, and it had been excruciatingly uncomfortable for her whenever she went home for a family dinner, which usually happened once a month.

Mimi had finally been the one to give up and apologize and admit that yes, her mom's *donburi* was ten times better than Jenn's (which was so obviously untrue that Mimi worried a bolt of lightning would strike her down for telling such a blatant lie).

So she sat there, forcing herself to keep to her seat. She wasn't about to jump up and head to the dance floor, but if they spotted her and called her name, she was resolved to trudge up to participate.

Mimi sighed, ready to give in to the inevitable when she happened to catch Trish's eyes.

Trish casually stood up, moving around to the back of the seat even though there was hardly any room in between her chair and the table next to it. She leaned back against the chair and crossed her arms.

Mimi was about to ask her what she was doing when she realized that Trish very neatly screened her from the sight of the MC at the front of the restaurant.

The next second, Venus followed suit, urging Spencer and Drake to do the same.

Lex took a little longer to notice, blinking at them in confusion before exclaiming, "Oh!" She leaped up and hauled Aiden from his seat, making him drop the piece of fish that he was carrying to his mouth.

Soon, there was a wall in front of Mimi. To anyone else, it would look as though the cousins were simply standing to get a better view of the bouquet toss.

Venus suddenly moved out of place and instead planted herself directly beside Mimi, although still facing the dance floor. She made a hand motion to Drake, and the cousins shifted to fill in the gap.

"Why'd you do that?" Mimi asked.

"Auntie Meiko is sitting over there, and she was looking our way," Venus said coolly.

While Mimi was grateful that Venus had thought to screen her from Auntie Meiko, her proximity to Mimi's chair put her shapely rump right next to Mimi's face. Venus's discipline had ensured that she kept her hourglass figure even into her forties, which Mimi envied since her own metabolism had started to slow down in her thirties.

"You don't have to do this," Mimi said to Venus's backside. "I could have gone to the bathroom."

From above her head, Venus answered, "No, Trish's mom heard from your mom that she's very unhappy that you missed the last five bouquet tosses—"

"It was only three tosses," Mimi retorted.

"—and she expressly forbade you from hiding in the bathroom this time." Venus's voice took on un-Venus-like dulcet tones as she added, "Why, some of the aunties are going to think that you don't want to be married."

"Heaven forbid," Mimi answered in a monotone.

It wasn't that she didn't want to be married. It was that once she started seriously looking around, she simply couldn't find anyone she could stand—er, wanted to spend the rest of her life. It didn't help that she had dated so many men in her younger years—or perhaps it was *because* she had dated so many men in her younger years, the majority of them either losers or not marriage material. She had a habit of being attracted to men who were exciting, as opposed to those who might reasonably treat her well in a committed relationship.

The MC now started calling up young women by name.

"This isn't going to work," Mimi muttered.

"I'll *make* it work," Venus vowed.

"We would've had a better chance if it wasn't Uncle Charley," Jenn said in a low voice.

Uncle Charley was one of the cousins' older uncles on the Sakai side, so he had changed the diapers of every single female cousin present at the wedding. On the groom's side, he was aided by a middle-aged Chinese lady who would say something while pointing to a table so that Uncle Charley could shout out the unfortunate girl's name and nag her until she came up to the dance floor.

The old familiar feeling of anxiety was rumbling up inside of Mimi like nausea, but the sight of her cousins' backs acting as a stalwart bulwark to surround her made her feel … loved.

Yes, *real* friends saved you from the bouquet toss.

"Thanks, guys," Mimi said.

She wasn't as close to the four cousins as they were to each other, although she had been roommates with Lex for a time, and Jenn was technically her boss. But even among themselves, they were never particularly touchy-feely or affectionate with each other —mostly because Lex was still a bit uncomfortable with being touched in general. So they didn't respond to Mimi's thanks with a group hug, although Trish winked at her and blew her a kiss.

As Lex stared at the crowd of women gathered on the dance floor, her face had gone dark. "This was the reason I eloped," she said with a frown.

"This was the reason we got married in Hokkaido in winter," Venus said.

"This was the reason I made the pork dish extra spicy just before I did the bouquet toss," Jenn said.

"Ugh! It was so hot I was crying," Lex complained.

Jenn smiled in fond memory. "Exactly."

Mimi liked spicy food and thought the pork dish had been fantastic. "Was that the reason no one called me up for that one?" she asked. "People were crying so hard they couldn't see me?"

With a triumphant shaking of her fist, Jenn said, "I saved eight single female cousins from abject humiliation that night."

Mimi flashed her a thumbs-up. "Good going!"

"Now, honey," Edward said, grabbing Jenn's wrist and lowering her fist, "not every woman hates the bouquet toss. My relatives love to fight over it."

"That's true," Lex said thoughtfully. She glanced back at Mimi. "You liked the bouquet toss when you were younger."

"Emphasis on *younger*," Mimi said.

Mimi could see nothing except the zipper of Venus's designer dress, but her heart beat faster as she heard the MC say, "I think that's all the single ladies."

She hunched down even further in her seat, which was rather low already, so it put her face practically on the tabletop. She nervously sipped some cold jasmine tea as the MC called the bride up to throw her bouquet.

It wasn't the actual bouquet from the wedding because Mimi's cousin Paulette wanted to preserve the flowers (although why she'd want a bunch of dried flowers collecting dust, Mimi didn't know), and Auntie Noriko had very generously stuck a one hundred dollar bill inside of this alternate bouquet.

But even one hundred dollars of cold hard cash wasn't enough incentive for Mimi to get up there in front of everyone, reminding them that she was approaching forty and still single. So many of her younger cousins had already gotten married that there was a huge age gap between Mimi and the next oldest cousin on the dance floor.

There was shouting. There was squealing. (Unlike at Jenn's wedding, the squeals here sounded more like girls trying to avoid the bouquet landing on them rather than women scrambling to grab at it.) Then there was cheering and clapping.

It was over. Praise God, it was over!

The four cousins sighed, and their spouses did as well, although their sighs had more of a tinge of eye-rolling than relief. They started climbing back into their seats.

Amid all the conversation filling the restaurant, Mimi managed to hear Auntie Meiko's abnormally loud gasp.

Thundering footsteps, and then Auntie Meiko was at Mimi's side. "Oh! Mimi! We forgot about you!"

"It's fine, Auntie Meiko," Mimi said, trying to plaster a smile on her face, although she had a feeling it looked like a rictus grin.

"No, it's not fine," Auntie Meiko said. "We should tell them that we forgot you—" Her words cut off as she looked down at Mimi, and suddenly her cheeks turned pink. She stuttered, "Oh, you're probably too ol—" Her mouth worked open and closed a few times before she finished, "… not interested."

Mimi's smile at her aunt grew a little feral. "Exactly," she said in biting tones. "I'm not interested."

Auntie Meiko scurried away.

She knew Auntie Meiko didn't intend to be insulting, but at the same time, it *was* insulting. Mimi had been the next oldest single female cousin after Jenn, and there was a seven-year age gap. And her younger cousins had somehow simply been much more motivated to get hitched.

Mimi caught her cousins' sympathetic looks. "It's not that bad," she mumbled. "Some of the aunties are starting to give up entirely."

But in some ways, that was almost worse. It made her feel as though hope was slipping away. It made her feel like she no longer had any worth because she was getting too old.

No, forget that. She might be almost forty, but she refused to think she was past her prime. Besides, not all women wanted to be married.

Except that Mimi *did* want to be married. And she struggled with doubt and insecurity that there was something wrong with her.

She found herself more often fighting the fear that perhaps her inability to find someone was just a consequence of her flirtatious and promiscuous past. She was starting to believe that maybe she deserved this kind of loneliness.

Mimi saw Trish looking at her strangely, which jarred her out of her morose thoughts. What was she thinking? This wasn't like her. The wedding had made her mood go in a maudlin direction.

She wasn't going to simply sit here and feel sorry for herself. She grabbed the empty plate at the place setting next to her, which had been empty since she hadn't brought a date, and started loading food onto it.

"What are you doing that for?" Venus asked.

"I'm making a plate for Chester," Mimi answered.

When the plate was heaping and nearly spilling over, Mimi made her way around the other tables toward the entrance.

The front foyer of the restaurant was separated from the rest of the space by just a few standing screens, which did little to muffle the din of conversation. The cashier for takeout food stood to one side, and Mimi was shocked to find a line of people in front of it. The restaurant was still allowing takeout orders even though they were busy with the wedding.

On the other side of the foyer stood the reception table, only sparsely decorated with two tablecloths, one placed over the other at an angle, in the bride's colors of amber and sage. The wedding guest book lay open in the middle, and on the side was a collage of photos of the bride and groom.

Behind the table sat her cousin Chester, a tall, wide man whose hair was starting to look more gray than black these days. He was quite athletic, playing football with his friends almost every weekend, although he had also started to develop a slight paunch from all the beer and pizza they ate afterward.

Poor Chester was always asked to man the reception table, and he was always stuck with the job when everyone else was seated and began to eat. His large size was a good deterrent against anyone trying to steal gifts or envelopes, and he was so good-natured that he never told anyone no.

He gave Mimi a toothy grin as she approached the table. "Hey, Mimi."

"Here, Chester." Mimi placed the plate, chopsticks, and napkin in front of him.

"Oh! Thanks."

"I'm sorry you have to do this." She waved a hand at the mountain of gifts he was protecting.

His smile became broader. "Naw, you don't have to worry about me. I like doing it."

"You do?" Mimi glanced at the empty table, where his only companion was the specially decorated box that held the envelopes of money for the married couple. "You like being by yourself?"

He stared at her in disbelief. "We have four kids. Of *course* I like being by myself."

Mimi laughed. "You're right, my bad."

"Besides …" He picked up the chopsticks and then gestured under the table. "Look under there."

Mimi hesitantly bent down and lifted the edge of the tablecloth, wondering if Chester was simply going to release a fart like he used to when they were kids. Instead, she saw three empty plates that had been scraped clean of food, along with three sets of chopsticks and three dirty napkins that had been piled haphazardly on top.

As she straightened, Chester said around a mouthful of walnut prawns, "Whenever I do the reception table, my wife brings me a plate of food, and then my mom brings me another plate of food, and then Grandma always sends one of the cousins with another plate of food for me." He swallowed and grinned at her. "I get to eat way more than I would have sitting at a table."

"And you're still hungry?"

"Of course." He circled his arm around the plate as if she was going to snatch it away.

"How are your kids doing? Is the baby walking yet?" Mimi asked.

They chatted for fifteen or twenty minutes, occasionally needing to shout over the voice of the MC and the clapping of the wedding guests.

Finally, Mimi glanced at her watch. "I think it's late enough that I can leave now."

Chester leaned down to deposit his empty plate under the table. "Make sure you say goodbye to Grandma, too."

"Of course," Mimi said, offended. "I don't have a death wish."

Mimi went back to the table to grab her purse and said goodbye to the cousins. Then she managed to shout her goodbyes to the bride and groom, who were on the other side of a nearby table, doing their rounds of visiting all the guests.

Mimi gritted her teeth, then steeled herself as she made her way toward the front of the restaurant. She needed extra fortitude to run the gauntlet.

As she passed tables, she tried to move quickly, but she was inevitably noticed by some of the guests. Her cousins usually only nodded or waved at her, but aunties and uncles would often reach out and grab her arm to stop her and say hello.

"Oh, Mimi, we haven't seen you in so long. How great that you're still looking so good."

"Hey, Mimi, have you got a boyfriend yet? Uncle is working with this new hire at the company, and he's a nice boy…"

"Oh, Mimi, you weren't up there for the bridal toss, were you? Although I guess there's no point for you to go up there by now…"

Mimi gave all of them a bland smile paired with a chilly stare before peeling them off her like leeches and making her escape. She wasn't *that* old. Thirty-eight was not old! And it wasn't the end of the world for her to still be single!

Just as she thought that, she caught a snatch of conversation from a table she had just passed. It was one of her cousins, who was a little drunk and thought that his "indoor voice" was a lot quieter than it actually was.

"Yeah, poor Mimi. She's getting a little overripe, and all the good ones are already gone. Well, at least her parents will have someone to take care of them when they get older."

Mimi considered ignoring it, except that she recognized the voice. She slammed to a stop, then turned and directed an ice-pick glare that stabbed her cousin Bobby between the eyes. "*What* did you say, Bobby?" she demanded. Her voice might have been a little bit shrill.

Bobby paled, his eyes going as round and white as the steamed *bao* bread buns accompanying the Peking duck. "N-n-nothing, Mimi."

"Then I'm sure you'll understand that the next time your family needs a last-minute reservation at Jenn's restaurant, we'll be too busy to be able to seat you," Mimi bit out.

His wife, sitting next to him, frowned and slapped him on the arm, even though she had been nodding in agreement as she listened to him bad-mouthing Mimi.

Mimi spun around and continued toward the front of the

restaurant. Ultimately, it was simply pettiness, and it didn't make her feel much better. But she was getting tired of all the times that Bobby would come to Jenn's restaurant without a reservation and expect them to somehow seat him and his four kids—and their boyfriends or girlfriends—at a moment's notice, and offer them a discount on top of that.

She made her way to the large circular table to the side of the dance floor, which had been designated as the head table for the bride and groom and their immediate families.

Grandma Sakai managed to look like a queen on her throne as she sat in her chair. She seemed a little smaller every time Mimi saw her, but she still wore her neatly tailored suits and dresses with panache. Tonight, she wore a black silk dress with screen-printed kimono designs around the neckline and hem.

"Hi, Grandma. Hi Auntie Noriko! It's good to see you again." Mimi hugged her auntie, who owned a high-end cosmetics store in Hawaii but would naturally fly to California for the wedding of her youngest daughter, Paulette.

Mimi sat down in the empty chair next to Grandma Sakai, which she guessed was the bride's chair. "Are you both enjoying the party?"

"The food is very good," Auntie Noriko said.

"Yes. I haven't had good Chinese food in a long while," Grandma said.

She used to eat out quite often when she had numerous business meetings, but Grandma had given control of the bank to her oldest son just before Jenn's wedding. Since then, she had slowed down a lot.

"How is PT going?" Mimi asked. Grandma had had hip replacement surgery in both hips several years ago, but she hadn't recovered as well from the last surgery.

"I'm still going to PT every week, but I still have to walk with a cane." She gestured to the beautiful ebony cane hooked onto the back of her chair. Mimi had heard from several of the aunties that Grandma really should be walking with a walker, but her pride would not allow her to do so. After a great deal of arguing, she was

23

allowed to walk with a cane, but very slowly, since it wasn't quite enough for her to maintain her balance.

"Are you and your mother coming by on Wednesday?" Grandma asked. "I'm having lunch with Mrs. Matsumoto a little later that day, so come by around seven or eight instead."

"Sure thing." Mimi and her mother, or sometimes just one of them, would bring some food over for Grandma once a week and eat dinner with her. Sometimes they would tag team with Jenn, and Jenn would bring not only the food but also her family. Mimi always liked those weeks because the food was always better, and she liked playing with Jenn's kids.

"Where are you sitting?" Grandma asked, her eyes scanning the crowded restaurant.

Mimi pointed toward the far corner. "They stuck us way back there. I'm sitting with Lex, Trish, Venus, and Jenn."

"What about their kids?" Grandma asked.

"They all chipped in and paid for a few of Edward's cousins to watch them tonight," Mimi said. "The kids are sleeping over at their grandparents' house at the winery."

"Is Castillo Winery still doing well?" Auntie Noriko asked.

"I think so," Mimi said. "They're expanding the restaurant next summer, and they just finished renovations on the tasting room."

"Are Edward's parents still running the business?"

"Yes, but they've also started handing over portions of it to Edward, his brothers, and a couple of his cousins."

Grandma's eyes suddenly narrowed as she regarded Mimi. "I don't recall seeing you out there for the bouquet toss."

"Oh, yes, I was out on the dance floor," Mimi said. She had been out there when she was helping to set up the audiovisual equipment and the wedding cake, not the bouquet toss, but it was still perfectly true.

To distract her grandmother, she quickly asked, "Did you teach the kids at the Japanese school this past Thursday?"

"Oh yes, Mrs. Matsumoto's son picked me up." Once a month, her grandmother and her best friend, Mrs. Matsumoto, volunteered at the local Japanese school, which was run by the Buddhist temple as an afterschool program. Grandma taught *keigo*, or business Japanese, which involved different vocabulary and sentence construction.

Grandma tilted her head. "You speak business Japanese, don't you, Mimi?"

"Sort of," Mimi said hesitantly. "I haven't spoken it in a long time." She had learned it so that she could speak politely to Japanese customers who came to her mother's restaurant, but ever since she started working at Jenn's restaurant, she hardly needed to use it. She only used it once in a while if a Japanese-speaking couple wandered in.

"Oh, you'll pick it up again quickly," Grandma said blithely, then turned to Auntie Noriko, sitting beside her. "Noriko, you should ask Mimi to help you out."

"Help with what?" Mimi asked.

"Oh, it's nothing," Auntie Noriko tried to say, but Grandma interrupted her.

"Just tell her. Mimi might be able to help."

"Of course, I'll help if I can," Mimi said immediately. She was closest with her Auntie Noriko out of all of Grandma's children, even though she and her family lived on Oahu. She was Mimi's favorite aunt because she had taught her how to make lotions and salves to help prevent her skin from scarring after she had been in a car accident in her teens. Because Mimi already knew how to cook, thanks to helping her mother at the restaurant, it had been easy for her to pick up the chemistry that her aunt taught her.

Auntie Noriko had not only shown her how to make the lotions to reduce scarring, but she had also given her samples of very high-end lotions from her competitors which she knew would also help. Mimi had discovered that she had liked making the lotions quite a bit, and she'd given some to Lex to prevent post-ACL surgery scarring several years ago.

"Well..." Auntie Noriko sighed. "I've been having staffing problems at the store. I discovered some of the employees were stealing cosmetics or just being generally lazy."

In many ways, Auntie Noriko was very similar to Jenn, who had a difficult time firing employees unless they had done something blatantly rude or illegal. Auntie Noriko was both generous and softhearted.

"Are you going to fire them?" Mimi asked.

Auntie Noriko winced. "I already did, but I'm short-staffed right now, just as it's about to become busy with Thanksgiving and the Christmas holidays. I could use someone to help out in the store."

Mimi was torn. She hadn't visited Auntie Noriko in Hawaii in several years, but Thanksgiving and Christmas were also the busiest times at Jenn's restaurant.

"Do you still remember how to make the lotions?" Auntie Noriko asked Mimi.

"Of course. I make them for a few of the cousins."

"Yes, I heard about that," Grandma said.

"Venus was the one to start it," Mimi said. "She got a sudden allergic reaction to a facial lotion that she had been using for years. Apparently, the company had done something to change the formula. So I gave her a lotion to soothe the reaction, and Venus liked it so much that she told me she wanted to buy more from me. After that, several of the cousins started buying their face creams and night creams from me."

Ever the businesswoman, Grandma said, "You should open your own shop. Couldn't you sell them online?"

"The creams only last a couple of weeks before going bad," Mimi said. "They're essentially the same recipes that Auntie Noriko taught me."

Auntie's lotions were made with fresh herbs and oils and had a very short shelf life since they used a minimum of preservatives. Because they had to be consumed quickly, they were only sold in small containers, and Auntie Noriko had to constantly make new batches.

Her auntie nodded. "We have to make it very clear that the lotions have an expiration date, but we still get people who come back into the store and complain."

"I didn't want to have to deal with the hassle of customers who ignored the warnings about the shelf life, especially since it takes a few days for the lotions to be shipped to them," Mimi said.

"If you're still making those," Auntie Noriko said, "then I could use your help making some of the more complicated lotions at my shop. We subcontracted out some of our products, but I'm still the only one who can make the special formulas."

"I thought you were teaching Trinda to make that?" Grandma asked.

Auntie Noriko sighed again. "Trinda is a terrific businesswoman, but she's not very good at making the lotions."

"But both your daughters grew up helping you make them," Grandma said.

"Trinda knows *how* to make it, but she's very inconsistent—her products tend to vary in quality." Auntie smiled at Mimi. "You were always very good at that kind of stuff, Mimi."

She felt as though she couldn't say no to Auntie Noriko. Mimi owed her a great deal, and Auntie had always been very kind to her.

But Mimi also admitted to herself that another reason she was tempted to go was because another cousin's wedding was scheduled for early December, as well as two birthday parties in the same month, and she wouldn't mind having an excuse to skip them. Plus, if she could stay in Hawaii until past the middle of January, she could also miss another cousin's Red Egg and Ginger party. That wasn't even counting the large family parties at Thanksgiving, Christmas, and New Year's.

Mimi might not have been so eager to miss the holiday season and all the family parties if she hadn't been so annoyed by the aunties and uncles who had spoken to her as she headed toward Grandma's table, even if she ignored her cousin Bobby's idiocy. Being in Hawaii for a few weeks would be a nice change of pace, and while she would always have weddings and birthdays and family gatherings, there weren't any other weddings or red egg parties scheduled (yet) for at least the next year.

She would have to ask Jenn. It might be difficult, but Jenn might be able to bribe a couple of Edward's cousins to help out in Mimi's place.

"Let me ask—" Mimi began.

She was interrupted by a loud, very drunken voice. "Hey! Mimi wasn't in the bouquet toss!"

Mimi turned in horror to see Mariko bearing down on her. Her cousin's cheeks were flushed red, indicating that she had drunk too much of the wine or whiskey bottles that had been set out at each of the tables.

Mariko reached the chair where Mimi was sitting and gripped the back of it to steady herself. Then she turned and yelled toward the room at large, "We have to do the bouquet toss again!"

"Mariko, don't be ridiculous," Grandma said severely. "They're not going to do the bouquet toss again."

Mariko blinked at her for a few moments, then said, "Oh, I know how to fix this." She ran off.

Mimi was going to take advantage of this and escape. She stood up. "I think I'm going to go now, Grandma. I'll call you, Auntie Noriko."

Mimi had underestimated how fast Mariko could run. Or perhaps she had underestimated how much resentment Mariko still bore over the fact that she had been the Oldest Single Female Cousin for so many years and had suffered so much, while Mimi was better at making it appear that it didn't bother her at all.

Mariko came rushing back, holding the bouquet in her hands. At the same time, amongst all the conversations in the restaurant rose the piercing wail of a child.

"Here, Mimi," Mariko said triumphantly.

Mimi leaned away as if she were handing her a plate of sheep intestines. "Did you steal that from whoever caught it?" she demanded.

Mariko waved a hand. "Oh, it's fine. One of the cousins was holding one of the babies who caught it." Mariko apparently couldn't even be bothered to remember the names of her relatives. "She won't mind giving it to the Oldest Single Female Cousin instead. How old are you now, Mimi? Are you forty already? You need to get a move on. It's as if you don't want to be married."

Mimi's cousin Esther came hurrying up, holding her youngest

daughter, Sasha, who was crying so violently that she was starting to hiccup. "Mariko …" Esther said, frowning.

Mimi plucked the bouquet from Mariko's hands and handed it to Sasha, who immediately stopped crying.

Esther gave Mimi a grateful look. "Thanks, Mimi." She directed a single glare at Mariko—who was too drunk to notice—then stalked away.

Mariko was looking at her empty hands with a confused expression as if wondering where the bouquet had gone.

Mimi pointed to the back of the room. "Look, Mariko, they're serving the cake. I heard it has zero calories."

Mariko immediately perked up. "Really?" She turned and stumbled away.

Mimi turned to Auntie Noriko. "I'd be happy to come to Hawaii for the holidays, Auntie."

2

Mimi loved Hawaii.

What she didn't love was the fact that she never seemed to be able to travel there without two carry-ons and a giant box full of gifts for her relatives living there. Half of the stuff in the box wasn't even from her or from her family. It was from her cousins, her grandma, and anyone else who happened to hear she was flying there.

She exited the plane and staggered in the blast of heat before she stepped into the range of the jetway air conditioning. She would have moved quicker if she hadn't been loaded down with a huge duffel bag carrying sponge cake (from her cousin Jenn), Chinese pastries (from her mom), and cream puffs (which Mimi herself had filled just before going to the airport this morning). And that was just her left shoulder. Her right shoulder held another carry-on tote bag that held not only her laptop and wallet but also some bubble-wrapped bottles of essential oils that Grandma had decided at the last minute to send to Auntie Noriko (via MPS, Mimi's Parcel Service).

Mimi waddled her way to baggage claim, hoping to find a

luggage cart soon … but she was out of luck. The entire rack was empty of carts.

She bowed her head in abject despair for a moment, then picked up her two bags (which she'd dropped as soon as her feet stopped moving) and dove into the huge crowd around the baggage carousels.

Since the plane from San Jose arrived at midday, Mimi had told her aunt and uncle that they didn't need to park and meet her in the baggage claim area. Instead, Mimi would head out street side, and they could swoop in for a drive-by.

All the same, she felt a bit like a pariah to be standing around the baggage carousel by herself while groups of people greeted friends or relatives who had arrived with hugs and laughter. In a strange way, it reminded her of Paulette's wedding, the feeling stirring in her gut as she sat at the banquet table while surrounded by family members who had been accompanied by their +1s. While Mimi was just one.

Mimi had some extended family living in Hawaii whom she'd visit, but thankfully none of them were close enough to Mimi to feel comfortable jabbing her with the Dating Inquisition. It was already bad enough that at every major family gathering, her relatives would nag her about settling down, reminding her that "You're not getting any younger." As if she could forget it.

What, did they expect her to pull a husband out of her pocket? These days, most of the single men that she met were younger than her and often a bit immature, or else they were around her age but had some sort of baggage, such as a nasty divorce or grieving the loss of a wife. Half the time, Mimi wasn't entirely sure if these older men weren't interested in her solely because they needed someone to help them take care of their kids.

Mimi didn't mind kids. In fact, she wanted some of her own, but she also wasn't going to compromise and marry just anyone. Her parents didn't hate each other, but she saw the mismatch in their personalities and how the rough edges were constantly banging against each other. On the flip side, she saw the loving relationships between some of her other aunties and uncles and knew that a happier marriage was possible if she found the right person.

No, not quite the right person. Jenn had told her that there was someone out there whom God wanted for her.

Mimi's prayers these days often went like this: *Dear God, I'm pretty sure You have someone planned for me. That's really nice. Do you think I might be able to meet them before I hit menopause?*

She shook herself out of her thoughts. It was hard to stay gloomy when she was in Hawaii. Maybe it was the laid-back atmosphere—even here at the airport, people walked at a slower pace as they traveled to and from the gates. Rather than a plethora of business suits like she'd seen in the airport in San Jose, most people wore casual clothing, punctuated by garishly bright Hawaiian print clothes that had probably been bought at the ABC store.

It could be that she was just getting older and appreciating ways to decrease her stress. Look at her, talking like an old woman. *Thirty-eight is not old.* If she chanted it like a Buddhist priest, maybe it would suddenly be true.

It wasn't so much being thirty-eight. It was being thirty-eight and single when all her cousins above marriageable age were, well, *married*.

She made it to her baggage carousel, and her carry-ons dropped like rocks at her sides.

Then she yelped as she realized that the box on the conveyor belt was hers. She leaped forward to try to wrestle the heavy cardboard box off of the belt, but her arms were shaking from the strain of carrying her two heavy bags across the length of the airport. The box tipped back onto the belt and threatened to drag her with it as it continued on its merry way.

"Hey, let me give you a hand there, sister," a man's voice boomed from high above her.

In the next moment, a tanned local man with a worn, wide-brimmed fishing hat had pulled her box off of the carousel for her and set it down next to the two carry-ons she'd abandoned on the floor.

"Thanks." Mimi smiled at him and the woman next to him—his wife, maybe?—but she was afraid it looked more like a grimace because she was still panting from her exertions.

"No worries. You got anything else?"

"Yeah, one suitcase."

He nodded at her. "Just point 'em out to me."

Luckily, her suitcase came drifting down the carousel within a few minutes, and the man retrieved that for her, too.

"Thanks," Mimi said again.

"Any time, sister," the man said.

His wife looked dubiously at her as she balanced the box on top of her rolling suitcase. "You going to be okay? You should get a luggage cart."

"I couldn't find any. I'll be fine, I just need to make it outside and then my auntie will pick me up."

"Okay," she said, although she still looked doubtful. But Mimi waved at the two of them, then lumbered away.

She probably looked ridiculous, a tiny woman less than five feet tall, a bag full to bursting on each shoulder, carefully wheeling a suitcase with a big cardboard box balanced on top. The top of the box was almost taller than she was.

But the encounter with the man with the fishing hat had somehow raised her spirits. She had forgotten how friendly local people could be. Not everyone was like that, of course, but she always seemed to be more likely to find someone willing to give her a hand here in Hawaii as opposed to California.

As she exited the baggage claim, the hot, humid air attacked her like a giant, sticky spiderweb that weighed down her limbs, and she staggered a little. Mimi didn't often visit Hawaii during the winter months—she was more likely to spend several weeks during the summer—and the temperature usually wasn't that different from San Jose. But now, going from California cold to Hawaii humid made her drag her feet as she got out of the way of the automatic doors. This was pathetic! She needed to toughen up or she'd *melt* before Auntie Noriko picked her up.

She suddenly started vibrating, which startled her so much that she nearly lost control of her moving mountain. She grabbed at it before it could roll down the slight incline of the sidewalk and shoot out onto the street.

What in the world? What was going on?

Belatedly she remembered her phone tucked into her bag—correction: tucked into the *bottom* of her bag, where it was causing the container of peach-strawberry jelly dessert that Jenn had given to her to jiggle wildly. She hustled to one of the concrete pillars and leaned her box and suitcase against it while dropping her bags to grope frantically inside the one vibrating so hard it looked blurry.

It was Auntie Noriko. "Hi, Auntie! I just picked up my bags. Are you and Uncle Milton at the cell phone waiting area?"

"No, I'm—" *Munch, munch.* "—almost at baggage claim. Oops! Hey! Why aren't you letting me in?" *Munch, munch.* "Oh, I'm not signaling. There, I'm signaling. Thank you!"

Cold sweat dripped down Mimi's back despite the hot ambient temperature. She had expected her uncle to be driving because Auntie Noriko was, quite frankly, a *terrible* driver. Eating and driving at the same time was like begging for an accident. "Auntie! Stop eating and watch the road!"

"I'm not—" *Swallow.* "—eating."

Mimi needed to get her off the phone or she'd hit something. "Auntie—"

"I couldn't help it! Henk's was on the way, and their gourmet hot dogs are so good! I bought you something."

"That's not going to matter if you crash the car! I'll be waiting out on the curb!" Mimi disconnected the call and hoped her aunt would make it there soon.

She heard the honking of horns from irate drivers long before Auntie Noriko's SUV appeared. Mimi had maneuvered her suitcase close to the edge of the sidewalk and put the box down with her carry-ons sitting on top of it (the box was wide enough to hold both bags with ease), so she was unburdened and could jump and wave her hands to get her aunt's attention.

Auntie brought the vehicle to a screeching halt (the front

bumper nearly went up on the curb) and flung open the driver's side door to run toward Mimi, arms outstretched and a wide smile on her face (decorated with a smear of mustard on her lip). "Mimi! My savior!"

"Aren't you exaggerating?" But Mimi hugged her aunt, feeling comforted by her loving arms. Unlike the rest of Grandma's children, Auntie Noriko was a hugger.

"Absolutely not! I'm putting you to work as soon as we get home."

"The shop is that busy?"

Auntie nodded while Mimi dug a tissue out of her jeans pocket and wiped the mustard off for her. "Oh, thank you, dear. Yes, we ran almost out of stock last night. I had to leave Trinda to run the store while I made more lotions."

Mimi loaded her bags into the back of the SUV, then confiscated the keys from her aunt. "Where's Uncle Milton?" He usually drove when picking Mimi up from the airport.

"Emergency at work. He couldn't leave." He was a supervisor in charge of medical supplies for Leilani Medical Centers, a collection of specialized hospitals across the state.

Mimi climbed into the driver's seat but found she had to back up to get some space between the right front tire and the curb before she could pull out into the street.

"Oh, just hop up on the curb a little," Auntie Noriko said blithely.

Mimi paused to glare at her aunt. "I am not going to hop up onto the curb."

"There's no one there." She gestured in front of the car, which was indeed empty of people, but only because they'd scattered in panic when Auntie drove up.

"You are a menace," Mimi told her as she backed up. "I don't know how you still have your driver's license."

"I rarely drive. Milton likes to do it, usually."

More like, Milton *had* to do it, usually, if he didn't want his wife to get into a fender-bender. "I'm honored by the rare privilege of being your driver," Mimi said. She didn't want to get into (another) accident with Auntie Noriko behind the wheel. The last one had been a relatively minor fender bender when she was in college, but she still had shoulder problems that cropped up occasionally because of it.

As they got onto the freeway, her aunt turned to her. "So, you're staying just until after New Year's?"

"If you need me to stay longer, I can change my ticket. My boss says it's okay."

Auntie Noriko smirked at her. "Jenn is your boss, right? Considering I changed her diapers, the least she can do is be flexible."

Mimi started cackling. "Jenn said almost the exact same thing. 'Auntie Noriko changed my diapers. You can stay as long as you want.'"

Auntie grinned. "That diaper argument always lets me get my way." She gave Mimi a sidelong glance. "Speaking of children, any new boyfriend you're leaving in tears in California?"

She raised an eyebrow at her. "That's a completely obvious and unrelated conversational detour."

"Who cares! Well?"

Mimi sighed. "No, no boyfriend. I haven't dated in a few years."

She waited for the inevitable *You're not getting any younger* type of comment, but instead, Auntie Noriko said, "Nothing wrong with that. Do you want to get married?"

"That's the problem. I do. Except ..." She gave another gusty sigh. "Sometimes I think I'm only wanting to date someone to shake things up in my life, and that's not a good reason." In truth, lately she'd felt like things in her life were getting stagnant, but she couldn't figure out what to do about it.

"Move to Hawaii!" Auntie said cheerfully. "I'll give you a job."

"As grateful as I am, Auntie, you know that I would start insulting the customers if I had to work at the store for longer than a few weeks."

Auntie frowned. "Yes, you're right. You're too much like

Paulette. Both of you have too smart a mouth to be any good at customer service."

"I consider it an asset for my mental health, but that's probably a bad thing in your line of work."

"Regardless, I was serious about moving. When you were younger, you wanted to live here."

"That was before I realized how much it cost to rent an apartment here."

"You can stay with me! And I'm sure you'd find a good job. You graduated in … what did you graduate in again?"

"Business." And she'd taken extra years, which her mother never forgot to remind her about.

"Oh, that's right. It was such a waste that you took all those temp jobs after graduating."

Back then, she hadn't been sure what to do with herself, which was why she'd aimlessly taken on all that temp work, but nothing had induced her to want to stay past the end of the contract. "At the time, I still wanted to please Mom, and in between the temp jobs I worked for her restaurant when she needed help."

"Your mother is the only person I know with worse staffing problems than I have."

"Maybe that was my fault?"

"What do you mean?"

"Maybe I did Mom a disservice. She bullied me into giving her a hand since no one else would agree to work for free, so she started expecting all her staff to be the same way."

Auntie scoffed. "You kids these days. Thinking you ought to be *paid*."

Mimi grinned. "Yeah, Mom didn't like it when I started working for Jenn at the restaurant at Castillo Winery, but I'm happy there." It had been the first place she'd ever found with such a close, healthy work environment. Even if the work wasn't completely fulfilling in terms of her ambition, the good atmosphere more than made up for it.

"I wasn't that surprised. I think if your mother had taken the son-sized blinders off her face, she'd have seen you were better suited to taking over her restaurant than anyone else. Who's she grooming as heir now?"

"My brother Rick. He couldn't decide what he wanted to do—kind of like me, so I guess it runs in the family—and Mom nagged him until he agreed to take some business classes and start helping her with running things. He seems happy about it, though."

"Well, at least *someone's* happy." Auntie's voice was slightly bitter. She and Mimi's mother had never gotten along, and it was exacerbated by their disagreements about how Mom treated Mimi.

"Aw, don't be like that. I'm glad not to work at Mom's restaurant. If I think about it, Mom and I would have killed each other within a few years."

Auntie Noriko reached over to stroke Mimi's hair. "She never saw your blazing talent."

"As much as I appreciate your unconditional love, I don't have blazing talent."

"You got a culinary degree! At your age! Oh, sorry, that was rather tactless of me. But still!"

"It was probably a mid-life-crisis project." To get off the double-disaster topics of her age and her mother, Mimi said, "By the way, I made some things for you to try. Empanadas, macarons, and truffles."

They talked about food all the way until they got to her aunt's house. The street was the same—mostly quiet, the houses about 20-30 years old, the older ones having had renovations in the last decade or so. Some front lawns were meticulously cared for, others were wastelands of weeds, but all were large.

Her aunt and uncle's house was a little larger than their neighbors' since they had originally bought an extra big lot and they had added extensions over the years. The largest extension had been her aunt's industrial-grade stillroom for making the lotions and salves she sold at her store.

Mimi's first order of business was unpacking the perishables she'd brought with her. After sticking the cream puffs in the fridge to cool, Auntie insisted on making some expensive Japanese green tea and tasting all the food Mimi had carefully packed into the box. Mimi had made tuna-mayo-filled rice balls to eat on the plane, so she wasn't very hungry, which left more food for her aunt to eat.

Thanks to her culinary degree, Mimi had experimented with macadamia nut truffles spiced with chili powder, as well as a dark chocolate ganache flavored with passion fruit. The mini empanadas were also unusual, filled with Japanese chicken curry or Korean bulgogi simmered beef. The macarons alone were relatively normal, although Mimi had included a guava flavor and a mango flavor.

"These are delicious!" Auntie Noriko popped another macaron in her mouth. "You should open a restaurant."

"I know exactly how much work a restaurant is—it's not just cooking the food, it's hiring the staff, balancing the books, and marketing it enough to gain customers. I'm not ready for that kind of responsibility." Mimi drained the last of her tea. "Besides, I don't like doing entrees. I like doing snacky things like this." She enjoyed using her creativity to come up with different kinds of mini-bites, both savory and sweet.

"I should stop eating or else I won't want to leave any for your uncle." Auntie Noriko stood up, taking away the empty plates. Mimi helped her put away the uneaten food.

"Did you need my help making lotions now?" Mimi asked her when they were done cleaning up.

"I am normally a cruel and ruthless slave driver, but in this instance, I'll let you unpack first. That reminds me, we have a box for you to go through."

"A box of what?" Mimi followed her aunt, rolling her suitcase into the guest bedroom, a.k.a. Paulette's old bedroom, where Mimi would always stay when she visited. When they were kids, Mimi had slept on the floor on a futon, but when Paulette moved out of the house after college, it became a permanent guest bedroom and Mimi had graduated to the bed.

The room had been cleared of boy band posters and stuffed animals, but it still had the same faded blue carpet and white four-poster bed that somehow made Mimi suddenly feel twenty years younger. "You took out Paulette's desk," Mimi commented. Her cousin had gotten a large, beautiful desk in high school.

"The last time she came home, just before the wedding, she cleaned the room entirely and figured out what she wanted to take with her back to California. The desk was the first thing." Auntie Noriko opened the slatted closet doors, revealing that all the stuff once jam-packed into it had been almost entirely removed.

Mimi gasped in surprise. "Did Paulette take all her old clothes, too?"

"No, of course not. Half of that stuff was from her grunge phase—or was it her hippie phase?—and she's no longer into revealing glimpses of parts of her best left unseen."

Mimi shuddered. Some of Paulette's clothing choices back then had been enough to send her screaming and running for her life like a slasher flick heroine.

Auntie Noriko pointed to a box on the bottom of the closet. "Paulette tossed almost everything, but she found a bunch of things that she says might belong to you."

Mimi grimaced, remembering some of her own fashion phases that she'd rather forget about.

Her aunt gave her a sly grin. "Milton was highly amused by some of the things Paulette found."

Mimi groaned. "Uncle Milton is never going to stop teasing me about some of it, is he?"

"Not for the entire eight weeks you're here."

"Maybe I'll leave early …"

"No, don't do that! I'll make him stop … after a week or two."

"No way! I'm not spending more than a day being nagged about my pink-winged unicorn T-shirt."

"How did you know that was in there?"

"It is?! Aargh!" Mimi put her head in her hands.

In reality, she was willing to tolerate a substantial amount of ribbing from her uncle. She'd been a flower girl at their wedding, and Uncle Milton had treated Mimi like a daughter even after his own two daughters were born. But that didn't mean she'd let Uncle

Milton terrorize her for the entire time she was here. "Well, I did bring a lot of snacks this time. Maybe I can blackmail him."

"And there she goes, falling into a life of crime ..."

Mimi glanced around the small room. "By the way, did you get Lex's email about the Honolulu Marathon?"

"You mean her last-minute groveling for me and Trinda to house her and your other cousins?"

"That would be the one."

Lex's husband, Aiden, was a runner and had decided to enter the Honolulu Marathon, set for the second weekend in December. Trish, Venus, Jenn, and their husbands were all traveling to Hawaii with them to cheer him on, and they'd asked to stay with Auntie Noriko and Trinda so they wouldn't have to find lodging. Probably two of her cousins would sleep here on the floor while their husbands slept on an air mattress in Uncle Milton's office. The two couples staying with Trinda would have to navigate the war zone (i.e., the living room where her kids scattered their toys) to find a place to lay down futons or air mattresses.

Mimi gave her auntie a stern look. "What are you charging them, Auntie?"

Auntie Noriko pretended to look shocked but failed to hide her smile of mercenary glee. "I would never charge my relatives. But they are bringing some expensive bottles of sake, canned abalone, and dried Hokkaido squid."

"Auntie!" Mimi scolded her. "Talk about falling into a life of crime!"

"What?" she asked innocently. "I need the abalone and squid for New Year's."

It was true that she did use the canned abalone and dried squid to make her traditional New Year's mochi soup, but they were also the most expensive ingredients. "Hokkaido squid? Really? It has to be from Hokkaido?"

Auntie Noriko shrugged. "Lex was the one asking. It's not my fault she knows almost nothing about Japan. Trish was on the email too, and she didn't say anything."

Trish didn't often speak it, but she understood Japanese because she'd taken classes, like Mimi. She also knew more about Japanese culture than the other cousins, so she would have known exactly how expensive those squids were. She must have been okay with the outrageous ask either because she felt bad they were all crashing at Auntie Noriko's and Trinda's homes, or because someone else was footing the bill—probably the latter, and it was probably Lex.

"I'm just glad they're not bringing all their children, too," Auntie Noriko said. "We wouldn't have room for everyone."

"If they brought their entire families, they'd get hotel rooms rather than bunking with you and Trinda," Mimi said. While their parents were here, all the kids would be staying with Jenn's in-laws, who loved having all of them around.

"I don't know how they managed to even plan the trip without a full-scale rebellion from the older kids," Auntie said.

"Oh, they bribed them with a trip to Disneyland during President's Day weekend."

"Ah. That'll appease the rabble." Her aunt headed out the door. "Well, unpack and then go through the box. Any old clothes you don't want, set them aside for me to use as rags in the stillroom. I'll be there when you're done."

It didn't take Mimi long to unpack her suitcase, but she rather dreaded going through the box, certain only embarrassment awaited her. She wasn't entirely wrong.

The pink winged unicorn shirt was folded conspicuously on top, but the other shirts she'd left here were local Hawaiian brands. She had left several swimsuits that she only used in Hawaii, and she was surprised to see one that she hadn't been able to find when she was fourteen, prompting her to buy a new one.

She set aside some rubber slippers, which still fit her, and the pair of running sneakers she'd left the last time she visited because she hadn't had room in her suitcase. She also resurrected an old Hawaiian print canvas backpack that she used to use to hold her things when she went to the beach.

There were many items that she hadn't seen in years and must have been shoved into the back of the closet. She wasn't certain if she should be happy or dismayed that some of the T-shirts and shorts she wore as a teenager almost still fit her, being only a little tight. She found an old snorkel set that she'd used as a kid, and under that was a woolen tube scarf in chocolate brown and snazzy burnt orange that she'd knit one summer—suffering through the discomfort of knitting with wool in Hawaii's heat and humidity— intending to take it with her on a Tahoe ski trip, except she'd forgotten it here. Under that were some old paperbacks—a copy of a truly awful vampire romance along with *Moby Dick*, which had been a summer reading requirement for school one year.

And then at the bottom of the box was a plastic bag from a Japanese bookstore in Tokyo which looked familiar to her, but she was certain she'd never been there. Curious about what was inside, she reached in and pulled out a large, rather dense book.

As soon as she saw the manga art on the cover, the memories enveloped her. She could have almost sworn she smelled a whiff of green kiawe wood, beach grasses, and lime.

It was a Japanese book, so it opened in the opposite direction as an English book. The size was also tall and wide, filled with thick color-printed pages that were a bit glossy under the soft light from the ceiling fan. Mimi translated the Japanese words on the spine: *The Art of The Ritual Metallurgist* by Sanae Komori.

The Ritual Metallurgist was a manga series she'd read as a teenager. It hadn't been translated into English at the time, and Mimi had been so hooked that she had been learning Japanese so that she could read it. This beautiful book was filled with color artwork from the entire series, including extra illustrations never previously published.

The sight of the book both thrilled her and, at the same time, caused a sickening pain in her stomach.

Suddenly she was sixteen again, and it was the summer before her junior year in high school. The memories came flooding back— including the stupid things she'd done. The regret was so strong that her gut clenched with nausea as if she had food poisoning.

She sat there with the book in her hands, her breath coming fast and sharp. This book didn't belong to her. It belonged to Tosh.

Mimi, accompanied by her brothers, had been visiting Auntie

Noriko here in Hawaii since she was five years old, ever since her parents had discovered it was a convenient way to get the kids out of their hair for the summer. They'd fly here at the start of the summer, and then her parents would leave after a week. At the end of the summer, Auntie Noriko flew back to California with them so she could visit her other relatives.

Mimi didn't mind because she had a beloved playmate, a boy who lived a few houses down the street.

She and Tosh were the same age. When they were kids, his younger sister and her older and younger brothers would play with them, but as they grew older, her brothers stopped coming to Hawaii, and it was just Mimi.

Tosh was the reason Mimi became secretly interested in Japanese media. He had been born in Hawaii, but his parents were both from Japan, and he was fluent. He also loved anime, manga, and light novels back before they were popular in American culture. When they were kids, very few of the books were translated into English, but he had been sent to Japanese school since he was young, so he could read Japanese as well as a boy his age in Japan. He would read Japanese books that his grandparents sent to him, and when his family visited Japan once every couple of years, they would buy lots of manga and light novels for him to read.

He introduced Mimi to these Japanese stories, translating them for her. Unlike some of her other cousins, she hadn't grown up learning to speak Japanese because neither of her parents spoke it at home, although they both understood the language to an extent. But suddenly she wanted to learn Japanese so she could read these books as well. It hadn't been too difficult to convince her parents to enroll her in an after-school Japanese language program.

She would look forward to visiting Hawaii so that she could discuss manga and light novels with Tosh. She borrowed books from him and watched anime in Japanese with him. For his part, he seemed to enjoy having someone else to talk to about them, since he didn't have many friends who could read Japanese either.

Outside of her visits, they tried to write letters to each other, but neither of them was very good at correspondence. But they always made up for it when she came to Hawaii and they could talk with each other.

However, in middle school, she started hiding her interest in manga and anime. Her school had a Japanese club, and there was a group of creepy boys who liked the gory battle manga and nasty R-rated *ecchi* stuff. She didn't want to be associated with them.

But it also meant she hid her interest from her friends and family members. Many of them visited Japan every so often, but she was too embarrassed to ask them to buy Japanese books for her. So she borrowed them from Tosh, who was always able to get his family to buy new ones for him.

The book in her hands was one of those. He had let her borrow it, but soon after, the two of them had had a falling out. A few days later, Mimi had returned to California.

She came back to Hawaii the following summer, prepared to apologize to Tosh, but his family had moved away from their house down the street. She had never returned the book to him.

Mimi traced the beautiful artwork on the cover. She shouldn't have forgotten to give it back to him, but at the time, she had assumed she could simply return the book the following year.

But more than the book, she regretted the words she had flung at him the last time they argued. She regretted everything about her behavior then, even though she had been just a stupid teenager.

Mimi sighed as she slipped the book back into the bookstore bag. She had been feeling regret more often as she got older. Or was she fixating on her age because of everything that had happened at Paulette's wedding?

At the very least, she needed to return this expensive book to Tosh. But how?

Auntie Noriko's eldest daughter, Trinda, still lived in Hawaii. She was a few years younger than Mimi and Tosh, but she had gone to Laniloa Academy, the same private school that Tosh and his sister had attended for middle school and high school.

Would Trinda know how to find him after all these years? But Mimi didn't know any other way to find out what had happened to him.

Auntie Noriko was grooming Trinda to eventually take over her cosmetics store, and Mimi would start working there tomorrow. She'd find a way to bring the subject up with Trinda.

Her stomach twisted again at the thought of seeing Tosh, but she knew she had to return his book to him.

And after all these years, if she apologized to him, he would surely forgive her ... wouldn't he?

3

Mimi felt like an elementary school student wearing her mother's clothes.

It wouldn't have been so bad if her cousin Paulette's old uniform had simply been too long for her. To add insult to injury, Paulette was small-boned and as skinny as a broom (not unlike Mimi's other cousin Lex), so the tight waistband of the skirt felt like it was going to cut her in half at the torso.

Auntie Noriko's cosmetics store, Miwaku, required uniforms for all the staff, just like at department stores in Tokyo, and the similarity to Japanese stores did seem to encourage a lot of Japanese tourists to enter the shop. It also made the store look very upscale, which matched many of the stores around it in that section of Ala Moana Shopping Center.

Unfortunately, she'd updated the uniforms a few years ago, so Mimi couldn't use the old uniform that had been made for her when she volunteered to help at the store in the past. She'd been forced to borrow the one worn by Auntie Noriko's younger daughter.

The two other employees who worked the front retail area were entirely different from the last time Mimi had worked at Miwaku, so she smiled and nodded politely to Effie and Waite while trying not to tug yet again at her pale blue pencil skirt.

"I guess you're doing most of the heavy lifting when it comes to running the store these days?" Mimi asked her cousin Trinda.

"It works out because Mom can spend more time making the products." Trinda tucked a strand of hair behind her ear. She was sporting a seventies vibe these days, with a slightly poofy bob haircut and glasses with a cat's-eye shape to the lenses. "I'm honestly glad you're here to help out, not just with the front area but also with helping her make the specialty lotions. Our stock has been low, so Mom's been overworking herself like she used to."

Mimi caught herself tugging at her skirt again, and Trinda noticed it.

"I'm sorry we couldn't get another uniform made for you before you came."

"No, there's no need to go through the expense if I'm here for only a few weeks." The uniforms were quite a bit nicer than the last style. The employees still had to wear white button-down shirts or blouses, but the icy blue vest and pencil skirt trimmed in sage were made of a bamboo fabric that was a lot cooler than the previous polyester version. There was also a subtle hibiscus design on the vests in ice-blue thread, which Mimi thought was pretty stylish. Waite, the only male employee, wore ice-blue slacks.

The only thing really annoying about the uniform—aside from the poor fit on Mimi—was the fact that women were required to wear skin-toned or white pantyhose and low-heeled sage pumps. It wasn't so bad in the spacious, air-conditioned store, but once she stepped outside, she'd immediately explode into sweat. Even in the wintertime, Honolulu weather wasn't really cool.

"Well, but it kind of hangs on you," Trinda said with a wince and an utter lack of tact.

Despite the too-small waistband, the skirt hung at Mimi's mid-calf instead of her knees, and the vest looked more like a tunic. Mimi had also been forced to wear a sports bra to flatten her chest since her bra size was a bit larger than Paulette's and she didn't want to burst the tiny buttons of the vest, which were there more for decoration than function.

"How about I bring you one of my uniforms tomorrow?" Trinda said. "It'll be even longer on you than this one, but the waistband and the bust size will fit you better."

"I'd appreciate that," Mimi mumbled. She was used to things like this by now, though—practically every garment she bought had to be shortened.

Trinda explained her work duties, but it was still basically the same as the last time Mimi had volunteered at the store a few years ago. Some of the lotion formulas were new, and Mimi did her best to memorize the new products, but she hadn't quite gotten it done before the store opened and the first customers came in.

There was a steady stream of people all morning, although some simply browsed the products on display tables, reading the descriptions—and the prices—without buying anything. Mimi stood beside the table on the right side of the front door, while Effie stood beside the table directly across the store from her. Waite and Trinda manned the longer display table directly facing the glass front double doors.

The entire front wall of the store was glass panels, but there were pots of bamboo and Japanese Aralia directly in front of Mimi's station, so she couldn't see through them very well. But she had a clear view through the front doors and the other walls, which was why she noticed the man.

He was dressed like a local in a Hawaiian shirt, but it was a nicer, more expensive Hawaiian print shirt than the tourists wore, and he had on slacks rather than shorts, so he looked more like a businessman. He wouldn't have caught her attention if he hadn't passed the front of the store *twenty times* in the space of thirty minutes.

People passing back and forth weren't unusual, but something about the man's posture seemed nervous, and Mimi was at an angle where she could see that he glanced inside the store every single time he passed. Then she started counting how many times she spotted him. By the time she reached ten, she knew something was up.

Mimi glanced at Trinda, but she was ringing up a customer. As soon as the woman left with her products, Mimi was about to go speak to her cousin, but then she paused. Really, what could she do? She was pretty certain that barging out the doors to go confront the creepy man was probably against the policies of the shopping center.

The choice was taken away from her when the man *finally* entered the store.

Trinda greeted him as soon as he came inside. However, he completely ignored her and made a beeline for Waite, who was on the left end of the long display table. Then again, Waite was the only male employee, so maybe it wasn't that strange. Also, Mimi had noticed in her years working for the store that some repeat customers preferred to work with certain employees whenever they came in, so maybe he was one of Waite's regulars.

Trinda came up to Mimi's side of the store. "I'm going in back to do some paperwork. Effie should be back from her break in about fifteen minutes, but if it gets busy, just run back to get me." She normally wouldn't leave during the busiest times of the day, but since the man was the only customer, she probably figured it wouldn't hurt this time, and Mimi knew she'd been swamped with accounting work.

"Okay."

The store had hardly been empty for more than a few minutes all day, and sometimes customers were browsing or waiting for one of the four employees to finish up with the customers they were waiting on. So Mimi hadn't had time to be bored before. Now, she cleaned up her area and then stood there, stealing glances at Waite and the Creepy Customer.

Since Auntie Noriko had been concerned about her employees lately, Mimi had been studying their work throughout the day. Effie was friendly, and her age—she looked to be in her early- to mid-twenties—made her popular with younger customers. Mimi looked young, too, but only because of her height, so she got a mix of people, including several of the rare male customers. Trinda often had regulars coming up to her, and she'd chat with them not only about the products but also about how her mother was doing.

Waite wasn't unfriendly, and he was always extremely polite, but he wasn't quite as outgoing as Effie. Mimi didn't consider herself particularly extroverted, but even she smiled at the customers more than Waite did. Trinda was good at making suggestions if a customer was undecided about something, but Waite was usually silent as his customers made their choices. Mimi supposed some people might like that better, but it made him seem disinterested in the very products he was selling.

Now, however, Waite had his head bowed closer to the Creepy Customer, and they were speaking in extremely quiet voices. Creepy Customer had looked so suspicious before coming in—as if he'd been scoping out the store and waiting for it to empty before entering to talk to Waite. Maybe he'd needed to speak to him about a personal matter? Which Waite really shouldn't be doing during work hours, even if there was a lull.

But both men had serious expressions on their faces. That, combined with the customer's strange actions, made suspicions rise like nausea in her stomach.

After all the staffing problems Auntie Noriko had been having, the thought of yet another one involving Waite only made Mimi more certain something was wrong. But the two men were too far away for Mimi to hear the conversation, and it would look too obvious if she moved closer to try.

Suddenly the door opened, and Mimi immediately bowed. "Welcome to Miwaku," she said.

Strangely, the new customer was another man. At first glance, he looked like any other Japanese tourist walking through the shopping center. He was in his late thirties or early forties, neither handsome nor ugly, but Mimi could tell that his short haircut had an overseas Asian-style sculpting, different from typical American styling, sweeping his hair forward and partially covering his eyes. His shirt and jeans were unremarkable but had a quality to the fabrics that hinted at a high price tag.

Most of the Japanese tourists came as couples—a man and his girlfriend or wife, or maybe two girlfriends—or sometimes as a family. Men by themselves, like this man, rarely came into the store, and it was already unusual for two men to be there at the same time.

Which was perhaps why she studied the Possible-Japanese-Tourist a bit more closely than she normally would, and which was why she saw when the man glanced directly at Creepy Customer talking to Waite. Possible-Japanese-Tourist's gaze lingered perhaps a tiny bit longer than normal for an indifferent stranger.

But then Possible-Japanese-Tourist had swiftly moved toward Mimi's table, and she had to get to work.

She bowed again, but this time she spoke her greeting in Japanese. "Welcome. How may I assist you?" Then she straightened from her bow and froze.

The man was staring directly at her face. His gaze was rather more intense than was polite—certainly more intense than a typical man from Tokyo.

There was a strong possibility that Mimi might have been so shocked that she stared back at him wide-eyed like a stunned fish. But then she came back to her senses and said uncomfortably in Japanese, "Is there anything in particular that you are interested in?"

He cleared his throat and looked away, then said in perfect American-accented English, "Aren't you a little young to work here?"

Rude! She pasted on an exemplary employee smile, although Auntie Noriko would probably take one look at her and rush forward in panic at what Mimi was going to say. "I can assure you, sir, I am fully knowledgeable about our products. Also, I'm a bit older than I look. However, if you wish, I can fetch my manager Trinda to help you. What sort of product were you looking for?" She wasn't about to bother Trinda if the moron was just going to ask if they sold something like body glitter.

Not-Japanese-Tourist brusquely replied, "No, I'm just looking," and then bent down to examine the lotions on the table.

Mimi tried not to hover, but she wanted to hurry the jerk out of the store, so she might have invaded his personal space a bit. Or maybe a lot.

Her proximity happened to cause her to study the side of his face. Something about his features seemed familiar to her. Maybe he simply looked like someone she knew. He wasn't ugly, but the shape of his lips and jaw showed that he had a strong overbite. Perhaps he'd never had orthodontic work done.

Not-Japanese-Tourist also had slightly rounded cheeks that would have made him look a bit pudgy, but they contrasted strangely with the corded muscles on his neck and the shape of his shoulders under his shirt, which seemed to indicate that while he wasn't Captain-America-ripped, he worked out quite a bit.

She still rather disliked him, but now her curiosity was piqued, and if Mimi had been a cat, she'd have died a million deaths by now. She studied the side of his face discreetly as he looked down at the table.

It was precisely because of her angle that she noticed it. His ear was more tanned than his face.

It wasn't anything obvious, but Mimi had always been perceptive to detail. She had also worked at Auntie's store ever since it started selling foundation several years ago, so Mimi had gotten very familiar with makeup shades. The shade of the man's ear was slightly darker than his face.

Mimi leaned in closer, *absolutely* invading his personal space. "Does anything interest you, sir?" she asked, but she barely listened to his stammered answer as she studied his skin, noticing the freckles on his ear.

Yes, Not-Japanese-Tourist was almost certainly wearing makeup, thick enough that it changed the shade of his skin to make him appear more pale. It wasn't unheard of for a man to wear foundation, but his makeup extended down his neck below the collar of his shirt, so he wasn't wearing it to smooth the pores of his face.

Not-Japanese-Tourist didn't look at her, but he shifted away from her in a jerking, uncomfortable motion.

Mimi didn't take the hint and moved along with him.

She studied his hands and arms, resting on the top of the table. They were the same pale shade as the man's face—the *exact* same shade. Usually, a person's arms were a bit darker than their face, and the skin tone had variations between the top and underside of the arm. But this man's arm was entirely pale, with no gradations— just as if he'd also used makeup on his arms.

Why would he change the shade of his skin tone all over his body?

He had probably forgotten to put makeup on his ear, and if he hadn't, she might not have noticed it. But then again, she might have, since the shade of his arms was so unnaturally even.

But what was the point?

His pale skin, haircut, and clothing made him appear to be just like any of the other Japanese tourists walking around the shopping center. She wouldn't have been able to pick him out of a busload of visitors straight from Tokyo.

What was going on?

She didn't realize she was leaning in even closer and staring fixedly at his face until he cleared his throat, his eyes blinking rapidly several times. But he still didn't look at her. Instead, he zipped away to the far end of the display table where Waite and Creepy Customer #1 were still talking in hushed tones like women gossiping in the grocery store.

Mimi followed at a more sedate pace, although she felt a bit like a hunter stalking a deer.

Creepy Customer #2 had wandered closer to Waite and Creepy Customer #1, but just far enough away to not be rude. Mimi realized that he provided her the perfect opportunity to get closer to Waite and overhear the conversation.

Creepy Customer #2 seemed to be staring at the lotion on the table. That meant he was interested in it, right?

Mimi decided he must be absolutely obsessed with it. She stepped closer. "Would you like to try a sample of that lotion, sir?"

He glanced up at her, and when she caught the surprised look in his eyes, she again had that strange sensation that she knew him. But all too quickly, he looked back down at the lotion. After a few moments, he muttered, "Sure."

Mimi held up the sample tube and motioned toward his hand, which he extended, palm up. As she squirted some lotion, she noticed callouses on his fingers and palm.

He had held out his right hand, which she assumed was his dominant hand. There were small callouses on his index finger and, to a lesser extent, his middle finger. Thicker callouses clustered at the base of his fingers and in the webbing between his thumb and index finger, and the texture of his palm was tough and rough.

She had seen that particular pattern of callouses before—on the hand of Bernardo, the son of Mimi's cousin Melinda.

Bernardo was a policeman.

Her entire body tensed as if a live current was coursing through her. She could only stand there stiffly as Creepy-Customer-Who-Uses-Guns calmly smoothed lotion on his hands.

She was right, however, and drawing closer to the customer now enabled her to hear snatches of words from Waite's conversation.

"… break out …" Creepy Customer #1 muttered softly, and she couldn't hear his entire sentence.

It was the same for Waite's reply. " … how much …"

The customer paused, then shrugged. "Normal amount?"

Mimi couldn't hear anything useful, and the little she could hear sounded vaguely criminal. She took a step closer to them under the pretext of giving space to Creepy-Customer-Who-Might-Be-a-Cop-or-a-Criminal.

Waite seemed to be thinking for a moment, then he asked, "Did she apply about the same amount you'd use when applying sunscreen lotion?"

Creepy Customer #1 considered it, then said, "No, maybe a bit less."

"Hmm," Waite said. "Sometimes using too much lotion with certain botanicals can irritate your skin, but if your wife didn't apply a lot and she still broke out in a rash, then she probably is a bit sensitive to something in it. I can suggest this line of products …" He pointed to some lotions on the far end of the display table.

Mimi felt vaguely let down. Only *she* would take a normal conversation about a wife's allergic reaction to some other product and turn it into plans to rob a bank.

That was why the conversation had seemed so serious—the customer was trying to be careful about what he bought for her. It still didn't explain his impression of windshield wipers going back and forth in front of the store, but maybe he had a good reason to wait for the store to empty before he entered it.

Just as she downgraded Creepy Customer #1 to Peculiar Customer #1 in her mind, Creepy Customer Cop/Criminal suddenly straightened. "Thank you," he muttered curtly, then walked out of the store.

She stared at him as the doors closed and he turned toward the center of the shopping center. It was almost as if Creepy Customer Cop/Criminal had come into the store simply to try to overhear the conversation between Waite and Peculiar Customer.

No, she must have been imagining things. Except … why had he worn makeup all over his exposed skin?

Mimi didn't have any other excuse to remain standing near Waite, so she returned to her station at the other display table. Within a few minutes, Peculiar Customer had bought a line of lotions and left the store. It had been simply a normal transaction.

She hurried up to Waite so she could talk to him before another customer came in. "Do you know why that guy waited until the store was empty to come talk to you?"

Waite blinked at her in surprise at her abrupt question. "Uh … he did?"

"Yes, he did," she said impatiently.

"Uh … I don't know. He didn't say."

"Was he …" What would make a customer act like a spy meeting his secret contact? "… embarrassed to be in here?" It was a predominantly female sort of store, after all.

Waite shrugged. "Maybe? He just seemed worried about his wife."

Mimi was about to ask him something else when a pair of

women entered the store. She had to break off her conversation to turn to them with a smile and welcome them.

While she assisted one woman, she eyed Waite as he assisted the other. Had Creepy Customer Cop/Criminal entered the store because he was interested in Peculiar Customer or Waite?

She didn't know Waite very well, and she was concerned about whatever that was that had just happened. Or was she just being paranoid because of all the problems her aunt had been having lately with her staff?

Still, Mimi couldn't dismiss the uncomfortable feeling she had. What had Waite gotten into?

4

Mimi considered telling Trinda about the two strange customers today, but in the end, she didn't. Mostly because when she thought about what she'd say, she realized she sounded like one of her crazy, embarrassing aunts whom everyone avoids at family parties.

Mimi's shift ended earlier than the other employees because she'd gotten up early to help Auntie Noriko make lotions in the stillroom before coming to work at the shop. But today she stayed after her shift ended and helped out in the retail area so that Trinda could finish the paperwork she had to do. When Auntie Noriko arrived at five o'clock to manage the store for the last few hours, Mimi left with Trinda.

They headed to where they'd parked their cars in the employee parking area.

"How did things go today?" Trinda asked.

"Well, I didn't bite anyone."

Trinda laughed. "It's only the first day. You got your rabies shot, right?"

"Hey! I'm not *diseased*. How do you think I did? You know,

compared to your *regular employees.*" Maybe Mimi could subtly bring up Waite.

"It was like when Paulette subs in to help out. Except that your Japanese doesn't sound like you've got fizzy candy in your mouth."

"Wow, she's that bad, huh? The new employees seem to speak it pretty well, though. How long have they been here?"

Trinda paused to think. "Effie was hired in the spring and Waite in the summer." Mimi didn't miss the fact that she grimaced slightly as she said his name. "And you met Gladys when she arrived for the late shift—she was hired at the same time as Effie. The one you haven't met is Flora—she's another part-timer who comes in on weekends. She was hired just last month."

"Everyone is entirely new from the last time I worked at the shop. Auntie said there were problems with laziness and stealing?"

Trinda sighed and rolled her eyes. "Mom has too soft a heart and kept giving them second, third, fourth chances. I finally told her that they needed to be fired and I'd do it for her if she wanted."

"I'm sorry."

Trinda shook her head. "It had to be done. But I made sure to help conduct the interviews for the new employees."

"What do you think of them?"

"Well … there are a couple people I wouldn't have hired, but I understand why Mom chose the ones she did."

Was Waite one of those?

Trinda went on to ask, "What did you think of them compared to the employees from the last time you worked at the store?"

"It's been a couple of years since then. I remember the old employees were friendly to the customers, but not very attentive. Effie and Waite seem more capable and professional. Effie is very active in serving the customers. Waite is … polite. He doesn't ignore the customers, but he's not overly outgoing and considerate, either."

Trinda nodded. "They're both better than the old employees, at least."

Mimi was going to ask more about Waite when Trinda got a text on her phone and slowed her pace to answer it.

They had already reached the parking garage, and Mimi wanted to ask about Tosh while they were alone (in other words, without Auntie Noriko around).

As soon as Trinda put her phone away, Mimi asked, "Do you remember the Kusunokis who lived down the street from you?"

Trinda frowned as she tried to remember. "I think so. They had two kids, right?"

"Tosh and Tomoko. You went to Laniloa Academy with them, didn't you?"

"Yeah, but Tosh was older than me while his sister was younger. Our classroom buildings were completely different, so I never interacted with them at school."

When Tosh's family moved away, Trinda would have been in seventh grade at the private school while Tosh would have been in high school.

"I'm trying to get in touch with Tosh again. I have a book I need to return to him."

"Hmm." Trinda's brow furrowed as she thought. "I could try asking my friend Kelani. You know her, right?"

"Yeah. I haven't seen her in a few years." Kelani, Trinda's classmate, was the kind of outgoing person who knew a lot of people. "But she's your age, right? Do you think she knows Tosh?"

"She might, but I was thinking more of her two older siblings. I think they're a couple years older than Tosh, but they're pretty sociable. They might know what happened to him, or they might know who to ask about it. Let me message her."

Trinda stopped walking to type out a message on her phone. Mimi stood nearby, looking around, and happened to notice Waite.

He'd left a few minutes before they did, so she had assumed he'd be long gone by now, but he was talking to someone on his phone as he opened his car door. He was some distance away so Mimi couldn't hear what he was saying, but it was obvious from his thunderous expression and the way he was shouting that he was arguing with whoever called him. The inarticulate sounds of his anger echoed in the covered parking garage.

Waite hadn't noticed her and Trinda, but Mimi took a step to the side so that she was partially shielded by one of the concrete weight-bearing pillars. She also managed to nudge Trinda (who didn't look up from her phone) so she'd be out of sight, too.

It was only because Mimi had moved that she noticed the other man.

He was casually leaning against another cement pillar behind Waite, but because of the angle, even if Waite turned around, the man would probably be just out of his sight. Something about him reminded her of the man with makeup on from earlier that day, although everything about him was different.

His long hair was that orangish color that results when Asian black hair is bleached badly, and it swirled around his face like feathers in the light breeze. He wore large dark glasses and had an expression on his face that said either, *I'm too cool to speak to you,* or *If you so much as look at me funny I'll pull a katana out of my trenchcoat and decapitate you.* Not that he wore a trenchcoat, which would have been ridiculous in the hot Hawaiian weather, although it would have matched his black jeans, biker boots, and black T-shirt.

He also didn't have the other man's overbite or round cheeks—he had a long face, hollow cheeks, and a small, mean-looking mouth—and yet she couldn't shake the feeling that he was just like the man from earlier.

But why would the same man change clothes and put on a wig … unless it had something to do with Waite?

The Wannabe Yakuza didn't seem to be paying any attention to Waite, even though he likely was close enough to overhear the argument. Instead, he ignored everything as he casually lounged against a pillar.

"Is that Waite?" Trinda asked, her voice hushed. She had moved so that she was even further blocked by the pillar that Mimi was cowering behind.

"I think so." Mimi matched her low tone. "How much do you know about him?"

Trinda gave another grimace just like the one she made before when she mentioned Waite being hired. "I wouldn't have hired him because he didn't have much experience in retail, and at the interview, he seemed kind of apathetic about the store. It was like he only wanted a job and it didn't matter where. But Mom knows Waite's auntie and hired him as a favor to her."

"Oh, I see."

"But to be fair, he's been a decent employee. He arrives on time and doesn't try to leave early or take long lunch breaks. He's competent and responsible. He's not quite as outgoing as some of the others, but some customers like his quiet nature and keep coming back to him when they revisit the store."

Mimi looked at her and felt kind of silly to be hiding behind a pillar, but there was no way—no way!—she'd walk out there for Waite to notice her when he was obviously having a fight with someone.

And while a small part of her did want to get closer to that Wannabe Yakuza to see if he looked like the Creepy Customer Cop/Criminal from earlier, well ... *wannabe Yakuza*. She hadn't lost all sense of self-preservation.

Waite had sat in the driver's seat with his window down to let the hot air out of his car, which made it obvious he was continuing the argument. But suddenly he shouted something and disconnected the call. Within a few minutes, he'd started the engine and peeled out of the parking lot with a squeal of tires.

Mimi released a sigh of relief. But then she remembered Wannabe Yakuza and hesitated in moving toward her car.

Trinda had no concerns and started marching toward the monstrosity that she called an SUV. Mimi had to hurry after her before she noticed her strange behavior.

The man was gone from the pillar. When had he left? Now she just felt stupid.

Her cousin suddenly pulled out her phone and read a message. "Oh, Kelani texted me already. She says it's okay for you to call her."

"Great. Thanks."

Mimi inputted the number into her phone, then waved goodbye to Trinda as she drove away.

She sat in her parked car—an ancient pickup truck with a

manual stick shift that stuck as if she was trying to stir mochi. She had borrowed it from one of her cousins living in Hawaii, but she was seriously reconsidering just marching into a car rental place and slapping down her credit card for something automatic. With a better air conditioner.

The handle to lower the window was a harder workout than at the gym, and she was bathed in sweat before she got it down. Then she crawled over to lower the other window to try to get a cross breeze and blow the hot air out of the cab.

She dialed the number and Kelani picked up right away. "Hi, Mimi! It's been a while. How've you been?"

Mimi had seen a lot of Kelani when she and Trinda hung out with the same group of people in high school, but the two hadn't been as close after graduating, so in the years since, Mimi had only happened to run into her once or twice during her trips to Hawaii. But Kelani's chatter was bright and warm, as if they'd only seen each other last month.

After filling Kelani in with her plans to help Auntie Noriko for a couple of months, Mimi said, "At Auntie's house, I found an old book I borrowed from Toshiro Kusunoki back in high school that I want to get back to him. Do you happen to know how to get a hold of him now?"

"Tosh?" Kelani's voice suddenly took on a subdued tone. "I wasn't that close to him, but my older sister was in the drama club with him. I guess you didn't hear what happened to him?"

A pain seemed to stab her in the heart and begin to spread like cracks in a mirror. "What happened? Did he ... pass away or something?"

"No, but ... in his Junior year in high school, his father caused a car accident and killed a girl."

"No way ..." Mimi's throat was dry. On the one hand, her worst fear hadn't come true, but on the other, the truth was even more awful.

"His dad died a few days later, and Tosh and his sister left Laniloa Academy to go to another school. My sister lost touch with him."

"Oh. So she doesn't have his number?"

"No, but ..." Kelani's voice took on a brighter tone. "I think I know someone who might. Last year, my sister's friend Minnie Chou posted a photo on social media, and she was with her boyfriend and Tosh."

"You're sure it was him?"

"Not unless a second Toshiro Kusunoki is hanging around."

"Yeah, his surname's not all that common in Hawaii."

"The only reason I even saw the photo is because my sister saw it and commented that she went to school with Tosh. I remembered him because of the whole scandal with his father."

"Did Tosh comment on the photo, too?" Maybe she could somehow find his social media profile. Mimi had looked Tosh's name up online last night, but strangely she hadn't found any social media accounts that seemed to belong to him.

"No, but Minnie replied that her boyfriend used to work with Tosh. I can ask my sister to get in touch with Minnie for you, but there's a faster way. I looked up Minnie's social media profile and she works at Kukui Cove—it's a Hawaiian wear store in Honolulu. If you call the store or drop by, you might catch her there or at least find out when she'll be working next."

"Thank you so much, Kelani."

"No problem! Let's get together for drinks or something before you leave."

Mimi agreed and hung up. In many ways, Kelani's friendliness reminded her of her cousin Trish. When they were younger, Mimi hadn't gotten along with Trish—as in, a lion and hyena level of not-love—but she'd secretly always admired how Trish's outgoing nature always made people feel welcome and included.

Except, of course, for Mimi. She couldn't blame Trish for some of their antipathy—Mimi had both accidentally and also deliberately stolen a few of Trish's love interests. She hadn't had a good explanation for why except for the perverse reason that she could.

Their relationship improved after Mimi had offered a place to stay for Lex and had then started working for Jenn, both of them

Trish's close cousins. She knew Trish wasn't the type to hold grudges, but she knew they'd never be close because of the conflicts of the past that stood between them.

It was another reminder of how there were so many things in Mimi's past that she regretted. So many things that made her ashamed of who she had been, and that made her doubt if she had grown wiser or better. Maybe all she'd grown was older.

Now she was just wallowing in negativity. She had more important things to do.

She looked up Kukui Cove on her phone and called the store.

"Hello, Kukui Cove."

"Hi, I'm looking for Minnie Chou."

A short pause, then, "This is Minnie."

What luck! "My name is Mimi Sakai. I'm sorry to call you like this, but Kelani Johnson suggested I contact you."

"Oh?" The voice was a bit less wary.

"I need to return something to Toshiro Kusunoki. Kelani said your boyfriend used to work with him and might know how to get in touch with him again."

"Oh, Tosh! I haven't talked to him in months. Sure, I can ask Raymond about him. Oh, I know what'll be better—I'm meeting Raymond for dinner when I get off work. Why don't you join us?"

Minnie's chattiness made Mimi feel a bit like she had verbal whiplash, but it was better than being stonewalled. "I don't want to interrupt your date or anything."

"I'll ask him first, but I'm sure he won't mind. Plus we're eating at a Filipino food truck, so nothing fancy. I get off in thirty minutes. Is that okay?"

"Sure. Thanks a bunch."

"Oh, don't worry about it. What's your number?" After Mimi gave it to her, Minnie added, "It'll be good for Tosh to reconnect with old friends. From what Ray says about him, he hasn't been doing so good."

Wait, what? "What do you m—"

"I'll talk to Ray and then text you. Bye!"

Mimi stared in confusion at her phone for a long minute. After what she'd just learned about Tosh's father, Minnie's description of him concerned her.

She had been looking forward to meeting Tosh again, but now she wasn't so sure he'd be the same boy she remembered. And after she had hurt him, would he even want to see her?

5

Minnie had texted Mimi with the address of a food truck called Elenita's, which was parked near Sandy Beach. It was a little far from Ala Moana, so when she finally found parking and made it to the truck, she was a few minutes late.

She had told Minnie what she was wearing, and as she approached the truck, a woman standing at the front of the line smiled and waved at her. She had long, dark, curly hair and a bright yellow T-shirt with "Kukui Cove" on the front in a fancy graphic design. Next to her stood a shorter Asian man with features that reminded Mimi of her Uncle Howard—largish nose and kind eyes under thick, slightly wavy hair.

As she approached the truck, she belatedly realized she should have taken a few minutes while she was in the parking garage at Ala Moana to strip off the confining pantyhose, but it was too late now. Luckily, there was a breeze blowing off the ocean that made her butt a bit less sweaty.

"You're Mimi, right?" Minnie said as she approached. "Good timing. What do you want to eat?"

Mimi glanced at the menu, which was largely Filipino food. "What do you suggest?"

"Adobo fried rice."

"I'll get that then." Mimi dug in her purse for some cash.

Minnie waved it away despite Mimi's protests. "No worries. Ray already said he'd pay for it. This is my fiancé, Raymond. Ray, this is Mimi, Kelani's friend."

"Nice to meet you," Raymond replied with a toothy smile.

"Hi," Mimi said. Kelani had said he was her boyfriend, not her fiancé. "Congratulations. When's the wedding?"

"Thanks!" Minnie said. "Not until late next year. We're still trying to figure out the venue."

The food arrived quickly, and the three of them walked the short distance to a nearby beach, which had fewer tourists since the shoreline was all black rocks. They were able to find a spot on the small stretch of sand above the high-tide line, and Raymond had brought a foldable stadium blanket to spread out for them to sit on.

It was a little awkward for Mimi to sit down with her skirt, but once she did, she paused to look out onto the water. Here on the south side of Oahu, the waves were smaller during the winter, but the fresh air coming from the ocean seemed heavier with salt at this time of year. She could smell the seaweed from the debris line, although it seemed a little less pungent. All she could hear were the waves, which drowned out the sounds of traffic from the nearby boulevard.

Minnie and her fiancé were already digging in—they had apparently all gotten the same dish. "What do you think?" Minnie asked her.

The adobo fried rice was covered with a thin, smooth layer of scrambled eggs, similar to Japanese *omurice*, but without the ketchup on top of the eggs and with lots of chunks of pork adobo in the fried rice. The braised meat was incredibly tender and full of flavor.

"Wow, this is good adobo," Mimi said.

"I know, right? This is our favorite place to eat." Minnie turned to Raymond. "Mimi had some questions about Tosh."

"His family used to live near my aunt, and I have an expensive book I need to return to him, but I lost touch after he moved. I'd like to get a hold of him."

"Do you have his number?" Minnie asked her fiancé.

Raymond looked confused. "No, why should I?"

"What do you mean?" Minnie asked. "You worked with him, didn't you?"

"Well, yeah ..." Raymond put down his wooden disposable chopsticks and turned to Mimi. "I work in accounting at Kahiko Gemstones, and Tosh was in security, but he was laid off two years ago because of budget cuts."

"Has it already been two years?" Minnie paused in her eating to think. "It didn't seem that long, I guess because I saw him a few months ago." She told Mimi, "Tosh happened to see us at a restaurant and came up to say hi."

"You're the one who invited him to come sit and eat with us." Raymond's voice was a bit sulky.

Minnie didn't even try to avoid the issue. "What's the matter? It's like you don't want to talk about Tosh."

Raymond heaved a sigh so large it seemed to come up from the pits of his stomach. "Well ... I think he had a crush on you."

"What?" Minnie and Mimi said at the same time.

Raymond only sighed again.

Minnie recovered from her shock first. "No, no way." She gave a little laugh.

But Mimi wasn't quite ready to scoff at the idea. Minnie was tall and slender, with a cute round face and freckles. Pair that with her outgoing, friendly personality, and Mimi could see how any guy would have been attracted to her, but especially the quiet boy she'd known.

"You always got along well with Tosh," Raymond said.

"He's easy to talk to—he listens and he asks intelligent questions —but I never flirted with him."

"You were always friendly with him."

"I was never overly friendly," Minnie shot back, irritation sharpening her voice. "Why would you think I was encouraging him?"

"I didn't, not really, but ... well ..." Raymond seemed to be having a hard time putting his thoughts and feelings into words, but to Minnie's credit, she stopped and waited for him to answer. He finally said, "Tosh is athletic and confident. If he'd thought he had a chance ..."

Athletic and confident? *Tosh?* Mimi stared at Raymond as hard as Minnie was doing. Were they talking about the same person?

"So? What does that have to do with anything?" Minnie demanded. "Did you ask me out just so that Tosh wouldn't have me, or something stupid and caveman like that?"

"No! It's just that I've loved you since we were both dorky freshmen in high school. I know the person you are inside, both your strengths and your flaws, and I love you for all of it."

In a flash, Minnie's anger evaporated and she beamed at him. "That's so romantic!" She threw her arms around him and kissed him.

Forgotten by the two lovebirds, Mimi sighed gustily.

Raymond's impassioned declaration had been a bit awkward, but she could tell it had also been entirely heartfelt. She was happy that Minnie seemed to appreciate such a sincere guy, but she also felt a bit depressed.

She'd dated a lot of guys, but she'd never found one she liked so much that she wanted to know who they were inside, their strengths and flaws. And she'd never found one who had wanted to do the same for her. Her relationships had all been relatively short—the longest had been a year. She didn't even know if she was capable of loving someone for so long, like Raymond loved Minnie.

Was it simply that she hadn't bothered to try to make the effort to get to know one of those guys better? It didn't help that she hadn't chosen her boyfriends very well, and maybe that's why she hadn't wanted a deeper relationship with any of them.

What had she been doing with her life? Why had she wasted so much time in frivolous pursuits? And while she regretted her past self, she'd come to realize that it was too late for her by now. She was getting older.

Good, single men whom she might seriously consider as potential partners seemed to be scarce—they all seemed to have too much relationship baggage. Mimi simply didn't want to have to deal with that because she had enough stress from her relationship with her family. There was also the fact that she hadn't liked anyone enough to want to tackle another person's concerns. She had talked about this issue with Jenn several times, mostly right after breaking up with someone after discovering something like two nasty divorces and four kids he never saw, or a rather disturbing slavish devotion to his mother.

Jenn had told her that God forgives our past mistakes and doesn't hold grudges against us for past behavior. It should have made Mimi feel better, but somehow it was too difficult to believe. While God might not punish her for her past, she also knew she still had to face the consequences of her actions. Maybe her loneliness now was simply a consequence.

The couple's romantic nothings were becoming too sickly sweet for her to withstand. Mimi coughed once, then again more loudly. Finally, she reached out a stockinged toe and prodded Minnie's butt.

"Oh, sorry," Minnie said with a giggle. In contrast, Raymond remembered Mimi's presence, and his face turned bright red.

Well, that was his fault for saying something so adorably earnest to his fiancée and making Mimi feel like a cobweb-coated spinster. She cleared her throat. "So … Tosh?"

Raymond's expression grew uncomfortable again, but it seemed to be for a different reason this time. "Did you know about Tosh's father?"

"Kelani mentioned he got into a car accident and, uh, killed a girl."

"It's a bit worse than that," Raymond said. "I made the mistake of teasing Tosh about something when we were out to lunch one day, and he kind of reluctantly told me that his dad fell asleep at the wheel and happened to kill Tosh's girlfriend at the time."

Minnie gasped.

Mimi froze in horror. "His girlfriend?" she asked.

Raymond nodded sadly. "It explained a lot about what happened to Tosh. His dad died a few days later from his injuries, and things were really tough for his family. So they moved from Honolulu to live with his uncle in Haleiwa."

"I can imagine the gossip about his father killing a young girl must have been awful," Minnie said. "It's too bad they had to move."

"Tosh said it wasn't too bad. He's grateful to his uncle for helping the family out and taking care of them while he was in the National Guard."

"He joined the National Guard?" Mimi asked. She remembered Tosh hadn't been a jock, but then again, he also hadn't been unhealthy. He had enjoyed doing drama, and while he couldn't dance, he had been comfortable enough in his body to carry himself well on stage.

"Right out of high school," Raymond said. "He went to college after that and got the job at Kahiko Gemstones."

"You two hung out together, but you didn't get his phone number?" Minnie asked.

"We went out to lunch and for drinks after work a few times, but we weren't all that close. Actually ..." Raymond grimaced. "We probably didn't get as close as we might have after you started joining us for drinks."

Minnie protested, "I never encouraged him."

"I know, I know." Raymond looked faintly ashamed. "But I was still secretly a little relieved when Tosh was laid off, and we stopped hanging out."

Mimi started to wonder if she'd get any information about how to contact Tosh now since she couldn't see Raymond keeping in touch with a guy he thought had a crush on his fiancé. "So you don't know how I can get a hold of him?"

"No, but ... one or two months ago, I saw Tosh."

Minnie nodded. "Ray told me about it. It was in Haleiwa, right?" she asked him.

"At the Molokai Red Restaurant. Our department had a retirement party there for one of my coworkers, and Tosh was working as a waiter. He told me his uncle owned the restaurant."

"The uncle his family moved in with?" Mimi asked.

"Yeah. The restaurant's been getting more popular since it was featured in some online articles and blogs."

Mimi was relieved his family seemed to be doing well. At first, it sounded troubling that Tosh had gone from doing security at a big company in Honolulu to being a waiter, but it sounded like the restaurant was successful.

"The Molokai Red Restaurant?" Mimi asked. "I could stop by tomorrow night to see if he's working."

Raymond's brow furrowed. "I don't know if you want to see him."

"No, I think it will be good for Tosh," Minnie said to him.

"What do you mean?" Mimi asked.

"When I saw him," Raymond said, "he'd lost a lot of weight, and it looked like he wasn't sleeping well—he had bags under his eyes, and he seemed kind of worn down."

Privately, Mimi thought that didn't sound much different from how Tosh used to look after he'd stayed up too late reading manga or light novels.

Raymond continued, "He was different from how he used to be when he worked at my company—he was always kind of quiet, but he used to be cheerful and confident. I was shocked when I saw him."

"What happened to him?" Mimi asked.

Raymond shook his head. "I didn't have much time to talk to him, and I didn't know if I wanted to ask him. He looked in bad shape emotionally."

Had something terrible happened to him to change him so drastically?

"I don't think you should go see him," Raymond said.

"I think it's even more important for Mimi to go see him," Minnie said. "He might need a friendly face."

Mimi squirmed uncomfortably in her seat. The sight of her was more likely to make his sanity snap, and he'd start throwing olives and little paper umbrellas at her.

"No, he's probably really changed from when Mimi knew him in high school," Raymond said. "It might be better for her just to remember the fun times they had as kids."

"That's Mimi's choice to make," Minnie said.

All she had wanted was a way to contact Tosh, but now she was even more worried about what she'd find when she finally talked to him.

"I have to see him," Mimi finally said. "The book I borrowed is really expensive, and I don't feel right keeping it."

The book seemed to be a reasonable enough excuse for the two of them, and Minnie changed the subject, asking about Mimi's job. She told them about visiting from California and took the opportunity to plug her aunt's store.

But she knew that the book wasn't the real reason she needed to see Tosh, no matter how much he might have changed. She had hurt him all those years ago, and that book seemed to draw all her regret up to the surface of her mind, like petroleum sludge on water.

She needed to finally apologize to Tosh for how she treated him the last time they spoke. She needed to clean away the sludge of regret.

And then she'd never see him again.

6

Mimi stood there frozen, staring at the bartender and trying not to freak out.

That was Tosh! He had been at the store yesterday. He had been at the store *in disguise* yesterday. What was going on?

How had she not known it was him when she first saw him? She had always been good with faces and names, and she never thought she'd fail to recognize someone, even if they did have makeup on. He'd had an overbite and a rounded face yesterday, too—probably false teeth, a flexing of his jaw, and something stuffed in his cheeks to balloon them out. Was that why she hadn't realized it was Tosh?

He hadn't recognized her, either. Or at least, he hadn't greeted her by name. Did the reason he was in disguise have something to do with that?

Or was it that she'd just changed so much?

She was frustrated to have so many unanswered questions, so she stomped rather than walked up to the bar and sat down, waiting for him to finish serving another customer. He seemed to be taking an inordinately long time, chatting casually with the man long after serving his drink.

If she was a suspicious sort of person (which she *totally* was), she'd think Tosh was trying to avoid her.

Finally, the customer left the bar with his drink, and Tosh came up to Mimi, a polite smile on his face. "How can I help you?"

"It's me, Mimi. Do you remember me?" She had been trying for a bright, friendly voice, but her jaw was clenched, so she probably sounded like she was chewing on tacks.

Or that she wanted to punch him in the face. Which she kind of did.

He gave an exaggerated start of surprise. "Mimi! Hey, it's been a while."

That's when she knew she had been right, and something was up.

While Tosh liked theater, he wasn't an incredible actor. He certainly hadn't been terrible, but he didn't have the presence or personality to be a powerful leading man (and, being Japanese, he was a bit shorter than average, so some actresses towered over him and treated him a bit like a pet).

His strength was in supporting roles, making himself almost invisible on stage to emphasize the leading actors. His best role had been in a murder mystery where he played the villain, skillfully making himself almost disappear amongst the ensemble cast and surprising everyone in the audience when he was finally revealed.

So it was his mediocre acting, or maybe it was because Mimi had known him so well, but she immediately knew something fishy was going on. His surprise looked entirely natural at first glance, but something about his eyes gave him away.

Now that she thought about it, after he came into the store, he'd stared at her for a moment right after she'd greeted him.

She planted her hands on the smooth wood surface of the bar and leaned forward, skewering him with her glare. (Unfortunately, she probably looked like a little kid having a tantrum.) "Did you recognize me when you came into the store earlier?"

"What? What store?" He tried to look confused but failed.

"Why did you have a wig on? And makeup? And you did something to your jaw and mouth."

"I don't know what you're talking about."

She gave him a flat look. "I might have been inattentive at the time, but I'm not stupid. I know you came into my aunt's cosmetics store yesterday. You should have told me it was you."

Or had he not identified himself because he hadn't wanted to talk to her? She paused.

Why hadn't she thought of that before she shot off her mouth? She seriously needed a muzzle.

He took a step back away from the crazy woman (probably a wise thing to do), but then his gaze flickered behind her, and he tensed. Tosh suddenly whirled, and she got an eyeful of the back of his shoulder.

She was about to hiss at him to demand what he was doing, but then she realized what was going on. She inhaled and casually turned around, surveying the rest of the lounge area.

It didn't take her long to spot her coworker, Waite, as he entered the room with a shorter, younger man.

Mimi wanted to whirl around as fast as Tosh had done, but she forced herself to move slowly, although she twisted her head away first to hide her face.

"Why is Waite here?" she hissed at his deltoid.

"Why are you asking me?" he hissed back, although since his back was turned toward her, it sounded like his voice was coming from his armpit.

"And why are you panicked about it?"

"Why are *you* panicked about it?"

Actually, that was a good point. "I'm going to go say hi."

"No, wait!" He pivoted slightly so that he could grab her wrist to stop her. "Follow me into the back," he said tersely, then walked away toward a door behind the bar.

Mimi slid off the barstool and followed him along the outside of the long counter. It was not enclosed at the end, and there was an opening for her to slip through and into a door marked Employees Only.

The storeroom was brighter and quite a bit cooler than the lounge area, lined with metal racks of bottles and cases of wine. A narrow aisle between the racks led to a section at the back of the room where she could see a round table surrounded by chairs and a short counter against the wall with a microwave, a toaster oven, and a sink.

Mimi remained a few steps beyond the door after Tosh closed it behind her. "What's going on?" she demanded, then thrust a finger at Tosh's face. "And if you lie, I'll poke my finger up your nose like I used to."

He jerked his head back. "You're so immature!"

"I'm entitled to be! You came into my auntie's store in disguise like *Mission: Impossible!*" She gasped. "Are you a spy?"

"I'm not a spy!" But then he paused and his eyes slid away from hers, just a fraction.

"You *are* a spy!"

"I'm not a spy and I wasn't at your auntie's store."

"Don't bother to deny it when my coworker just appeared in your lounge!"

"It's not my lounge, it belongs to my uncle."

She threw out her hands in frustration, picturing strangling him. Then she took a breath and put her hands on her hips. "I'm going out there to ask Waite about you." She turned around, but he grabbed her elbow.

"I was hired by a private investigator," he said quickly.

Mimi studied him, raising an eyebrow. "Why would a private investigator hire *you*?"

Tosh looked down at himself. "What's wrong with me?"

"Well, you're not exactly Academy Award material."

"Rude! I played a great—"

"I don't want to hear yet again about your brilliant performance as a *murderer*."

He paused. "Okay, fair enough. Look, I work for a security consulting firm called Mahina Security. One of our clients is a PI who sometimes hires me to shadow people because I'm good at not being noticed."

That made sense. Tosh had worked in security at Kahiko Gemstones, and he had experience acting. She had just been thinking about how he could make himself almost disappear on stage. "That's why you were in disguise?" she asked.

"I was hired to shadow Waite and try to overhear conversations with suspicious people who talk to him."

"You were staking out my auntie's store all day?"

"It's not that hard. The front walls are all glass, and I can see anyone who talks to him and take photos of them."

She remembered the man who had been talking to Waite when Tosh came into the store. "Did you know that customer who kept walking back and forth in front of the store before he came inside?"

Tosh shook his head. "His behavior was suspicious, so I took a chance and went inside to try to overhear them."

She suddenly remembered the parking lot. "Waite was arguing with someone on the phone in the parking lot. Were you that emo Yakuza wannabe behind the pillar?"

"I was not an emo Yakuza!"

She smirked at him.

He sighed gustily and dropped his head, letting it hang in defeat. "Why, yes, I was the long-haired man—wait a minute! How did you know it was me? You were too far away to see my face clearly."

Mimi wasn't about to admit that she recognized the shape of his body. "I didn't know at first, since your hair and clothes were different, but the way you, uh, slouched reminded me of the customer who came into the store."

"You recognized me as two complete strangers, but you didn't recognize me as me?"

She untangled that question and bit her lip. Yeah, that was kind of awful of her. "When I first saw you, you looked so different. You were like a pale vampire with an eating problem."

"What?"

Mimi stuck her teeth out at him. "Overbite. By the way, next time remember that people are paler on their underarms."

Tosh looked at his arms, then grimaced. "Oh. Good point."

"And don't forget to put makeup on your ears."

"You were suspicious of me because of my *ears*? Why were you looking at my ears?"

"I wasn't looking at your ears!" Except she kind of had been. "Well, maybe I was. But remember, vampire with an eating problem? Who wouldn't be suspicious?"

"Nearly every person who passed by me at Ala Moana." He gave her a superior smile that made her want to smack it off his face.

"Okay, vampire with an eating problem who walked into a cosmetics store."

He opened his mouth and stuck his finger out at her, but then stopped and snapped his mouth shut. "Okay, yeah, that does sound kind of weird."

"It was creepy! You were a creepy customer." She remembered the moment he first saw her. "Did you recognize me when you walked in?"

He winced as he scratched the back of his head, and only then did she notice the huge muscles of his triceps. "I didn't know you were working there because I couldn't see you clearly from outside the store. You were standing on the side, behind those potted plants."

And unfortunately, some of the potted plants were taller than she was.

"I pretended not to know you because I was working," Tosh continued. "I was relieved you didn't recognize me and blow my cover—it would have ruined my job of shadowing Waite."

His words might have been meant to make her feel better, but they only caused a heaviness in her chest, like a sopping wet beach towel. They'd known each other for so many years, and she should have known him instantly.

While it might be true that he was glad she didn't recognize him and jeopardize his case, was he also perhaps glad she didn't recognize him because he didn't want to talk to her? She wouldn't blame him if he felt that way.

"Why were *you* the one hired to shadow him?" she asked Tosh. "Why couldn't the PI do it?"

"Because your auntie knows her. The PI's a customer of the store."

That threw her for a little bit of a loop. "I guess I never considered that PIs need facial lotion."

"She runs a day spa in Waialua and they use some of your auntie's products. But yes, she also uses her facial lotions."

So that's why the PI hired someone else to do this kind of work. "What were you shadowing Waite for, anyway?"

He stilled, and his face grew serious. "I'm not allowed to say. I've probably already said too much."

"Oh. Yeah." She glanced back at the closed door to the storeroom. "I'm sorry for interfering with your undercover work."

"Technically, I'm not supposed to be following Waite right now. It's my undercover work that's interfering with my job working the bar tonight."

"Do you know that man with Waite right now?"

Tosh raised his eyebrows at her. "Wouldn't you know better since you work with him?"

"He's been my coworker for all of two days!"

"Oh." Tosh's gaze wandered away from hers. "When did you fly into Hawaii?"

"Three days ago."

His brow furrowed as his attention snapped back to her face. "Your auntie put you to work the day after you arrived?"

"That's the whole point of my coming to Hawaii this time, to help her out."

"Oh," he said sheepishly. "Uh, no, I don't know that guy."

"You were in disguise in the store. You can't just go out there to listen in on them?"

He gave her an incredulous look. "Why do you think I ducked into the storeroom—to commune with the mezcal? I had to avoid being seen. I can't risk having Waite recognizing me because I still have to follow him for the next few days, too."

Mimi probably wouldn't have even considered the insane idea in her head if she hadn't been concerned about her auntie's staffing problems. But she was alarmed that Tosh's PI was investigating Waite for some reason, and she realized she was in a perfect position to help. It might or might not affect Waite's job at Miwaku, but shouldn't she do what she could to ensure Auntie Noriko didn't have any more issues with her employees?

"Wait here," Mimi told him as she unbuttoned the top buttons of her blouse and pulled off the blue vest of her uniform.

"What are you doing?" he demanded.

"Doing you a favor." She rolled up the waistband of her skirt to shorten it and show a bit of thigh, then pulled out her shirt to cover the roll. She cracked her neck and straightened her shoulders.

"Mimi, stop," he said, alarmed.

She ignored him and exited the storeroom.

There was an art to the sashay. She had figured out how to use just enough hip action without looking like she was wiggling her butt, and how to elongate her stride just enough to emphasize the line of her legs. The handles of her designer purse hung off a bent elbow, but she used the line of her hand and forearm to draw the eye to the deep V of her shirt. She walked slowly, coolly, glancing only briefly as men's eyes were drawn to the sinuous line of her body as she passed.

Waite and the man were sitting in comfortable leather chairs with a low table between them. They each had a tumbler of amber liquid in front of them, but they hadn't had time to drink much of it.

Mimi was about to walk completely past the two men when she stopped and pretended to be surprised. "Waite!" She gave a little laugh. "What a coincidence we both came here for dinner tonight."

"Mimi, I didn't realize you'd be here." Waite gave her a polite smile, but it didn't reach his eyes, and his mouth twitched. Was he nervous? Maybe he hadn't wanted to meet anyone he knew, which was why he chose a restaurant in Haleiwa, on the other side of the island from both his work and home.

"Oh, I'm waiting for friends to meet me here." Her gaze shifted to the man sitting with him, and she gave him a slow smile.

He returned the smile. He was younger than Mimi, probably in his late twenties or early thirties, with a mix of ethnicities in his features. He had a wide smile with pleasant laugh lines at the corners, a high, wide forehead, and dark hair shaved at the sides but in tight, short curls on top. He was handsome and he acted like he knew it.

"Hi, I'm Mimi. I'm Waite's new coworker." She dug into her purse and pulled out a business card for Miwaku, which Trinda had made this morning for her at a copy shop.

Her action prompted the man to give her his own card. "Nice to meet you. I'm Ivan."

She glanced at the card. Ivan Vierra, security at Pleiades Resort.

When Mimi looked up, she caught the way Waite's mouth thinned. He was annoyed with her for introducing herself or forcing Ivan to make her acquaintance. Why was that?

To be honest, Waite and Ivan formed a strange couple here in the lounge. Waite had changed out of his uniform into a Hawaiian shirt and dark slacks, so he looked a bit like a businessman, while Ivan dressed in stylish clothing like some of her younger cousins wore when they were going out to a nightclub. Waite wasn't much older than Mimi, but with his narrow face, weak jaw, and thin brown hair, he looked much older. In contrast, Ivan was full of energy, and while not young enough to look like Waite's son, he could be a nephew.

"So how do you know Waite?" Mimi asked Ivan.

"Oh, we happened to meet at a bar—not this one," Ivan said smoothly. "We hit it off right away. We get together for a drink every so often."

"Mimi, I wouldn't want to keep you from your friends," Waite said with forced joviality in his voice.

She could have said she was simply waiting for them, but she didn't want to antagonize him. After all, she'd accomplished her goal.

"Of course. I hope the two of you have a nice dinner." She continued walking, but her slow pace enabled her to overhear Waite's next words to Ivan.

"I'm thinking maybe we should go to a different restaurant," Waite said. "The wait for a table might be too long here."

Maybe she hadn't been as subtle as she thought and her interest in Waite's business with Ivan had scared him off. Or maybe Waite was simply paranoid.

Ivan agreed affably, and the two men drained their drinks. Mimi sat in an empty chair in the lounge area, looking for all the world like a woman simply waiting for her friends to appear. Waite and Ivan passed her chair on their way out the door, and Ivan raised a hand and flashed a smile at her in goodbye. Waite didn't even look at her, simply marching stiffly out of the lounge.

Mimi gazed out the cut glass windows of the lounge to the front of the restaurant, seeing the two men as they made their way down the walkway flanked by hibiscus bushes. Once they were out of sight, she rose and went back to the storeroom.

The door was cracked open and Tosh was watching. He opened the door wider for her, and once it shut behind them, she handed him the business card.

He read the name, then gave her a rueful smile. "I'm impressed despite myself." The dimple at the corner of his mouth flashed, and she realized this was the first genuine smile he'd given to her since she had arrived.

Granted, she'd started their conversation with an accusation, and they'd done nothing but snipe at each other when she wasn't pulling potentially confidential information about his case out of him.

His praise flustered her for some reason. "Never underestimate the power of a cute face and a glimpse of cleavage," she said.

Tosh's face turned lychee red.

She wasn't exposing very much—her bridesmaid's dress for a cousin's wedding had had a neckline that plunged like Niagara Falls —but his embarrassment suddenly made her self-conscious. She hurriedly buttoned her shirt back up. Had she only made things worse between them?

The door to the storeroom flew open, and the female bartender looked in on them. "Tosh! There you are. A large order just came in from the restaurant side."

"I'll be right there." Tosh pocketed the card and glanced at Mimi. "Thanks." Then he was suddenly gone.

She was left alone in the storeroom, feeling a bit awkward to be there. Then she screwed up her face as she realized she hadn't talked to him about the book, much less apologized. She had just been so shocked when she realized he'd come into her aunt's store in disguise, and she reverted to her old habit of saying whatever came to mind when she was with him.

But since he was working, she shouldn't have expected him to be able to make time to have a conversation with her anyway. He probably thought she was still the vain girl she used to be.

Was he wrong about that? He'd just watched her flaunt her legs and charm a business card out of a total stranger. She collapsed against the wall, feeling depressed.

It took her a few minutes to straighten out her clothes and put her vest back on—Tosh had folded it carefully and laid it on an open space on one of the shelves. She exited the storeroom and walked out of the lounge. When she looked behind the bar, Tosh and his two coworkers were busy making drinks that they placed on large serving trays on the counter, and he didn't even look up at her.

At the restaurant reception desk, Mimi asked the young woman for a pen and paper and received a pad of paper with the restaurant logo at the top.

Mimi stared at the blank page, unsure what to write. She should have thought of the possibility earlier that she might need to simply leave him a note and planned what she would say. Finally, she wrote the lamest note in the world:

> *Tosh,*
> *I'm sorry for how I acted toward you when we were kids. I came to return this to you.*
> *Mimi*

She would have tried again, but a noisy group of people had entered the restaurant, and the receptionist was looking impatiently behind Mimi at the new customers. She took the book, still in the bookstore bag, slipped the note under the front cover, then handed it to the receptionist.

"Please deliver this to Tosh."

"Sure." The woman took the bag and placed it under the desk.

"Thanks." Mimi turned to leave but couldn't resist peeking back inside the bar lounge. Tosh was mixing something in a shaker while saying something to one of the other bartenders.

He had said he would be following Waite for another few days. Mimi wondered if she'd see him again before she left Hawaii after the holidays.

7

Tosh had completely lost his cool.

It seemed he always did when he was with Mimi. He'd already done several jobs for Edytha since he was good at tailing people, and he'd been surprised by unexpected snags in a plan.

But a couple days ago, he entered the store and got just one look at Mimi, and then he froze.

Even when he'd forgotten his lines in a play, he'd been able to smooth things over and get back on track. He had never freaked out or fumbled around.

Except the day before yesterday. Except with Mimi.

He looked down and realized he'd poured too much Vermouth into the Manhattan he was mixing. He groaned.

"What is it?" The bar manager, Elizabeth, came up to him. "Whoa! That smells like a lot of Vermouth."

"Sorry." The only way to salvage this would be to add more whiskey and bitters to bring the ratios back to the right amounts.

"That's okay. The Manhattan is for Mrs. Cadang, and she always tips well. No harm in supersizing her drink."

Tosh went to work fixing the drink, determined to concentrate on work. Out of the corner of his eye, he saw someone take a seat at the bar near him—someone short. He looked up, his heart suddenly speeding up.

The woman wasn't Mimi. She was a few inches taller and about half his age. When she smiled sweetly at him, he gave a cool smile in return and said, "I hope you're willing to show me your driver's license."

The sweet smile disappeared behind a sour expression. The girl flounced away.

Tosh sighed, feeling old.

Had he been hoping it was Mimi? Was that why he had looked up so quickly?

When he saw her at the bar last night, he hadn't expected to still feel the old tug in his gut. Maybe it was just gas.

But he'd felt that tug every time they hung out together throughout the summers of his childhood, when they had sat talking for hours, not just about anime and light novels but about everything both serious and stupid.

And that tug had been twisted into pain when they argued that last summer before his family had moved. Before his father had died.

His argument with Mimi was nothing compared to the loss of his father and the suffering his mother and sister had gone through because of the gossip and social stigma. After so many years, after so many other things had happened to him, it wasn't as if he was still upset that Mimi had hurt him.

But he had expected he'd only be indifferent to her. He hadn't expected to still feel attracted to her instead.

It had been over twenty years. Shouldn't he be over her by now? She was a weakness he thought he'd weeded out, only to find the weeds were too insidious. It frustrated him that he couldn't seem to root her out of his thoughts.

It didn't help that she'd surprised and impressed him. He'd been surprised when she decided to help out with his investigation by going up to Waite and finagling an introduction to his companion. He'd been impressed at how quickly she'd gotten his business card.

No, he had no reason to be impressed by her ability to charm men. She'd always been good at that, he reflected bitterly.

Except that he shouldn't complain because she'd gotten Ivan's information, making Edytha's job easier.

Tosh finished the supersized Manhattan and set it on the serving tray. He might have just created a monster—knowing Mrs. Cadang, she'd ask for another supersize the next time she came in.

As another customer came up to the bar, he realized that maybe he'd been working too hard. Yes, he definitely had been working too hard because he was hallucinating.

It was probably because he'd been thinking about Mimi, but he was seeing her right in front of him again. But why would she come back to the restaurant? She had no reason to want to see him again.

He was most certainly seeing things. He tried not to grimace as he looked at the girl who looked like Mimi and asked politely, "What can I get for you?"

Not-Mimi's eyes narrowed into slits, and her jaw hardened. Then she shattered his hazy delusion that this wasn't Mimi when she said in Mimi's voice, "You don't have to look like you're constipated when you see me, you know."

"I'm not constipated! What are you, nine years old?"

She lifted her chin, which he knew she did when she was trying to look taller. "According to Auntie Noriko's neighbor, now I finally look like I'm ten."

He pulled at his hair. "Argh! I can't handle talking to you. I wish you really had been a hallucination."

She wasn't offended, but she did take a second to unravel what he meant. "You thought I was a hallucination? You're working too hard."

Tosh peered at her in suspicion. "Why did you come back?"

Her expression turned as cold as an Arctic wind. "I know you're thrilled to see me, but I need to speak to you about the *new friend* I made last night."

That guy, Ivan Vierra? So that's why she'd come back to the restaurant. Of course she wouldn't come to see Tosh. "Come with me."

He led the way back into the storeroom again.

As he closed the door behind her, she frowned and folded her arms. "People are going to think we're coming back here to make out."

And that would be the last thing pretty, popular Mimi would want, to be associated with a loser like him.

Then he stopped that thought in its tracks. Now he was the one acting like he was nine years old.

To rub out his annoyance with himself, he glared back at her. "We're not going to be back here long enough. What is it?"

She didn't stop frowning, and her arms tightened. He suddenly realized that she was unsure, not irritated.

"That guy called me at work today and asked me out on a date."

Tosh wasn't proud of himself, but he gaped like a goldfish. "A date?"

"A date."

"But ... he's like, ten years younger than you."

She exploded at him. "Rude! He is not ten years younger than *us*, he's probably only ... five years younger."

Tosh pictured Ivan's handsome face. "Maybe eight years younger ..."

"Besides, I look like I'm ten, remember?"

"So he's a lolicon?"

"That's not even funny!" she shrieked at him.

When he considered it, he shouldn't be surprised Ivan asked Mimi out. Last night, she had been blasting her flirtatious powers like a lighthouse beacon—all for Tosh's sake, not because she was interested in Ivan. Or was she? "You're not interested in him?" he asked.

"Of course I'm not interested in him! He's like, ten years younger than me!" She started gnawing on her lip. "But ... well, I told him yes."

Tosh did the goldfish thing again before demanding, "Why in the world would you do that?"

"It's only one date. And you work for a *security company*, right? So I figured you could handle some undercover *security* on the date."

"Did you miss the part where I was hired to help *investigate* Waite and anyone he met? This isn't a game."

"Waite's meeting here with Ivan was super suspicious—he was as jittery as a squirrel on caffeine. So when I had a chance to find out more about Waite's friend, I took it. It'll help you and it'll help my auntie, who's been having staffing problems at the store."

"So you decide to just put yourself in danger? You don't know anything about Ivan."

"And I'm assuming the PI who hired you looked into the guy. What did she find?"

"He's totally suspicious! You shouldn't be going out on a date with him!" Tosh yelled at her.

Why was he so upset about the date? He didn't know. Or maybe he did know, but he didn't want to admit it to himself.

Mimi's face, already a bit paler than most Hawaiian girls, went white and pasty like a jellyfish. "Is he a murderer or something?" she whispered.

Oh, great, now he'd scared her. *Good going, Tosh.* "I don't think so …"

She regained a little color high in her cheekbones as she retorted, "Oh, that makes me feel so much better."

Tosh let out a sigh. "Look, my shift ends tonight in about forty-five minutes. I want to take you to see Edytha."

"Fine." She abruptly turned and headed out of the storeroom.

He had kind of expected more resistance. "Where are you going?"

"To sit at the bar." She glanced over her shoulder at him. "And I fully expect you to pay for some of those fried wonton appetizers for me while I wait."

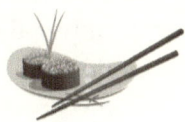

Mimi was always rather impulsive. It was why she'd always gotten into trouble when she was younger.

As she got older, her mom still nagged her about being too impulsive, but she had been hoping it was subtly different now.

It was her cousin, Jenn, who helped her see the difference. Jenn encouraged her to trust her instincts, and so she'd been learning how to listen to her gut. It helped her do a better job working for Jenn at the restaurant, such as when determining the plating arrangement for a new dish or refreshing the plating for an old recipe.

She wanted to say that she had gone with some mysterious instinct when Ivan asked her out on a date. But she was starting to wonder if she had simply been her old impulsive self.

However, after she'd hung up the phone with Ivan, she knew that the date might be helpful to her aunt because it would reveal more about Waite as well as his friend. And, of course, it would be helpful for Tosh's investigation into whatever Waite was doing.

All day, she'd been vacillating between regret at being impulsive and trying to talk herself down from the ledge, telling herself she'd been listening to her instincts.

Those instincts told her she would like the owner of the large plantation house as soon as she saw it. Much of the grounds were in darkness, but the walkway up to the front door was illuminated by twinkling lights woven through dozens of hibiscus bushes.

The massive house had a wide central section flanked by wings on either side. It was a lavish manor home that looked to have been built by one of the ancient pineapple or sugar cane barons from the turn of the century. As she parked her truck in the small parking lot in front of the house, the front door opened, and a woman was silhouetted by the light from the inside.

Tosh walked with Mimi through the lines of hibiscus bushes toward the front door. "I told Edytha we were coming," he said.

"Welcome," came the deep, musical voice from the woman on the front porch. "I'm Edytha Guerrero."

"Hi. I'm Mimi Sakai."

She felt like a child again in front of the tall woman. Edytha's warm smile and the stylish but casual clothes she wore gave off an older sister vibe, with her long, sun-lightened brown hair pulled up into a clip at the back of her head.

"Sorry we had to come so late," Tosh said as they entered the house. The entrance hall had been turned into a small waiting area for the day spa, with a receptionist's desk opposite the front door. Hallways branched out on the right and left sides of the entrance hall, while a wide open archway directly behind the receptionist's desk led into a larger room that was too dimly lit for Mimi to see clearly.

Edytha led them to the right, all the way to the north wing of the house, and then into a small conference room. As soon as she opened the door, Mimi smelled mint.

The mint was from the pot of tea on the table. Edytha poured the steaming liquid into teacups as Mimi and Tosh sat in the padded chairs. "Here. Have some tea made with fresh mint from the atrium garden," she told them as she set the cups in front of them.

The tea tasted like green summer sunlight, and it seemed to soothe Mimi's anxiety over whether she should have accepted the date or not. The tea seemed to be crooning to her, *It's okay—after all, you've made worse decisions about who you should go out with, and you're still around.*

No, on second thought, that sounded more like her grandma's voice.

Edytha smiled at Mimi, and she suddenly felt like her nagging relatives were thousands of miles away ... Wait, they *were* thousands of miles away.

Well, Edytha made Mimi feel like her nagging relatives couldn't just pick up a phone to call and nag her some more.

"I saw you last night at the Molokai Red," Edytha told her. "I was tailing Waite from work and followed him into the restaurant. Thank you for getting Ivan's business card, and in such a way that neither of them would be very suspicious. Excellent work."

"Oh. Thanks." It felt nice to be so appreciated.

Edytha paused in confusion, glancing at Tosh. "Did he not thank you properly?"

"He dished out a backhanded compliment," Mimi said.

"Hey!" Tosh protested. "I thanked you. I was very complimentary."

"'I'm impressed despite myself.' Your gratitude was *gushing* out."

"Tosh, I'm so disappointed in you." Edytha shook her head.

"We were teasing each other. Like we always used to. If I'd given you a sincere thank you, you would have looked at me like I'd been abducted by aliens."

Mimi opened her mouth to protest but then closed it again. "Okay, fair enough. I probably would have."

She admitted—but only to herself in the deepest, most secure part of her heart—that it had felt nice to be trading quips with Tosh as they had as kids. It had always been so easy to trade barbs in good fun. She hadn't even realized she'd missed it until they had fallen back into old habits again.

Edytha's smile turned a bit playful as she said, "Tosh mentioned you hadn't seen each other in years, but you went all the way to Haleiwa simply to return a book."

Tosh's face was calm as he answered, "I'm grateful to Mimi because the book was expensive. I got it in Japan."

"Well, I'm grateful you happened to be at the restaurant when Waite walked in with Ivan," Edytha said to Mimi. "What you did was very clever."

"No, it wasn't," Tosh said, his voice tight. "It's gotten her into trouble."

"Did you just insult me again?" Mimi demanded.

Edytha's playfulness vanished. "What happened?"

Mimi explained about Ivan calling her at work and asking for a date.

"You should have told him no," Tosh said.

"It's only one date," Mimi shot back. "I've gone on dozens."

"I told you we were investigating Waite. You should have known that anyone who'd meet with him in such an out-of-the-way place might be bad news."

"Haleiwa is not out of the way," both Mimi and Edytha said at the same time. Edytha held out her knuckles and Mimi bumped fists with her.

Tosh was doing that squiggly thing with his eyebrows where one was lowered and one was raised and twitching, so Mimi continued, "*Ivan* was the one who reached out to *me*, and I'm only Waite's coworker. It was the perfect way to get information on both Ivan and Waite, and it won't look like I'm fishing for anything if I ask him questions."

"Why would *you* need to ask him questions?" Tosh demanded.

"Waite is working for my aunt's store," Mimi replied. "Why wouldn't I want to help you find out more about him and his friend?"

"You should call him back and tell him you changed your mind."

"Why? What have you found out about Ivan?"

Tosh hesitated, his eyes sliding to Edytha.

Edytha sighed. "Well, I suppose Ivan has gotten you involved in all of this," she said to Mimi.

"Mimi got herself involved in all of this when she agreed to the date," Tosh grumbled.

"You might have prevented it if you had just told me what you were investigating Waite for," Mimi argued with him. "It's your fault I was in the dark."

"It's probably my fault," Edytha said. "Tosh is under contract not to say anything about the case."

"Is Waite in some sort of trouble?" She had assumed that if it were something criminal, it wouldn't be a private investigator looking into Waite, it would be the police.

"It's what we were trying to find out. I was hired by Waite's wife because she suspects him of using drugs. She wanted to know for certain before trying to get help for him."

"Drugs?" Mimi was surprised. "I thought Waite might've been cheating on his wife or something like that."

"I don't like taking too many of those cases," Edytha said with a grimace. "Luckily, I don't get too many of those because I tend to get clients who can't afford PI work, and so I work for barter."

"What kinds of barter?"

"One client has chickens as pets and gives me eggs. Another client gave me half a pig he butchered."

"Do you always barter for food?" Tosh asked her.

"Of course. Why would I barter for anything else?" Edytha replied, looking at Tosh like he was an idiot.

Mimi was thinking about what she'd been reading in the newspapers lately. "I've read about large drug busts in Waikiki and Honolulu, but I don't remember any in Haleiwa."

"When I saw Waite meeting Ivan in the Molokai Red Restaurant, I remembered a conversation with one of my friends who works for the Waialua Police Department," Edytha said. "There have been rumors of more cocaine popping up on the North Shore recently."

Waite certainly hadn't acted like a drug addict at work. Then again, Mimi's only exposure to addiction was an occasional over-caffeinated cousin and the shows on TV. But he had traveled all the way here to meet with Ivan. "Do you think Waite is not just using drugs, but dealing them?" Mimi asked.

"Just because Waite met with Ivan doesn't mean it has anything to do with drugs," Edytha said. "But after Tosh gave me his business card, I looked into him. I checked old yearbooks, social media posts and photos, and Waite and Ivan don't seem to have anything in common. So I don't know how they're close enough friends to meet together for dinner."

"Ivan's business card said he worked at the Pleiades Resort," Mimi said. "Is that true?"

Edytha nodded. "He works in security for the resort."

"They must have first met in Honolulu," Mimi said. "Waite lives there, and from what I remember him telling me, his family and his wife's family all live nearby."

"I would think that if they were doing something criminal, they'd meet in Honolulu or Waikiki, where they'd be less likely to be noticed in all the crowds," Tosh said.

"Maybe they just had to meet close to the resort because Ivan was working," Edytha said. "But it's why I thought about the rumors of cocaine on the North Shore."

Mimi groaned. Her impulsive nature had gotten her in trouble again! She certainly didn't want to go on a date with a drug dealer.

But at the same time, the date might help Edytha's investigation into Waite, and might even help the Waialua police investigation into cocaine. "Do you not think you could protect me on the date?"

Tosh gave her an incredulous look. "Are you still considering going out with him?"

"He asked me out on a date, not to try to sell me drugs."

"How do you know that?" Tosh argued.

"He doesn't know anything about me. One wrong word and I could tell the police about him and get him arrested. He's not going to risk all that for a cute face."

"And remember, we don't know for certain he's even involved with drugs at all," Edytha said. "I was just speculating."

"Also, I've gone out on lots of dates with men I know even less about," Mimi said. She wasn't proud about that, but at that moment, she was glad she had those past experiences. "I'm not careless. I know how to stay safe when I meet with a stranger. And in this case, I won't be alone because the two of you will be tailing me, right?" She eyed Tosh and Edytha. "Unless there's something even more dangerous about him that you're not telling me."

Edytha shook her head. "I didn't find anything suspicious about Ivan."

"But we can't figure out how he and Waite know each other," Tosh said.

"You know, he may be simply having an affair with Ivan," Mimi said. The thought was distasteful, and she felt bad for Waite's wife.

Edytha sighed. "These days, that's entirely possible. And from what I could gather, Waite's wife is from a very wealthy family. He would hesitate to simply divorce her."

"Oh?" Mimi hadn't known that. "Then I wonder why he's working for my aunt's shop?"

"I'm assuming he's not passionate about his job?" Tosh asked.

Mimi shook her head. "He's not terrible, though. I don't want to imply he's a bad employee."

"Just because his wife's family is wealthy doesn't mean he doesn't have to work," Tosh said. "After all, they live in Honolulu, and it's expensive to live there."

"Well," Edytha said, "as you said, it's only one date and we don't know for certain Ivan is involved in drugs. And the two of us will be watching over you the entire time."

"Edytha!" Tosh objected. "I still don't think this is a good idea."

"I don't have a good reason to call Ivan back and refuse to go on a date with him," Mimi pointed out. "I could cancel, but what would I say when he wants to reschedule?"

"It might be better not to get Ivan upset," Edytha said. "Her refusal might make him suspicious."

"As long as it's only one date." Tosh glared at Mimi. "You do know how to make yourself disagreeable to men, don't you?"

"It worked with you, didn't it?" Mimi snapped at him.

Edytha's expression was amused.

8

Mimi gaped at the neon sign on the black glass building, which read "Kaiholo." She had asked Ivan where they'd be going, but a part of her still couldn't quite believe they were at the nightclub.

"Isn't it really expensive?" she asked Ivan as he drove up to the front door.

"Don't worry, I'm a member," he said proudly. "I come here all the time."

It would cost an entire month's salary for her to afford membership at Kaiholo, and that didn't include costs for drinks and food.

As the valet opened the car door, the muted thumping of a bass beat reached her. She had liked going to clubs when she was younger, but not as much recently. She knew she was getting old when she worried about hearing loss from the loud music and dreaded the ordeal of slithering between crowds of drunken people.

Mimi had taken a quick trip to the mall for a black bodycon dress with a high halter neckline, paired with expensive designer heels she'd happened to bring to Hawaii with her. She'd also borrowed some truly gaudy but real diamond earrings and a bracelet from Trinda, a set she'd received at her wedding as part of the Chinese tea ceremony with her husband's relatives. Trinda hadn't been able to get herself to ever wear the garish jewelry in public and didn't mind letting Mimi have the honors. The diamonds made Mimi look needlessly expensive, which would allow her to fit right in with the people at the exclusive club.

"Will we be here all night?" She wanted to make sure she had a chance to talk to him and find out more about him, and she couldn't do that in a noisy club.

"Not long," he told her breezily. "I have to meet some friends. I'll introduce you."

It might be useful to meet his friends. "That'll be fun."

She wanted to glance around outside just before they entered the front doors but resisted the urge. She'd told Tosh and Edytha about the club and just had to trust that they knew how to follow her inside the crowded space.

Mimi and Ivan entered a small waiting area with a reception desk, and the walls practically vibrated with the dance music from the area beyond the double doors at the back of the room. While Ivan signed in, Mimi glanced around and saw that she wasn't the oldest person. She should have expected that, considering the high price of the cover charge. This would be a different experience from the nightclubs she went to in her twenties.

She fingered the pepper spray pendant on her necklace. Years ago, she had used it a few times while dating and now wore it whenever she went out. She had made sure it worked before meeting Ivan.

"Shall we?" Ivan grinned as he took her hand to lead her through the doors into Kaiholo.

The music hit her like a two-by-four to the eardrums, and she winced. However, she was glad to see that the club was well-lighted compared to some dives she'd gone to in her misguided youth.

"Wow!" She pulled out her phone, which she'd switched to a case with a wrist strap and card holder, and began snapping photos of the interior. Her awe wasn't entirely feigned—there was a huge glass art piece that covered the entire dance floor, looking like an ethereal jellyfish with crystal strands hanging down. She'd read that Kaiholo was famous for rotating magnificent pieces of artwork every few months, and this piece made full use of the colored dance floor lights to send prisms shimmering across the entire large space.

"Wow!" she said again, and then drew close to Ivan. "Take a picture with me." She took a selfie of the two of them with the crystal jellyfish as a backdrop. She was close enough to be able to speak in his ear without shouting, "My cousin will be so jealous when I tell her you brought me here."

He looked so delighted at her words that she resolved to make sure she told a few of her younger cousins to inspire adequate amounts of teeth-grinding jealousy.

Mimi continued to pretend to take pictures, falling behind Ivan a few steps. When he wasn't looking, she made a video call to Edytha, who answered with her own microphone muted and screen blackened.

It was partly for Mimi's safety, but also to allow Edytha to see the people she met tonight. Mimi casually held her phone so that when she folded her hands in front of her, the camera faced forward.

"Hey, Ralph! You made it!" Ivan clasped hands and came in for a manly hug with a man with hair cut short in a buzz cut. Ralph had a round, friendly face and eyes like crescent moons. He looked like a high school guidance counselor, except that Mimi could tell that his clothes were exceptionally high quality with an exceptionally high price tag.

The woman with him was tall and slender, dressed in a black bodycon with a plunging neckline, and her deathly pale skin contrasted her long raven hair, which shimmered like an ebony waterfall. Her pinched mouth and furrowed brow made her look like a disagreeable Morticia Addams.

Ralph leaned in to speak in Ivan's ear, ostensibly because the club was so loud, and Mimi wondered what he was saying. Ivan seemed to say something like, "Sure thing," but Mimi didn't hear him. The way they talked to each other seemed businesslike.

Ivan raised his voice to introduce the two of them, Ralph and

Louella. Mimi smiled and shook hands, keeping her phone tucked in her hand and resting against her stomach. Hopefully, Edytha was able to get a good look at his face. Ralph shook her hand warmly, while Louella barely gave her two fingers that felt like dead squid tentacles.

Mimi was just reflecting that she didn't look like a "Louella" when Ralph said to Ivan, "Why don't I take you to him and introduce you now?"

Ivan promptly turned to Mimi. "I'll only be gone a moment. You'll be fine with Louella."

For one thing, Mimi absolutely did not want to spend time alone with Miss Cheerful over there. For another, she'd been left "only for a moment" by more than one date (to her shame, she didn't learn the first time) only to be abandoned for over an hour before she went home in a huff.

And third, if she wasn't with Ivan, she wasn't finding out anything about him or his relationship with Waite. She wanted to know what he might be up to, if only to protect her auntie's store.

So she puckered her lips, which were slathered with Dragon Breath Blush lipstick (she bought it solely because of the name), and looked up at Ivan with Sad Puppy Eyes. "You're leaving me? Couldn't I go with you? I promise not to interrupt if you're talking about something important." Inwardly, she was thinking, *Please don't leave me alone with that woman who looks like the Evil Eclipse of the Demon Moon.*

Maybe her desperation came across and Ivan felt sorry for her, or maybe it was the Dragon Breath Blush that scrambled his brain cells for a moment. Regardless, he smiled down at her. "Well, if you want to stay with me …" He glanced at Ralph with his eyebrows raised.

Ralph just flashed his sunny smile (seriously, why was he with Grouch-face of the Living Dead over there?) and leaned in to ask Ivan, "How about I bring him by your table in the VIP area later?"

"That would be great. Thanks, Ralph." He grabbed Mimi's hand to lead her away, but turned to shout at Ralph, "I'll have a bottle of Padron waiting!"

Ralph looked even brighter, if that were possible, while Louella crossed her skinny arms and stared in displeasure off into the distance.

Well, unfortunately, that meant Mimi had to see Louella again, but she had managed to stay with Ivan.

They continued heading deeper into the club, but after only a few yards they were stopped by another man and woman, her hand tucked into his arm. They separated so the man could greet Ivan, and when Ivan greeted the woman, he leaned over to give her a friendly peck on the cheek.

"This is Janet and Albert," Ivan introduced them, then paused to speak to Albert.

It was too loud to do more than smile at Janet, not unless Mimi wanted to get close to her like the two men were doing.

They greeted more people, slowly making their way to the back corner of the club. Ivan didn't do anything as obvious as discreetly exchanging items with anyone. He was talking business-like things with some of his friends, but certainly not all of them. Nothing he said or did seemed to be secretive, much less illegal.

But Mimi decided to still be cautious in how she dealt with him. Something inside her was giving her warning bells, and she didn't want to ignore it.

Eventually, they made their way to the back corner, where a VIP area had been set up. It wasn't completely enclosed, but there were glass wall panels that partitioned out a section. The glass panels had space in between each of them, so some of the sound from the dance floor filtered in, but colorful silky swathes of cloth were draped behind each panel to screen the VIP area from the rest of the club.

The quieter area was like a shock to her eardrums. It took a few minutes to get her hearing back. In the meantime, she smelled delicious food and noticed waiters passing between clumps of comfortable sofas and chairs, serving what looked like appetizers and drinks.

Ivan led her to a group of two sofas and a couple of chairs around a low table. "There's a new charcuterie board every week. I usually get that. And then there's truffle fries, mini shrimp tacos, and dessert shooters."

Wait, truffle fries? Did he say truffle fries? She stopped herself from grabbing his collar and shaking him in excitement. Instead, she said calmly, "Um … the fries sound good."

"Sure thing."

A waiter came by within a few seconds of them sitting down, and Ivan ordered everything he'd mentioned to her, including the fries. Mimi had to admit the date had suddenly risen in her estimation by about 200%.

Even here in the VIP area, people constantly came up to say hi to Ivan and talk to him. Mimi could see why people liked him—he made everyone feel like they were a close friend and he was thrilled to see them. He shared his food generously and ordered more, including drinks, for the people who stopped to see him, even if they only stayed for a few minutes.

Some of the conversations Ivan had with various men and women were still too low for Mimi to overhear. She ended up talking to the date of whoever Ivan spoke with, making innocuous small talk so that they weren't bored. Some of the dates—mostly women—were happy to chat with Mimi, while occasionally they would simply ignore her and tap on their phones.

Mimi kept her phone in her lap, with the camera facing outward, leaning against her stomach. She didn't specifically aim it at each person, and she didn't want to fiddle with it too much to call attention to it, but she hoped the angle was good enough for Edytha to see everyone who came by.

Ralph eventually came by (sans Louella, thank goodness) and introduced two men who leaned in to have a low-voiced conversation with Ivan. Ralph spouted some aimless chatter to Mimi, but she only half-listened to him, straining her ears to hear what nefarious doings Ivan and the two men were up to, until she heard the words "keeper league," "PPR," and "fantasy points."

Fantasy football. That's what they were discussing as if the world were at stake. Maybe for them, it was.

Finally, the two fantasy footballers shook Ivan's hand and

headed off, and more people came by. After the eighth couple had left, Ivan leaned over to Mimi with a bright smile. "Are you having a good time? You seemed to have a lot in common with Merle," he added, mentioning the woman Mimi had recently been speaking with. "What were you talking about?"

"Oh, we both like the show, *Real Housewives of Fiji.*"

"There's a *Real Housewives of Fiji?*"

"Of course."

Then another couple came up to them, which was probably just as well because, no, there wasn't a *Real Housewives of Fiji* show, but Merle had been complaining about her bunions, and Mimi hadn't wanted to share that with Ivan.

In the next half hour, Mimi realized that Ivan must have simply wanted a woman to sit with him since almost everyone who came by had a date. Maybe he just didn't want to be alone, or maybe he didn't want his friends to pity him if he didn't have someone by his side. He had barely talked to her, which made her think that he wasn't all that interested in her.

Instead, he loved being around a lot of people. He grew more animated when more gathered around him, when there was a cluster of folks chatting with him and over him and with each other. He probably felt a bit like a rockstar with Mimi in the role of his groupie. It was rather demeaning.

She was suddenly reminded of one of the last times she'd gone to a Hawaii nightclub. It had been with Tosh and his friends, and it had been a far cry from this decadent place. They had gone as a group of people rather than paired off, and since the music was too loud for talking, they'd done a lot of dancing. She'd danced with everyone for the fast songs, and she'd made sure to dance with each boy for the slow songs, without favoritism. She'd enjoyed chatting with each boy during those dances.

She hadn't been an adornment on anyone's arm. She'd been herself, not needing to be polite, not even needing to be agreeable.

And she'd thrown it all away a few weeks later when she'd flippantly asked Tosh to date her.

She told herself it was all over. That God saw her past and

forgave her for it. But she had a hard time believing it. Those past events felt like chains still wrapped around her.

"Are you okay?" asked the woman Mimi had been talking with.

"Oh, yes, sorry. I just remembered something."

"It must have been sad," the woman said.

"It was, a little." Mimi put on a bright smile. "You said you worked at a bank? How did you decide you wanted to work there?"

She was simply sitting here, meeting people with him. She wasn't finding out anything about him, or even about his relationship with these people, since she couldn't hear a majority of their conversations.

It also occurred to her that the fact Ivan didn't want her to overhear these conversations was concerning. It might have been one thing if Ivan worked for a big tech company and was talking shop with fellow employees, and all of them were constrained by an NDA to not let any outsiders know about super-secret tech products that hadn't come out yet.

But Ivan worked in security at Pleiades Resort, and she knew from speaking to the dates of each of these people that they didn't work at the resort with him.

He was also so busy with other people that she hadn't had a chance to talk to him about himself or Waite.

Why had she thought she could help with an investigation by going out on a date? Granted, at the time, she had thought Edytha was only trying to suss out if Waite was cheating on his wife, so Mimi had figured that getting to know Waite's friend Ivan seemed an easy way to uncover information. After all, Mimi had always been good at talking with guys and drawing them out.

But now, there was nothing for her to do besides sit here and entertain the dates of the people who wanted to discuss something with Ivan.

And that was the problem. Since she'd accepted this date to help Tosh and Edytha, she was doing all she could to please Ivan, to get him to lower his guard. But essentially, she was trying to be someone she wasn't.

If she'd accepted an actual date from someone, she wouldn't be sitting here like a wart on a frog. Any of her cousins would be backing away in alarm at the Mimi-lookalike creepy porcelain doll squeezed into a body shaper with her feet crippled by stilettos.

Instead, she would be more interested in interacting with her date rather than simply meeting a bunch of people in a club, no matter how posh and expensive (and no matter how to-die-for the truffle fries were).

So what she should be doing was getting Ivan into the ideal situation where she could utilize her strength, which was getting the guy to talk about himself.

Unfortunately, at the moment he was surrounded by six people, all of them listening to him tell a story about a time he'd tried deep-sea fishing. So Mimi waited.

She got her opportunity when a couple said they had to go. As they left, Mimi leaned closer to Ivan with a charming smile. The Dragon Breath Blush was starting to rub off, but hopefully it still held its magic. "It's kind of loud in here. I'm afraid I went to too many concerts when I was in my teens, so I can barely hear anyone when they talk to me." She snuggled up closer to him. "Do you think maybe we can go somewhere more quiet so we can talk and I can get to know you better? That's the whole point of going on a date, right? Or do you have more people you need to meet up with here?"

His smile faltered with a bit of disappointment, but he was quick to tell her, "Sure, if that's what you want to do."

It took another fifteen minutes for the four people with him to finally disperse. Then, as they were making their way across the club back to the front door, he stopped to talk to two other clusters of people. Mimi tried not to be too annoyed, but for the second cluster of people, she sort-of not-accidentally stepped on the bare toes of a tall woman in scrappy bronze-colored heels and a slinky bronze dress.

"Ow!" the woman shrieked. "Watch it!"

"Oh, I'm so sorry," Mimi said. But the distraction had done its job and cut off the lengthy conversation Ivan was having with the two other people in her party.

They finally made it to the reception desk, and Ivan called for his car from the valet. Mimi furtively checked that Edytha was still on video call with her—she was, although she had darkened her side of the call so that Mimi's phone screen was black. Unfortunately, Mimi's phone battery was nearing 10%. She discreetly ended the video call.

After they got into Ivan's car, he asked, "How did you like the club?"

"It's amazing."

It wasn't a lie—the interior had been decadent and beautiful. But that probably hadn't been what he'd been talking about.

He obviously loved being in the midst of the crowd more than the decor, and she realized that he had probably assumed Mimi would enjoy it, too. Maybe when she was younger she might have.

"Where to now?" she asked.

"I know a bar with a great view," Ivan said.

"That sounds fantastic."

Mimi might have heard the name Leilani's Hideout or read it in an article in a magazine, but it had never figured into her plans of someplace she could afford to go. However, like Kaiholo, Ivan was greeted as a regular by the valet at the front door.

They entered through the double doors, and Mimi was taken aback to be in a tiny room with two elevators. When they entered, the elevator only had two buttons—"Ground" and "Leilani's."

The elevator opened into a wide circular room with glass windows all around. Tables and chairs had been set up against the windows so customers could enjoy the view, with only a few clusters of sofas in the middle of the room. The rest of the space was taken up by an extensive semi-circular bar.

They were led to a couple of chairs and a small round table next to a window with a breathtaking view of Diamond Head crater. "This is wonderful," Mimi gushed. She checked her phone. "I'm going to text my cousin to let her know where I am."

Mimi did better than that—she found herself on the map on her phone and shared the exact GPS location with Edytha and Tosh, using up the last of her phone battery.

A waiter came up to them, and Ivan ordered an expensive Japanese whiskey. "What do you want to drink?" he asked her.

Mimi had been able to avoid drinking much in Kaiholo. Despite her small size, she had always been able to hold her liquor pretty well, but since becoming a Christian a few years ago, she had stopped getting drunk. Now, however, she wanted to get Ivan to open up, so she ordered the same whiskey.

He smiled at her choice. "What do you want to eat? This place has terrific lamb skewers and homemade smoked sausages. If you want something sweet, they have homemade dark chocolate truffles and cheesecake."

Those were foods that went well with whiskey (well, maybe not the cheesecake, but Mimi wasn't about to refuse *cheesecake*), and she agreed to all of them.

"You have so many friends," she said to Ivan when the waiter left. "Do you go to other clubs with them besides Kaiholo?"

"We used to go to a few other places, but now we mainly go there. The food is great and the guest list is more exclusive." There was a hint of pride in his voice.

"I could tell. I was so impressed. What else do you like to do?"

She had suspected while they were at the club, but she now confirmed that Ivan loved telling stories to entertain his audience. At the moment, his audience was just Mimi, but he seemed okay with that since he'd met so many people in the past couple of hours.

So it was easy for her to keep the conversation rolling and draw information out of him. She asked what he liked doing with his friends, and all his interests seemed expensive. He listed a bunch of his favorite restaurants, and while he liked a few local favorites like Kua'Aina hamburgers and Liliha Drive Inn, he also mentioned Kai Keaupuni Terrace, which was extremely high-end. She had the feeling that the other places he mentioned were also very expensive.

He was also physically active, but even his weekend warrior stints cost a lot of money—extreme sports like paragliding and skydiving, and golfing at courses like Coral Crest Lagoon, an exclusive country club, and Pleiades Resort, although since he worked there, he got a discount on the golf course.

Mimi sipped the last of her whiskey. "Don't you ever like staying home for a quiet night?"

"Nah," he said. "I get too bored. I like being busy. Do you want another whiskey?" He'd already had a second glass.

He seemed to want to continue drinking with her, so she said yes. However, when the waiter arrived, she asked him to also bring her a glass of club soda on the side. When her drinks arrived, she started drinking the club soda first.

"Oh, you're not going to let me drink alone, are you?" Ivan teased her.

She had been on enough dates to know not to allow the man even the slightest bit of input regarding how much she drank. But she tried not to be mean about it. She gave him a sweet smile (which her cousin Venus would have said was impossible for her to do, considering how sour she was inside) and gestured toward herself. "It's just that I'm so petite…" She wasn't lying, but she also wasn't confessing that she could probably drink him under the table.

"Oh." He nodded, and for a moment, Mimi thought he might be one of the few dates she had had who wouldn't push her. Then he gave her a playful smile. "But you wouldn't have to worry. I'll make sure you get home all right."

She hoped her smile didn't look too feral as she gave him a wink. "I want to be able to talk to you and remember it."

He laughed. However, he looked like he might want to continue to try to persuade her, so she added, "Besides, I wouldn't want to have to go to the emergency room *again*." That incident had actually been a car accident in her teens, not alcohol-related, but the sentiment was still true.

Ivan paled a little bit, and she could almost see his anxious thoughts like an exclamation point hovering above his head.

She led the conversation to their jobs, talking about her aunt's shop. "How did you meet Waite?"

"We met at a small bar that used to be in this area—it closed a few months ago. Waite had drunk too much and was pretty sick, so I helped him home. We've been friends ever since. We have dinner or a drink together about once a month since he can't go out very often."

It seemed innocuous enough, but Mimi didn't know what Ivan would have in common with Waite. "You two seem so different. What do you talk about?"

He laughed. "You don't know Waite well enough yet. We like talking about sports."

Maybe they were like Mimi's cousin Lex. She worked for a sports news company and could literally talk about sports all day without stopping.

He asked her more about her job, which enabled her to turn the conversation to his at the security department at Pleiades Resort.

"Do you like it there?" she asked.

"I do." He seemed very sincere. "I met my best friend there."

She shouldn't have been so quick to assume that he only had shallow friendships with all the people he met tonight. "Oh?"

"John Hackett," Ivan said. "He's not the head of security or a supervisor, but the owner of the resort, Mr. Thayer, favors him. He's always sending him to do odd jobs for him. He brought me to Mr. Thayer's attention, too."

"That's great. Sounds like you two are close."

Ivan laughed. "Literally. His apartment is only a few doors down from me. Oh, well, actually, it used to be. He just bought a house."

"So you work together and also happened to live in the same apartment building? What a coincidence."

"No, no." Ivan chuckled. "The resort has an apartment complex for some of the employees, so I technically live on the resort premises."

"Is the rent expensive?"

"No, it's a great deal because the rent is discounted compared to housing around here. But I'd like a house on the beach one day like John just bought."

He'd bought a beachfront house? How much was John making at the resort? And how much was Ivan making that he was thinking of buying a house himself?

Ivan continued, "The only problem with owning a house is that

John and I don't hang out at the resort bar after work like we used to." He slid the small plate that held the chocolates toward her. "Here, take the last one."

"Thanks." The truffles had been delectable, although she felt that the ones made by her cousin Jenn were better.

"You know, I've never met someone like you, who's interested in who I am and really listens to me." His dark eyes shone with warmth as he gazed at her.

He had been reluctant to leave the club, so it surprised her that he seemed to now enjoy talking with Mimi. "Thank you. That's a nice compliment. But doesn't John listen to you?"

Ivan laughed. "We talk a lot, but men aren't great communicators."

So even though John was his best friend, he wasn't the sort to ask Ivan about himself and his opinions. Mimi felt a bit sad for him, that he seemed to only have surface acquaintances.

"You, on the other hand," Ivan said, "are a great communicator. I don't know if you realized it, but it was a big help to me that you chatted with the dates of some of my friends at the club."

She hadn't expected him to notice that, but it was nice to be appreciated. "I'm glad I could help you out."

As she finished eating the chocolate, he handed her a napkin, but his fingers brushed hers. She didn't jerk away, but she ignored the contact and smoothly withdrew.

She hadn't been trying to lead him on—she had only been trying to be congenial company—but maybe the fact that she, out of all his other friends and acquaintances, listened to him so intently had made more of an impact on him than she intended.

Or maybe he was indicating his interest for more mercenary reasons, since he had been able to converse with his friends at the club because Mimi was acting a bit like a hostess for him, entertaining everyone else when he was focused on only one or two people at a time.

Mimi had been trying to be careful to not encourage Ivan, but maybe she hadn't been careful enough. In the past, she hadn't cared about leading guys on, but once she hit her thirties, and especially since becoming a Christian, she'd tried to be more considerate.

So she did what she could—she continued to be polite and listen to him, but she consciously stopped herself from mirroring his movements and actions. She had once had a good laugh when trying this with Jenn, because her cousin absolutely couldn't stop herself from mirroring Mimi unless she focused so hard that it looked like she was trying to emit light beams from her eyes. But Jenn was the sort of person who always tried to be agreeable. Mimi, on the other hand, didn't have a problem being contrary.

She waited until a few minutes after eleven o'clock, then said, "Ivan, I've had fun, but I need to go home. I have to wake up early tomorrow morning for work."

It was gratifying that he seemed disappointed. "That's right, you told me you would need to leave by eleven." He signaled a waiter.

When the waiter arrived, Ivan told him they'd need the check, but before he could leave, Mimi stopped him. "Please call a taxi for me."

"Of course." The waiter left.

"No, no, I can drive you home," Ivan said.

"I'm in the complete opposite direction. It's fine—I always intended to take a cab home." Auntie Noriko had dropped her off at work this morning and she'd changed clothes and met Ivan at the mall.

"I don't mind driving you."

"I appreciate the offer, but it's really fine. If you drove me, it would take you almost an additional hour to get back to your place."

"If you're sure," he said reluctantly. "It wouldn't bother me."

There were moments when Ivan was sweet. It was too bad other things about him rubbed her the wrong way.

Oh, and he might be dealing drugs. That too.

The check arrived and she reached to pull some bills from the cardholder on her phone case, but Ivan reached out and grabbed her wrist. He didn't hold her tightly, but his grip was firm.

Mimi squelched her instinctive reaction to fight him and instead forced herself to remain relaxed and calm, sitting and looking at him inquiringly. She had met enough men to know that he was the type of personality where if she did fight him, he would respond like a hunter after prey.

"I never let a woman pay when I take her out," Ivan said.

"I'm used to being independent." She hadn't been able to pay for anything at the club—all the food and drinks were put on Ivan's tab, and the one waiter she had spoken to had refused her money. But in the past, she'd learned that it was better to pay her share so that her date never felt like he owed him anything.

"I insist," he said.

She looked him in the eye with a serious expression. "I know you have a strong sense of self, and you seem to respect others who do, too. You wouldn't want to change who I am, would you? This is how I am, and I won't apologize for it."

Maybe it was her tone of voice, or maybe he saw something in her eyes, or maybe he was touched by the compliment to his self-identity. He nodded and finally released her wrist. "I can respect that."

"Thanks, Ivan."

As she laid the money in the check folder, the waiter came up to tell her, "Your taxi is downstairs."

He tossed back his drink and stood up. "I'll walk you downstairs."

They exited the private elevator, and a cab had pulled up in front for her. Ivan smiled at her. "How about another date?"

"Um … I had fun with you, and I think you're a nice guy, but I don't think we have a lot in common." Mimi's cousins would have picked their jaws off the floor if they saw her now. She was usually more blunt in refusing—Lex had said Mimi was as brutal as a rampaging dinosaur—but this time, since she wasn't entirely sure if Ivan was involved in anything illegal, she had deliberately softened her reply and had even managed to be diplomatic, for a change.

"I enjoyed talking with you," Ivan said. "I'd like to see you again because I'm genuinely interested in you."

It was very flattering, but she couldn't budge. "I don't think it would be a good idea to go on more dates," she said gently. Then before he could say anything else, she added, "Thanks for a great night, Ivan," and stepped toward the cab.

"It was my pleasure," he said.

Mimi entered the car and gave him a little wave before the driver pulled away.

Once she was alone, she rubbed her wrist. For some reason, when he grabbed her, his grip had felt like a manacle trying to restrain her.

He hadn't been an utter monster. Compared to some of her past dates, he'd been stellar.

Still, Mimi was glad she'd never see him again.

9

Tosh's stomach twisted in knots even before the night began.

Because of the exclusivity of the club, they hadn't been able to scope out the place before the date. In fact, they'd been lucky his boss happened to have a voucher for Kaiholo that they could use, and he and Edytha had entered the club before Mimi and Ivan even got there. Edytha remained in sight of the entrance doors, and then Tosh did what he did best—he blended in, unnoticed, waiting for Mimi to arrive.

He didn't need Edytha's text because he spotted them as they entered the double doors. He had to force himself to look away from Mimi, who was stunning in a form-fitting black dress with diamonds at her ears.

Following them through the club ended up being more difficult than he had expected because Ivan kept stopping every few feet to talk to someone. But soon it became obvious that they were heading to the VIP area, so he went ahead of them, texting Edytha to keep them in sight.

He saw that once they entered the VIP area, it would be more difficult to keep an eye on Mimi. The section was partitioned with glass panels, but there were long curtains on the inside of the area to close it off from outside observers—like Tosh.

However, there was a small gap between each of the glass panels, and there were a few clusters of chairs right next to some panels.

Unfortunately, they were all occupied.

When Ivan ushered Mimi inside the sectioned-off area, Edytha joined Tosh where he stood next to a pillar. "There's no chance we could sneak in, is there?" she asked.

"I have an idea," he said.

A few minutes later, he was holding the insanely expensive bottle of wine he'd just bought at the bar and escorting Edytha, who was trying to walk normally despite the fact she'd deliberately broken the heel of her shoe. They approached the couple Tosh had decided to target, a pair drinking wine and sitting in some chairs next to the VIP section panels.

On cue, Edytha tripped and splashed her glass of club soda all over the poor woman. Her shriek felt a bit like a spear to his eardrums.

"Oh!" Edytha was on the ground, clutching her ankle.

"Are you all right?" Tosh asked her.

"My ankle hurts."

"You should sit down." Tosh helped her up, then looked pointedly at the man.

He reluctantly stood up to allow Edytha to sit next to the woman, who was ineffectually dabbing at her wet dress with a tissue.

"I'm so sorry," Edytha told the woman. "My heel broke." She held up the broken shoe. "And I think I've sprained my ankle."

"Just sit here for a few minutes," Tosh told Edytha. He turned to the couple and held out the bottle of wine. "It was only club soda, so it shouldn't stain. Here, take this. We're very sorry."

The couple recognized the excellent vintage and the woman's distraught mewling immediately ceased. She got to her feet. "The chair is completely wet," she complained to her companion. "I need to try to dry my dress." The two of them wandered away.

Mission accomplished.

Tosh threw his jacket down on the soggy chair, which was right next to the glass panels, and sat. Under the pretext of bending down to tie his shoe, he used his utility knife to reach into the space between two panels and snag the curtain. He slowly tugged at it until it revealed a narrow view of the inside of the VIP section.

He couldn't see Mimi at first, but he angled his chair until he got a good view of her and Ivan, sitting against the far wall. He studied her face to see if she showed signs of stress, but if anything, there was a subtle woodenness to her features that indicated she was rather bored and trying to hide it.

"Are you still on call with her?" he asked Edytha. Because of the acoustics of the building, this area near the VIP section was not as loud as the rest of the club.

She nodded and showed him her phone. He noticed that she had put tape over the cameras to darken her side of the call, and she had muted her phone's microphone.

The video jostled, but from the brief glimpses that Tosh could see, Mimi had stood up to meet someone and was shaking their hand. When she sat down, the angle was a little high, but he could see the face of a man who sat down kitty-corner from Ivan's chair. Then the angle shifted to the empty chair to the side of him, and he heard Mimi's voice speaking to someone. A woman answered her. She must be chatting with the man's date.

Edytha glanced at the slit in the curtain, but she wasn't sitting at the right angle to see Mimi. "How does she look?" she asked Tosh.

"She doesn't look frightened, stressed, or alarmed by anything."

"Would you be able to tell if she was trying to hide it?" Edytha asked.

"Yes," he answered, then reconsidered. It had been years since they had been friends.

He looked back inside again. Mimi had a pleasant smile on her face and was speaking brightly to the woman seated next to her, but he could somehow tell by the set of her shoulders and the way she moved her hands that she was merely being polite.

"I think I'll know if something starts to bother her," Tosh said.

Or was he mistaken? Perhaps she had changed, and her expression right now was her "interested" face.

As the minutes turned into hours, Tosh continued to watch Mimi while Edytha monitored the video call. It didn't take Tosh very long to realize that Mimi was acting like Ivan's perfect hostess. It was strange for him to see her like this because, in all his admittedly cynical memories of her, she was the center of attention, surrounded by a harem of men.

Mimi hardly knew Ivan, and yet she had managed to immediately become the person he needed her to be. In some ways, she was as much of a chameleon as Tosh was.

"They're leaving," Edytha said only a moment before he saw Mimi and Ivan stand up. The group around them dispersed, and they made their way out of the VIP section.

"Where are they going?" Tosh asked.

Edytha shook her head. "They haven't said yet."

"Head to your car." Tosh stood up. "I'll follow them in here and meet you there."

Mimi and Ivan exited the club the same way they had entered, stopping every few feet to talk to people. However, Tosh caught the exact moment when Mimi's perfect smile slipped, and she stepped forward directly on the toes of a woman in a brownish metallic dress.

Tosh snorted in laughter, which made a disdainful woman who happened to be standing next to him look at him as if he had suddenly belched the alphabet.

He considered apologizing, but it would probably be as insincere as the apology that Mimi gave to the woman whose toes she'd flattened. He wouldn't have had the chance anyway, as the disdainful woman quickly turned away from him.

After Mimi and Ivan left the club, Tosh waited a few minutes before following them outside. He hurried toward the parking lot across the street and a couple blocks down from the club, where he and Edytha had both arrived early to make sure they got parking spaces in case they needed to leave the club quickly.

Tosh suddenly received a text from Mimi with a GPS location

pin. They weren't far away, at Leilani's Hideout, an extremely high-end bar.

As he got near her car, Edytha spoke to him through her open window. "Let's ride together. It'll be hard to find parking for both cars in that area."

Tosh grunted assent and climbed into the passenger seat.

"I suppose it's a good sign that Ivan didn't mind that Mimi is keeping someone else apprised of where she is at all times."

"Just because he's considerate doesn't mean he's not a drug dealer," Tosh grumbled as he fastened his seatbelt.

"You sound like you want him to be a drug dealer."

"Of course I don't." But he couldn't quite explain why it annoyed him. Then he was distracted by the fact she was driving barefoot. "Sorry about your shoe."

"You can buy me a new pair." Her smile had way too many teeth. "And for the indignity and discomfort of walking out of the club barefoot, you're buying me chantilly cupcakes from Kilani Bakery."

"Fine, fine." He could have predicted she'd want her recompense in the form of some type of dessert that he'd have to pick up for her.

When Edytha pulled up in front of the bar, intending to hand her car over to the valet, he asked, "Do you have a Leilani's Hideout membership?"

When Edytha told him no, the valet said apologetically, "I'm sorry, but after nine P.M., only our exclusive club members can enter the restaurant."

Tosh stared hard at the closed doors as they drove away. They couldn't enter the bar, but they had to find a way to remain nearby in case Mimi needed help.

Unfortunately, there wasn't anywhere they could (legally) loiter outside within sight of the doors. All the businesses directly across the street were closed—a bank, a florist, an interior design company, and a nail salon.

"That store's open." Edytha pointed to a cigar shop and smoking lounge, but she then said, "No, it looks like the lounge is in the back of the shop and there's no way to stay and watch out the front window."

"I think that shop is open." It was hard to tell because the front windows were heavily decorated and not much light from the interior shone out. The store was located down and across the street from Leilani's Hideout, but it might have a view of the entrance.

It was a wine bar, and Edytha dropped Tosh off while she went to try to find parking. Luckily, there were seats next to the front windows and Tosh was able to snag two of them.

Unluckily, the wines were all rather expensive, and they had to order but wouldn't be able to drink since they were watching Mimi and had to drive.

Edytha arrived rather quickly, wearing a spare pair of shoes she must have had in her car, but she looked pained as they each ordered a glass of house wine and a charcuterie board to nibble on. She probably couldn't bill her client for the expense.

The window had artistic metal patterns covering most of it, but there were places where they could see through the glass. Tosh brooded as he stared down the street at the valets chatting as they manned their station. "Ivan is probably drinking a lot. He might try to get her to drink too much. Is she going to be okay?"

"Have some faith in her," Edytha replied.

"I mean, it wouldn't be hard for her to get drunk since she's so small. And she's not answering her texts."

In reply, Edytha kicked Tosh sharply in the ankle.

He would have shrieked like a little girl from the pain, except that it would disrupt the entire wine bar. He had to settle for glaring at her through the tears in his eyes. "What was that for?" he asked, although his words were slurred because he was gritting his teeth against the stabbing agony pulsing up his leg.

"Stop texting her," Edytha said calmly. "He might read them."

Sulking, Tosh said, "You didn't have to kick me so hard."

Edytha frowned at him. "What's the matter with you? You're acting like a creepy dad who stalked his daughter on her date and is getting ready to put the smackdown on the poor guy."

Tosh put up a finger. "For one thing, he is not a poor guy. He's got money flying out whenever he wiggles his toenails." He put up a second finger. "Second, if I'm the creepy dad, what are you?"

Without batting an eyelash, she said, "I'm the creepy older sister stalking her younger sister on her date to make sure he's not an ax murderer."

"Why does your cause sound so much more righteous than mine?"

She scowled at him. "Because you were being stupid and texting her."

He knew she was right, but ... "I'm worried about her. I've never worked with a civilian on an investigation like this."

Edytha stopped trying to freeze his bum to his chair with her glare. Instead, there was a fierce light in her eyes as she said, "That's why we are here. To protect her."

Tosh sipped his wine (ugh, that was good! If only he weren't working so that he could enjoy the entire glass). He tried to tell himself that he would be this concerned no matter who it was he was watching over, but he knew he was lying to himself. Even though Mimi should mean nothing to him, his jaw was tight with tension and he couldn't seem to relax it.

Maybe it was simply the uncertainty about how much danger she might or might not be in. He didn't usually feel this nervous when he was out on a job, and he knew the reason was because the job involved Mimi.

As soon as it turned eleven o'clock, Edytha kicked his ankle again. This time, a soft yelp escaped him because the toe of her shoe had hit the same tender spot that she had kicked before.

"I wasn't going to jump up and walk over there to wait for her to exit," he grumbled to her.

"I just wanted to make sure you *couldn't* do that," Edytha said blandly.

He scowled at her, which she simply ignored.

But as he crossed his legs and surreptitiously rubbed his ankle, he admitted that it kept his mind off the fact that it was now several minutes past eleven o'clock, when Mimi had told Ivan she had to leave.

Finally, a cab pulled up in front of Leilani's Hideout. Within a few minutes, the doors opened and two figures exited, one as short as a child. As soon as he saw her, Tosh felt like a band had been loosened around his chest, allowing him to breathe more deeply.

In the light from the valet's station, Tosh clearly saw the two figures talking and could tell the exact moment when Ivan asked her for another date.

However, her face was gentle and sweet as she refused him. It was completely unlike the arch, arrogant expression she'd had during their last argument in the summer before their junior years in high school.

He tasted bitterness in his throat, and he reached for his wineglass to try to wash it away. He was surprised to find that his fingers were stiff, and only then did he realize he had been gripping the armrest of his chair so tightly that his fingers had cramped.

He relaxed as Mimi entered the cab. At last, this aggravating night was finally at an end.

"I'll follow Mimi to make sure she's okay," Edytha said, rising. "You stay a few minutes to keep an eye on Ivan."

He nodded, partially relieved that he no longer had to fend off Edytha's barbs about his surly attitude, which he knew he probably deserved.

It was only after she had gone that he realized she had shafted him with the bill.

Ivan didn't remain long outside the bar. Tosh admitted he might have been watching a little too closely to see if Ivan would try to drive. But the man said something to the valet, and within a few minutes a taxi came to pick him up.

Tosh mourned the two glasses of wine that he and Edytha had barely touched, and he mourned even more when he signed the astronomical charge on his credit card. Then he called a cab himself to take him to where he'd parked his car outside of the nightclub.

But he tensed in a different way as he drove to Mimi's aunt's house. He easily remembered the way to the small residential street, even though it had been many years since he had been back here.

Many of the buildings had changed, but the library was still the same. As he drove past, he remembered meeting with Mimi there so the two of them could chat and hang out. The sight caused a hollow emptiness to resound in his chest, not simply because of the memory of Mimi but also because of the memory of his years in this neighborhood, which had been abruptly cut short.

He had been keeping watch to make sure he wasn't followed, but he was still alert when he parked his car on the side of the street and walked to Mimi's aunt's driveway. Mimi and Edytha were standing there, but she had apparently just gotten out of the cab and sent it on its way since it was nowhere in sight.

"Thanks for watching out for me tonight," Mimi told the two of them.

"Are you all right?" Edytha asked her.

Mimi nodded. "I turned him down for a second date."

"Good," Tosh said, although his voice was a bit harsh.

Mimi skewered him with a glance that was off the charts on the Annoyed Scale. "He was actually a rather nice guy. We simply didn't have much in common."

"Including his potential criminal activities," Tosh said.

Mimi bristled, and he could have sworn she started growling at him, but Edytha cut in, "Stop squabbling, you two." To Mimi, she said, "You look exhausted. You can tell us about it tomorrow. Tosh suggested Judy's Diner. Sound good?"

Mimi nodded.

Tosh had gone from being anxious for her safety straight to wanting to strangle her, and yet conversely he was now reluctant to leave her. But he had made sure that she came home from her date safely, and he had nothing else to say to her.

Mimi opened her mouth as she looked at him, and although it was hard to tell in the dark, he thought there was a strangely vulnerable expression on her face. But then she closed her mouth and simply nodded at him. "See you both tomorrow." She turned and headed to the front door, unlocking it with her key.

Tosh and Edytha turned to go as soon as they saw her close the door and lock it behind her. However, when they got to where they had parked their cars, Edytha crossed her arms and said to him, "I deserve a reward." She tried to look at him sternly, but he caught the glint of teasing in her eyes.

"A reward for what?" he asked warily. He already knew he wasn't going to like this.

"I didn't say anything when you came to me, obviously agitated that she showed up at your uncle's restaurant the first time. And I didn't pry when you were even more agitated that she came the second time with the news about her date with Ivan. And now you are circling her like a growling guard dog. I can't be expected to ignore you without some sort of reward. I'm thinking sushi."

He ignored the attempt to pilfer even more of his savings—because Edytha had the absolute most expensive tastes of any woman he'd ever known—and instead replied, "I am not a growling guard dog."

"You're growling, and you can't take your eyes off of her. You're either a guard dog or you're jealous."

He choked a little but managed to reply, "I am not jealous."

"Why don't you finally just tell me what's going on between the two of you?"

"There's absolutely nothing between us."

Edytha tapped her chin. "The sushi just got upgraded to *omakase* at Sushi Maruyama."

"That's two hundred dollars!" Tosh yelped.

She shrugged. "Talk or I'll start looking up even more expensive restaurants on my phone."

"I never agreed to take you out for sushi. And I paid that horrendous tab at the wine bar."

"Oh? Well, my mistake. I guess I'll just have to ask your *boss* about Mimi." She then pretended to gasp in delight as an idea hit.

"No, I'll ask your *coworkers*. One of them might know your sordid past."

"Sushi sounds good. I'll make reservations."

Edytha laughed, but then her face became serious. "Tosh, you know I'm not asking just to hear juicy gossip. I'm genuinely concerned about you."

"I know." He sighed.

Telling her about Mimi was the last thing he wanted to do, but he considered Edytha a friend. He'd worked with her several times in the past two years since he started working at Mahina Security Consultants, and she'd often request him specifically when she needed undercover work for her investigations. The two of them worked well together and even hung out outside of work. All joking aside, he couldn't ignore her entreaty now.

He pointed to a darkened house a couple of doors down the street. "I used to live there, until the middle of my junior year of high school. Mimi and I are the same age, and we would play together every summer when she came to Hawaii to stay with her aunt."

Edytha's eyebrows rose. "I had no idea you've known each other for so long."

"I hadn't spoken to her in twenty years, until the other day when I had to follow that suspicious customer into her aunt's store to listen in on the conversation with Waite."

"Did you know she was working there?"

"No, not until I entered the store and saw her."

"Why haven't you spoken to her for so long?"

He gusted another sigh. Thinking about it now, it seemed trivial, but it had been one of many things that caused the rift between them. "That summer before my junior year, just before Mimi had to leave to go back to California, she asked me to go out with her."

Edytha frowned and circled her hands in the air. "I fail to see why that would cause the two of you to avoid each other like the plague."

"Mimi has always been like this." He gestured toward her aunt's house. "Cute, friendly, skilled at charming men. I was a gloomy sixteen-year-old with bad skin, braces, and a haircut that was only fashionable in Akihabara."

"I still don't see why it was such a sin for her to want to go out with you."

"She didn't mean it. She asked in a breezy way, which told me that she wasn't really serious and she was just making fun of me."

"Maybe she wasn't."

"We were childhood friends—I knew her. I ... didn't respond very well."

Edytha grimaced. "I can almost imagine what that looked like."

Edytha was the guardian for her sixteen-year-old nephew, and while his haircut was normal, Shohei had bad skin and braces. She probably knew exactly how sixteen-year-old Tosh had responded.

"I was especially angry because I actually liked her," he softly confessed.

"Oh, that is not obvious at *all*," Edytha deadpanned.

He glowered at her. "Shut up. I was sixteen, embarrassed, and offended. All my old insecurities cropped up, and I felt like she was treating me like another guy in the string of boys she'd known."

"Is that what you said to her?"

"I don't remember what I said." Tosh rubbed the back of his head. "All I remember was feeling hurt and insulted, and also mad at myself. I knew she was good at getting guys to do things for her, and I could see myself doing the same, like a servant. I didn't want to be like that. I'd seen her treat men like pets. So I probably said something more cruel than I meant to. She yelled at me and stormed off. And then, well ... my dad died. And we moved. And reconnecting with her wasn't all that important to me."

"What she said to you can't still be bothering you."

"No. I hadn't even thought of her in years." But as soon as he said that, he realized that the latter portion was a lie.

He would think of her whenever he happened to see something from *The Ritual Metallurgist*, the manga series the two of them had enjoyed so much together. He remembered her whenever he heard of someone who was learning Japanese. He remembered her whenever he met someone also interested in

Japanese light novels featuring duke's daughters, princes, and magic, just like she did. It would only be a fleeting image of her face, her mouth wide with laughter, making her cheeks round and rosy and her eyes into dark crescent shapes. But he always remembered her, however briefly.

Then he realized he had been silent for too long. He cleared his throat. "I guess I'm just annoyed that I still think she's cute."

Edytha grinned and nudged his shoulder with hers. "You should tell her that."

"She would smile and then punch me between the eyes."

"Well, your grouchy attitude tonight didn't compare very well against Ivan, who is apparently rather nice despite the tiny little fact that he might be into drugs."

Tosh rolled his eyes. But despite Mimi's words about Ivan, he had been able to tell that she hadn't been all that interested in him. Her polite smiles and soft laughter were a far cry from the Mimi he remembered. She hadn't talked about anything with Ivan that made her eyes light up like he'd seen them do so often in the past. And that made him feel …

No, no, no, back up. Not going there. What did he care that Mimi didn't really like Ivan, and that Tosh had known what she used to look like when she was truly having fun?

"I'm sure she's different now," Edytha said.

"I'm sure you're right, but I still don't want to let her get close to me."

"Tosh, she's not poison," Edytha protested.

"I know that. What I meant was … When I was younger, it was easy for me to lose sight of who I was when I was with her because her personality overwhelmed me so easily. I don't want to do that again. I don't want to be attracted to her."

Edytha studied him. "Tosh, it almost sounds like you're *afraid* to be attracted to her."

"Maybe I am. Before, I would always give in and do whatever she wanted, and I don't want that. I want a relationship where the two of us are equals. But I don't feel like an equal with Mimi."

Edytha sighed. "I'm going to be frank with you. It sounds like you still need to deal with some lingering insecurities, and it's causing you to have assumptions about who she is now."

He could always count on Edytha to fearlessly tell him hard truths. He might think he knew Mimi, but he didn't. He didn't even know how she felt about him—she might hate his guts and would choose to jump into a volcano over breathing the same air as him.

But there was one thing he knew that drove him, that made him ignore the mess of his thoughts and feelings at this moment. He didn't want to be trapped in the past again, as he had been in the years after his father's death.

He had finally found a job that not only allowed him to help people but also to stay physically active and utilize his love of acting to do it. He felt stable, even though he no longer needed to have a steady income to support his mother and sister.

The last thing he needed was the kind of emotional mess of things thrown together like one of Edytha's (frankly vile) green smoothies. That was all from a time in his past that was especially difficult for him—and not only because of Mimi.

Which was why he'd do what he could to simply keep her at arm's length.

"I can see why you're uncomfortable with her," Edytha said, "but you should consider that maybe you should stop sniping at her."

Tosh groaned and scrubbed at his face with his hand. "I know. I can't seem to help myself."

"Maybe you just need more time to talk to her and get to know who she is now, rather than just remembering how she was twenty years ago."

"I know you're right—"

"I'm always right."

He ignored that. "—but I doubt I'll have a chance. Even if we find evidence Ivan is involved in drugs, that's for the police to investigate, not us. We're still just watching Waite."

"You never know," Edytha said as she turned to head to her car. "It could be that Mimi has been wanting to talk to you again all this time."

10

Mimi was so exhausted that she wouldn't be surprised if she did a faceplant into her dinner tonight.

She hadn't slept well. All night, she replayed the events of the date, and she tossed and turned and cringed in regret. Every time she thought she matured, she did something to prove she was still the same.

Mimi hadn't wanted to lead Ivan on, but she suspected that was exactly what she did. He had had a much more favorable impression of their date than she had.

If it had been a more honest date, if she'd been with him to get to know him and see what he was like rather than fishing for information, she'd have known soon enough that they didn't have a deeper connection. He loved surrounding himself with people who all knew and liked him. It was almost as if he collected friends like some people collected stamps.

But that wasn't what she liked. Even when she was younger, she preferred one-on-one interactions over being in the midst of a crowd. If she was with someone, she wanted to capture their undivided attention.

In her twenties, she would have simply said goodbye and walked out on Ivan in the middle of the club. Now that she was older, if it had been a real date, she would have more subtly indicated that she wasn't having fun.

Instead, Mimi had made Ivan think that she was okay with everything he was doing because she wanted to interrogate him.

As she blearily watched her bedroom lighten with the dawn, she reflected that while she thought she'd reached the age where she'd stop doing things that she was remorseful about later, apparently she hadn't grown up enough.

She hadn't been lying when she told Ivan she had to work early the next morning—she got out of bed at six to help Auntie Noriko make lotions in her stillroom. But on top of that, after the store closed, she and Trinda had to inventory and restock the shelves.

So she was a little late in meeting Tosh and Edytha at Judy's Diner, which was only ten minutes away from her aunt's house. When she drove into the parking lot around nine o'clock, despite the late hour, it was packed with cars just like it had always been.

She knew exactly what she was going to order—those gigantic, fluffy blueberry pancakes that they served at any time of the day or night.

Even though both Edytha and Tosh lived on the North Shore, he had suggested this little mom-and-pop diner for their meeting. She had assumed it was simply because it was close to her aunt's house and he was being considerate of her.

But maybe he suggested it because he remembered how much she enjoyed the food here. She hadn't expected him to be so kind to her, but then again, he had always been a kind boy, whether to his friends or strangers. Perhaps it was still just his nature.

And what was her nature? Still manipulative and heartless, she reflected bitterly.

There was a covered waiting area in front of the doors, open on two sides, and on the third was the wall of the restaurant building. Against the wall had been built a koi pond made of black Hawaiian rocks, with a waterfall trickling into it.

Edytha and Tosh stood in front of the pond, looking down at the fish inside. The owner of the restaurant, a tiny Asian lady who looked like she was a hundred years old, was fishing coins out of the pond and grumbling about the trash people threw in with her precious fish.

"Hi, Mrs. Kim," Mimi said as she came up to them. Her auntie and uncle came here once or twice a month at minimum, sometimes for breakfast and sometimes for dinner, so while Mimi wasn't quite a regular like them, she always got a warm welcome when she came to Hawaii for the summer.

The old woman squinted at her through her thick glasses for a moment, then broke out into a toothy smile. She gestured for Mimi to come closer and gave her a bony half-hug while holding the handle of the fishing net with her other hand. "Oh, you're back again. How long you staying?"

"Until after New Year's."

"Good, good. Come by for mochi soup."

"You bet, Mrs. Kim." Every New Year's morning, the diner made a special pot of mochi soup for their Japanese breakfast special. She turned to Edytha and Tosh as Mrs. Kim went back to cleaning out the fishpond. "Sorry I'm a bit late."

"No worries." Edytha leaned closer and whispered, "Is that the owner? Is she who the restaurant is named after?"

"She is the owner, but the restaurant is named after Big Judy." Mimi pointed to the largest of the koi in the pond, a fat white- and gold-colored fish that was swimming lazily in the still waters at the end farthest from the waterfall.

Edytha blinked at her.

"Wait, all this time I thought it was named after Mrs. Kim but it was named after her pet fish?" Tosh burst out.

"According to Auntie Noriko, there have been something like twelve Big Judys. The name passes to whatever fish happens to be the biggest in the pond."

Mrs. Kim didn't look their way, but she cackled. "One of these days, I'm gonna fry him up."

Edytha looked horrified, so Mimi whispered, "She won't really fry him up."

"Judy is a he?" Tosh asked weakly.

"Have your fond childhood memories been dashed to pieces?" Mimi asked him.

Tosh scowled at her.

The diner's distinctive smell of browned butter hit as soon as she entered the front doors and brought back memories of when she and Tosh had come here for a late-night snack, either just the two of them or with several of his friends. It was strange, like wearing her clothes inside out, to be here with Tosh again but to not be friends.

They were quickly seated at one of the round booths near the back of the restaurant, beside tall windows looking out onto the boulevard. At this time of the evening, the tinted windows acted like mirrors reflecting the busy diner.

Mimi didn't bother with the tattered menu. "I want the blueberry pancakes," she told the waitress.

"That sounds good. I'll get that too," Edytha said.

Tosh hesitated, scanning the menu. Mimi knew that he was tempted to also get the pancakes but was reluctant to order them.

He had always been embarrassed by his astronomical sweet tooth because he felt it clashed with his idea of what a man should be like. Mimi had needled him about it so much that he usually just gave in and indulged whenever he was with her. But when he was with his friends, he would order something he considered more manly, like super spicy chili or a loaded burger.

"You know you want to," Edytha teased him.

Tosh glared at her briefly but then ordered the pancakes along with a side of bacon, just like he always used to.

Seeing him order the pancakes somehow soothed Mimi deep inside, as if to reassure her that Tosh hadn't changed that much from when she knew him. Despite the terrible thing she did to him, and despite the tragedy that Minnie's boyfriend had told her about, Tosh's stupid pancakes gave her hope that he was still the same person and their relationship could return to what it had been.

No, she was just deluding herself. He might be the same person, but so was she, if her regrets over how she treated Ivan were any indication.

When they were teenagers, she had been excessively cruel and treated Tosh like a joke. Their relationship could never be the same. He had been her good friend, and she had burned him.

She needed to simply finish her work for Edytha, get a moment alone with Tosh to finally apologize to him, and then try to forget about him.

Mimi asked Edytha, "Did you take screenshots of the people I met last night?"

"I got good pictures of almost all of them, but unfortunately, the sound was muffled. Do you remember some of their names?"

"I remember the names of everyone I met." She pulled a piece of paper from her purse and handed it to Edytha. "I wrote this list after I got home last night. However, if you show me a person's photo, I should be able to recall their name."

Edytha's mouth dropped open. "This list is huge! Did you really remember everyone's name?"

Mimi wasn't sure how to respond to that aside from a lame, "Yes?"

But then she was surprised when Tosh said, "Mimi's always been like that. She's good with names."

Warmth spread through her chest … which was doused the next moment like hurling a slushy in her face.

Tosh continued, "Which is strange because she can never remember where she left her car keys. She always leaves them in a different place."

"You didn't need to add that," Mimi snapped at him.

Tosh opened his mouth, but Edytha interrupted their spat. "What are these places?" She pointed to the bottom of the list.

"Those are the bars and restaurants that Ivan mentioned he likes to go to, and also the things he likes to do on weekends. Those last two are the golf courses he likes."

Tosh leaned closer to Edytha to look at the list. He was so comfortable in invading her personal space—was their relationship purely professional, or were they closer than that?

But then she mentally slapped herself. She needed to focus. She knew almost nothing about Edytha—she wasn't wearing a ring, but she might be married already and simply didn't wear one.

And if she wasn't married, it shouldn't matter to Mimi if the two of them were dating. Besides, Edytha was a few years older than Mimi and Tosh, but she was still gorgeous. Mimi wouldn't blame Tosh if he had formed a relationship with her.

But the sight of the two of them with their heads so close together still made a tightness form in her chest.

Edytha pointed to the list. "All these bars and restaurants—even his leisure activities—are very expensive."

"I only recognized one or two restaurants, but I know they're high-end," Mimi said.

Edytha continued looking at the list and suddenly stiffened. "John Hackett?"

"Ivan said John is probably his closest friend," Mimi said. Edytha's pinched face alarmed her, so she asked, "What's wrong?"

"I admit," Edytha said slowly, "I'm becoming more personally interested in Ivan than in Waite."

"Because of that John Hackett guy?" Mimi asked. "Why?"

"This past year, a large percentage of the staff at the day spa have been quitting, and I discovered that they've all gone to work for the Pleiades Resort. If they're unhappy and want to leave—and especially if the resort can pay them the amount of money that they want—I'm not one to stop them. But then the resort started trying to headhunt some of my staff who had already refused them."

"Did they want to try an increased offer or something?" Mimi asked.

"No, their tactics turned aggressive." The line of Edytha's mouth was grim. "John Hackett stalked Lila, one of my best massage therapists, and approached her at her house, trying to bully her into working for Pleiades. Lila told me that she was pretty frightened. She doesn't know what might've happened if her boyfriend hadn't shown up videotaping John Hackett in the act of threatening Lila."

Threatening her? Mimi belatedly realized her mouth was wide open in shock, and she closed it.

"We haven't seen John Hackett around the spa or any of my other staff since the summer," Edytha said, "but it seems as though the Pleiades Resort is connected to the fact that some of my employees have been hired away."

"This man Ivan might be involved in all that," Tosh said.

"We don't have any proof that Ivan is connected with John's actions," Edytha said, "but I certainly don't trust him."

"It might be a coincidence that the two of them know each other," Mimi said.

"But now I'm even more concerned about the fact that you went on a date with Ivan," Edytha said. "We shouldn't have allowed you to go."

"I've been on plenty of dates," Mimi said, "and I know how to stay safe. Ivan didn't even seem to mind that I was texting to tell someone about where I was at all times."

"I'm just glad you turned him down for a second date," Edytha said.

"But he also seemed pretty disappointed. He's not the most observant and considerate guy," Mimi said bluntly, "but he appreciated how I entertained the dates of the people who spoke to him at the club. I think that's the only reason he wanted to see me again."

"Don't sell yourself short," Edytha said.

"He's a handsome guy," Mimi said, "so he'll probably get another girl soon enough. There's no chance that he's pining for me or anything like that."

They suddenly got their food, and the list was set aside so they could settle themselves with cutlery and napkins. Mimi slathered maple syrup on her pancakes, and Edytha did the same.

Mimi eyed Tosh, knowing he was going to pour his syrup on the side of his plate and dip both his pancake pieces and bacon into it. Which he did.

Then she wanted to drum at her head in frustration. Why did it matter to her what he did with his stupid maple syrup? Stupid pancakes. Stupid Mimi.

She took a huge bite of blueberry pancake and was slightly

mollified by the buttery, tender pancake and slightly tart blueberries tempered with just the right amount of maple syrup.

Mimi went over the date again, pointing out things she wrote down on the list that Ivan had talked about. She also went through the screenshots that Edytha had taken while she was on the video call with Mimi, matching each face with a name. It took them so long that Mimi had a chance to order hand-poured coffee—a new addition that the diner had never had when she was in high school —while Tosh ordered coffee and one of the restaurant's homemade cream puffs.

"This has been helpful," Edytha said just as the waitress delivered a paper bag filled with boxes of food. Earlier, she had ordered a chicken-fried steak and mashed potatoes to go. "You two can stay and finish your coffee, but I have to go back home and feed Shohei."

"I'm sorry to keep you from your husband," Mimi said. "We could have done this over a video call."

Edytha laughed and shook her head. "Shohei is my teenage nephew. He lives with me at the day spa because I'm his guardian and because technically he owns half the spa. He had his video game competition tonight, so he wouldn't even have wanted me to bother him until after that was done."

"Oh." Mimi was trying to decide if she was happier when she thought Edytha was married—which of course would have been thoroughly super-awful of her.

"Mimi, if I don't see you again, it's been nice meeting you."

"Same here."

"Tosh, I'll see you tomorrow."

"Bye, Edytha."

Mimi wasn't certain, but she thought she caught Edytha giving Tosh a wink just before she left. She tried to decide if she was amused or mortified. Probably mortified. Tosh looked like the custard in his cream puff had gone bad.

Regardless of what Edytha thought about the two of them, Mimi was grateful she left them together. She had been having such a hard time getting time alone with Tosh that she realized she needed to speak to him right away before he ran away or came up with some excuse to avoid her.

"Tosh, that argument we had as teenagers—"

"Don't worry about it," he said curtly.

"Let me finish, you jerk," she snapped, then immediately regretted it. She'd reverted to the casual way she spoke to him when they were kids. "I'm sorry, old habits," she muttered. "What I want to say is that I'm sorry about our argument. It was entirely my fault. When I came back to Hawaii the next summer, you had already moved away and I never got a chance to apologize to you." It was a profound relief to finally get it off her chest.

She could tell that Tosh was about to say something like "It's fine," but something stopped him. He rolled his coffee cup between his hands. Finally, he asked, "Why did you ask me out, or were you just messing with me?"

The shame over her past self was like both nausea in her stomach and pain jolting through her body. "I'm sorry you thought that. I was serious, but I was also embarrassed about it. That's why I came across like such a tramp."

"You weren't a tramp, Mimi," he said with a sigh. "You just didn't seem like you were sincere. I thought you were mocking me."

"I'm sorry. I don't blame you for getting so mad at me back then. When I found that art book I'd borrowed from you in my aunt's house, I felt like I was being suffocated by all the guilt and regret over how shallow a person I'd been the last time I spoke to you." She turned to face him fully. "I'm ashamed of how I acted toward you. I ruined our friendship. I want to think I've become a more mature and kinder person, but seeing the book and remembering the past was painful. It made me realize that I may not have changed in the way I wanted to."

For some reason—maybe the intensity of her gaze—Tosh flushed bright red. He mumbled, "It's fine. Thanks for returning the book."

There were a few awkward minutes of silence between them as Mimi sipped her coffee and Tosh finished his cream puff. She wanted to just say goodbye and leave, but was that too abrupt?

Should she say something more to him? If so, she didn't know what.

She inhaled, about to tell him she should go, when he blurted out, "Do you still read manga and light novels?"

"Oh. Uh, yeah." She was surprised he'd asked that. "Do you?"

"I never stopped."

She could tell he was still a bit embarrassed to admit that.

He asked, "Do you read them in English, or do you still read them in Japanese?"

Now it was Mimi's turn to be embarrassed that Tosh had remembered her efforts to learn Japanese just so she could read the books he'd lent to her. But she'd loved the series *The Ritual Metallurgist* and had wanted to be able to read new volumes as they came out.

"Yes, I read a few light novels in Japanese." While she didn't read as many novels as she used to, she read almost exclusively light novels, whether in Japanese or translated into English and published in the US. The only other books she read were the Christian romance novels she borrowed from Trish.

"It's a lot easier to buy books in Japanese these days, whereas when we were kids, they were so expensive," Tosh said.

Mimi nodded. "I'm glad that now there are websites where you can buy eBook versions." She remembered something she had always wanted to ask him, and the question tumbled out of her mouth before she could stop it. "Did you read the author's series after she finished *The Ritual Metallurgist*?"

"Do you mean *The Sword of Bunny Foo Foo*?"

"That's the one. The series just stopped, even though it had an anime and video game made out of it. Was it ever finished?"

"The artist Sanae Komori had some family issues. You didn't hear about it? It was on her social media account."

"She has a social media account?" It hadn't even occurred to her that the artist might be posting updates online. Back when they were first reading *The Ritual Metallurgist*, social media hadn't taken off yet, and the two of them were too young to be able to (legally) have a social media account anyway.

"She finally finished *Bunny Foo Foo* a couple months ago," Tosh said.

"Oh. I used to occasionally look up the artist on the website where I buy my Japanese books, but I haven't checked in a while."

"The ending seemed a bit rushed, and there was speculation that the publisher had pushed her to finish up the series quickly since she'd been on hiatus for so long. Maybe they worried that she'd have to go on hiatus again. The art was just as good, but the story …" Tosh trailed off, as though he'd suddenly realized who it was he was talking to and the hot mess of bad history between them. "Uh … well, I suppose you'll read it yourself," he mumbled.

Mimi couldn't stop herself from smiling. He was acting like he always did with her when they discussed Japanese media. "I'll look for the last volume."

"There were five more."

She stopped herself from asking to borrow his copies. She didn't feel close enough to do that with him again. And if she asked and he looked uncomfortable, that would make her feel like a bigger loser than she already did. She tried to convince herself that Tosh might only have eBook versions, but considering how he had liked seeing the volumes of *The Ritual Metallurgist* lined up on his bookshelf, she was only fooling herself—of *course* he'd have the physical books.

The silence between them was awkward again, so she asked, "So, um, why were you working at your uncle's restaurant if you have a job at that security consulting firm?"

"I only work in the evenings during busy seasons."

From her childhood, she dredged up a memory of a big man with a wide, toothy smile. "Does the restaurant belong to your Uncle Buster? Your mom's brother?"

"You remember meeting him?"

"He was so friendly. He kept buying me ice cream, telling me it would help me grow taller."

"The truth is that he likes ice cream, and if he bought it for us, he could eat it without getting in trouble with his wife."

"No wonder! I thought it was unusual that he was so invested in me growing taller." She felt a little stupid for thinking that all this time and cleared her throat. "I didn't know your family was so close to him. He didn't visit you often in those days."

"After my dad died—" There was a hardness in his tone as he said the words. "—my uncle took our family in. He helped us out a lot. So when he decided to open his restaurant, all of us pitched in however we could. During holidays, especially, he needs extra staff, so I usually work in the bar in the evenings, and my sister works as a waitress. My mom already works for him full-time, organizing his staffing and schedules and coordinating supply orders and deliveries." His eyes suddenly narrowed as he regarded her. "I never asked you how you knew I was working there."

Mimi felt her neck flushing. "I wanted to return the book to you, so I had my cousin Trinda reach out to her classmates to see if anyone knew how to contact you. One of them knew Minnie, the girlfriend of one of your ex-coworkers."

"Oh, yeah. I saw Raymond a couple months ago."

She watched his face at the mention of Minnie's name, but he didn't react in any particular way—certainly not like how she thought someone suffering from unrequited love would look.

Then again, what did she know? Was she expecting him to clutch his heart and groan about how he was pained by the name of the woman he had desperately longed for but couldn't have? He was probably over her by now.

"Minnie and Raymond are really nice." She tried to keep her face neutral because she wasn't sure if Tosh knew that Raymond suspected him of having a crush on Minnie. "He said you worked at his company. Honestly, I can't picture you as a security guard. I would've thought that you would go into teaching or theater."

"At the time, I wanted a steady job to help support my family, but with my uncle's restaurant taking off, now I don't need to worry as much. When I was laid off, I applied at Mahina Security Consultants and got the job right away." He grinned at her, suddenly looking like the teenage boy she remembered. "Basically, I'm paid to cosplay."

"What?"

"Most of my coworkers do general security consultations, but my specialty is security assessment. I disguise myself and attempt to infiltrate a company to test the weaknesses of the security system."

Mimi laughed. "So you get to act for your job."

"Yeah, but it's a bit more exciting because I'm out in the real world rather than on a stage, and I'm trying not to get caught."

She smiled at him. "I'm glad you got to do something you enjoy."

Mimi realized too late that she had been too sincere. She should have instead insulted his intelligence or taken potshots at the angsty cosplay he used to do. Because ironically, the kindness of her remark brought back the stilted silence between them.

He cleared his throat. "What about you? Did you end up working for your mom's restaurant like you wanted to?"

The bitterness fizzled like a sunburn on her skin, even though it had been years—decades, in fact—since Mimi realized her mother had no intention of allowing her to help with the restaurant.

"My mom wanted my cousin to work at the restaurant instead," Mimi said, trying to keep her voice neutral. "To be honest, Jenn is a much better chef than I am. But that also makes it ridiculous to think that she would work for my mom's restaurant. Jenn has the kind of skill where she needed a restaurant of her own. And in hindsight, I wouldn't have enjoyed working at Mom's restaurant, either. She's too controlling, and I would have wanted to try new things, which she wouldn't have allowed me to do." She grinned. "Instead, I went to work for my cousin Jenn."

"Was your mom upset?"

Mimi wasn't quite able to hide the grimace she made. "No, and I should've expected that. She didn't care that I'd chosen another restaurant over hers because she hadn't wanted me to work at her restaurant anyway. But she was upset that I chose to work for the restaurant of the cousin who had directly refused to work at *her* restaurant."

She tried to hide how her relationship with her mother was still strained and fraying, but Tosh had always known about how deeply her mother's words could cut her. He said softly, "I know it must've hurt, but I think you're happier this way."

He had always been far more sensitive to her feelings than even she was herself. His words touched her like an affirming hand on her shoulder, and she managed to smile at him. "You're right. I learned a lot in working for Jenn."

"Are you going to open your own restaurant?"

"Probably not …"

They talked long after finishing their drinks, and Mimi had a great time catching up with him. Perhaps he had forgiven her after all. She was glad she'd had a chance to apologize to him.

Judy's Diner used to be open twenty-four hours, but they had switched to closing at eleven o'clock a few years ago, so Mimi and Tosh found themselves chased out.

Out in the parking lot, Mimi hesitated before heading to her car. "Are you still going to be investigating Waite?"

Tosh nodded. "If you see me, don't say anything."

She rolled her eyes. "I'm not stupid, Tosh."

He gave her a half-smile. "I know you're not stupid. Your brain is sharper than your stilettos of torture."

That exact expression on his face and those exact words triggered a memory from high school. He'd said that to her once, and she'd forgotten the warmth that filled her when he said it, to have a boy who called her smart rather than cute or pretty. How often had that happened in her life?

And then he completely ruined it when he added, "Although there was that one time you wrecked my grand entrance at that Halloween party …"

"I was eight! And when are you going to accept that it was totally obvious it was you—"

"No way! My disguise was flawless—"

"If it was flawless, I wouldn't have recognized you. Immediately."

He had opened his mouth to protest, but shut it with a snap. "Just don't out me the next time. If there is a next time."

She would have retorted, except she hadn't recognized him at all when he'd been standing three feet away from her. "Fine, fine." She hesitated, then said, "I hope I can see you again before I have to leave Hawaii."

His face faltered. Not a lot, just a little bit. Then he gave a quick smile that didn't quite look sincere. "Sure, that'd be great."

Had Mimi misunderstood his friendliness as they chatted together? Was he hanging out with her just to be nice? Because he had been the sort of boy who would do that to a pathetic girl like her. In reality, did he not want anything to do with her?

She shouldn't be surprised. After all, she'd brought it on herself. She would respect his wishes and stay away from him. She owed him that much, at least.

They said their goodbyes, and she went to her truck for the short drive to her aunt's house.

She had been relieved when she left Ivan, knowing she wouldn't see him again. But in leaving Tosh, the thought made her feel as if her insides had been scooped out, and only shadows echoed within.

But maybe this was simply what she deserved after how she'd treated him, after how she'd treated their friendship as if it were worthless.

When she became a Christian several years ago, Jenn had told her that she was a new person in Christ. In general, she felt happier and more at peace with herself. But then there were moments like this that popped up, making her feel like the specter of her old self was going to haunt her over and over again for the rest of her life.

11

For an entire week, Mimi would look up every time a customer came in and hope to see Tosh in disguise.

A male Japanese tourist entered the store and Mimi tensed until she saw the woman—likely his girlfriend or wife—enter after him.

She reminded herself that she was trying to *forget* about Tosh.

Oh, and about the investigation.

Trinda sidled closer to her. "You've been kind of jumpy lately."

"Sorry. I haven't been sleeping well."

She had considered telling Auntie Noriko about the fact that Waite was being investigated by a private investigator, but she eventually decided not to. There still wasn't evidence he was into drugs, and she didn't want to slander his reputation.

Waite certainly didn't look like those drug addicts on TV—no bloodshot eyes or shaking hands. He was perfectly polite to the customers, although he did give Mimi a few strange looks until she realized she was staring at him.

She managed to quickly say, "You've got something on your face …" and gesture to her mouth, to explain why she was peering at him as if he was a particularly ugly bug under a microscope. She was starting to feel silly for suspecting him of nefarious doings.

The store was getting busy with Thanksgiving coming up, hosting several specials and sales, and Mimi found that when she threw herself into doing her job, she *almost* stopped thinking about Tosh. It had helped that she had needed to get up early all week to help Auntie Noriko make extra lotions and other products since their stock was flying off the shelves.

But keeping busy also made her more tired than usual. And that made her careless.

At the end of the workday, she said goodbye to Trinda, who was remaining at the store to do some paperwork in her office in the back. But as she headed to her truck in the covered parking garage at Ala Moana Center, she wasn't paying attention to her surroundings.

"Hey, Mimi!"

The voice made her blood turn to ice. Her heart fluttered uncomfortably and queasiness burbled in her stomach, but she managed to paste a smile (she hoped it was a smile and not a grimace) on her face before turning around.

Ivan was striding toward her, hand raised and face beaming. He wasn't exactly the picture of a man whose request for a second date had been rejected.

Had she been too gentle with him? She hadn't wanted to be rude because it wasn't like he'd been a total jerk during their evening together. Whenever a guy *really* hadn't treated her well and had asked for a second date, she had no qualms about bluntly refusing—as in, as obvious as Godzilla stomping a city to rubble.

Mimi hadn't meshed with Ivan's personality, but she had also done what she could to smooth his discussions with his friends. Maybe he'd interpreted that as, *She just doesn't realize how compatible we are*, or maybe he was simply thinking, *I need a chick like this at my side to support me and I'll do anything to get her there, including stalking her in a parking garage like a horror movie serial killer.*

"Hi, Ivan. I didn't expect to see you here." She did her best not to look nervous and to sound friendly. "Don't you work in Waialua? What are you doing in Honolulu?"

"Oh, my boss asked me to deliver something to Wanderlust

Pathways travel agency. I was going to stop by your aunt's store to say hi when I saw you leave, so I chased after you."

So maybe he wasn't stalking her? She was familiar with Wanderlust Pathways—they worked out of a tiny kiosk only a few hundred yards away from Miwaku. In fact, the name "Wanderlust Pathways" wasn't obvious since there wasn't a big sign anywhere on the kiosk, and for Ivan to even know the travel agency name might mean he had truly had business with them. It wasn't a stretch for them to have some sort of partnership with Pleiades Resort.

At the same time, why had he wanted to stop by her aunt's shop to say hi to her? Hadn't she refused him? Was he just trying to be nice to show there weren't hard feelings?

Or maybe he'd been hoping to try to convince her again to go out with him? Did he have an ulterior motive for talking to her or was she just being paranoid?

She would have said she was too cynical if he hadn't continued striding toward her, getting a little too close for comfort.

Mimi took a small step back. "How have you been?" she asked politely, while her mind was racing.

"Oh, just busy with work," he replied easily. He closed the distance between them again, his expression perfectly friendly.

But Mimi's breathing began to quicken. Something about his body language seemed almost … threatening.

Was she just imagining it? Maybe she was misinterpreting him. It could be that he simply wanted something from her and his desire was making him seem more insistent than he really was.

At moments like these, she wished she wasn't so short. Anyone in the parking garage would have a hard time even seeing the top of her head over the tall SUVs and trucks. If Ivan grabbed at her, would anyone notice, even if they were staring right at them? Or was she being silly to think that Ivan would try to hurt her?

Because she was small, for her entire life, she'd been creative and worked hard to maintain control of the situations around her. She didn't want to inadvertently become a victim of someone who thought she was helpless.

She'd been distracted when she headed to her car, so she

hadn't been as vigilant as she usually was. Now, belatedly, she reached her hand slowly into her purse. "I'm afraid I'm in a bit of a hurry—"

"Mimi!"

She took full advantage of the voice calling to her to step farther away from Ivan and look at the figure running toward her.

Mimi admitted she nearly cried in relief when she saw Edytha. The PI wore Hollywood-star sunglasses and a large floppy hat with a wide brim, and they would have screamed "secret agent surveilling a suspect" if she hadn't also paired it with a loose sundress and sandals, her dark hair streaming loose behind her. She looked even younger than Mimi in that outfit.

"I'm so sorry I'm late," Edytha said breathlessly as she approached them, taking off her sunglasses. "Are you ready to go?"

Mimi smoothly ran with Edytha's story. "In a minute. Can you wait while I talk to Ivan?" She gestured to where he still stood.

Edytha smiled at him in a friendly way, but Mimi could see sharpness like broken bottle shards in her green-brown eyes. "Sure. I'll be just over there." She moved barely a few feet away, close enough to overhear them.

Ivan shot Edytha an annoyed look and tried to cup his hand under Mimi's elbow, ostensibly to guide her out of earshot, but Mimi smoothly avoided his grip and remained where she stood. She regarded him impassively, knowing her silence would hopefully further clue him in that she wasn't interested in him.

He cleared his throat. "I was wondering if you'd like to go out for coffee sometime."

Mimi had probably been too apologetic and gentle when she refused him last week, so it wasn't entirely his fault that he hadn't gotten the message. She had to decide if she was going to be rampaging-elephant-mean and stomp all over his heart or simply be a little more forceful than the last time they'd spoken.

If she hadn't known that Waite was being investigated, would she have accepted his offer of a date? Maybe. Maybe not. She'd never know. But she had to take responsibility for the fact that she chose to be friendly with him in the first place.

"I don't think it's a good idea," she said. "I'm leaving Hawaii in a few weeks."

"That doesn't bother me. I'm … not all that interested in long-distance relationships."

His words made it more obvious to her that they were completely missing each other like bullets in cop dramas on TV. She had meant that she didn't want him getting more attached to her in the short time she had left in Hawaii when she was only indifferent about him. "I've reached a point in my life where I avoid short-term relationships." She hoped that being honest with him would help him to understand.

It didn't.

His face darkened. "Then why did you go on a date with me in the first place?"

Irritation flared, sizzling under her skin. "You're making it sound like this is all my fault. *You* asked *me*. I knew nothing about you, which was why I wanted to spend time with you. But now it's obvious we have nothing in common, including our feelings about long-distance relationships."

Ivan's voice rose in volume. "Listen, you—"

"Hey!" Edytha interrupted with a voice that was sharper than the tension between them.

But Mimi raised a hand toward her. "I appreciate your help, but I'll handle this." She turned to face Ivan and looked him firmly in the eyes. "I am *not* interested in a dating relationship with you."

His mouth had flattened into an ugly line. "You had to have known when I asked you—"

"No, I didn't have to know anything. I accepted a date from a stranger. There were no expectations."

"You acted like you were having a good time," he accused her.

"I was trying to be a pleasant date." Maybe she shouldn't have tried so hard to accommodate him. "I was trying to get to know you better."

"You were misleading me."

The flickering flames of her irritation *whooshed* into a conflagration. "I was not misleading you. Is there something wrong with trying to be nice to you and your friends?" A small part of her admitted that she might have been overreacting a bit because there had been times in her more sordid past when she had deliberately misled a date or two, but this was not one of them.

Ivan still looked mulish, but not as angry as before. "I thought we had something there."

Her anger was dampened by a few waves of regret. She hadn't intentionally misled him, but she *had* been guiding their conversation to find out more about him. "I didn't intend to give that impression, but I can't force myself to feel something I don't." She wondered if she should have been kinder in her words, but she didn't want to continue to water any more misunderstandings between them.

He frowned at her, and his tone was petulant as he said, "I don't understand. I did everything I could to show you a good time."

"I appreciated that, I really did. But why would you want to be with someone who doesn't enjoy the same things you do and who's leaving in a few weeks?"

He continued to glower at her, and while she kept her face cool and unmovable, inside she second-guessed herself. Should she have tried to stroke his ego a bit? Had she been overly harsh? She wasn't as diplomatic as some of her other cousins, a fact that often got her in trouble when her tendency toward sassiness went off the rails.

But if she hadn't been trying to help Edytha in the investigation, if this had been just a regular date … This was what she'd have said and done. If she hadn't tried to wrestle down her terrible temper, she might have even been more brutal.

And she would have had one more regret over her past actions. It was starting to grow longer and longer, like a stream of toilet paper stuck to her shoe after she left the restroom.

Her unhinged state of mind was apparently well-hidden, because Ivan finally huffed out, "Fine," and stalked away.

Mimi stared after him until she saw him leave the parking garage, then she let out a low, shaky breath. Her hands began to tremble, but she clenched them into fists, then loosened them.

She'd done it. She'd gotten through to him. He wouldn't bother her anymore … right?

Mimi should have been more afraid of him, but instead, she'd felt a desire to communicate with him, to try to explain, to try to make amends. The hurt in Ivan's eyes had reminded her of how Tosh had looked when she flippantly asked him to go out with her, of how other boyfriends had looked when she did or said something to wound them.

Was she cursed to do nothing but hurt men?

Edytha was suddenly beside her. "Are you all right?"

"Yes. Thanks for that. Were you watching my aunt's store?"

Edytha nodded. "It seemed to be like he said—he went to that travel agency kiosk, then headed to Miwaku and spotted you when you left. I had a bad feeling, so I followed him."

Mimi winced. "I'm sorry to pull you away from your job."

"Your safety is more important. Besides, Tosh is still watching Waite at the store."

"Waite's shift ends in about an hour," Mimi told her.

"Tosh will follow him when he leaves, but for the past week, he's only gone home after work."

"You haven't found anything else about him?"

Edytha shook her head. "There just isn't enough evidence that Waite or Ivan are involved in drugs in any way, but I mentioned it to a friend of mine who works for the Waialua Police Department anyway."

"You've been following Ivan, too?"

"No, It's hard to keep tabs on Ivan since he lives at the Pleiades Resort. We can't get on campus, and he could leave from one of several exits. We've been focusing more on Waite." She suddenly reached down to clasp Mimi's hand in a comforting grip. "I honestly didn't think Ivan would try to talk to you again. I'm sorry you've been pulled into this."

"I didn't think so, either. And there's nothing for you to apologize for—I wasn't pulled into this, I chose to involve myself."

"Still, you should be careful."

Mimi used her free hand to pull open her purse, revealing

pepper spray and a few heavy rings—in lieu of brass knuckles—rattling around in an inside pocket. "I always keep this stuff with me for protection."

Edytha's eyebrows rose as she peered inside, then at Mimi. "Ooookay, John Wick. You don't happen to have a gun in there too, do you?"

"I've just had my share of bad breakups," Mimi admitted. That long stream of toilet paper was starting to feel more like a ball and chain now. "And once in a while, a strange man will try to hit on me."

Edytha was still loosely holding Mimi's hand, but now she gave it a squeeze. Her other hand touched Mimi's face tenderly, making her feel the way she did when she looked at a Mary Cassatt painting. "You don't have to be strong and independent all the time," Edytha said.

"I'm not," Mimi said automatically. "I'm headstrong and impulsive."

"You stood up for yourself. That's not being headstrong."

"But agreeing to go on a date with Ivan was impulsive." Mimi gave a long, loud sigh. "It's all I know how to be. It's how I've been for most of my life. It's gotten me in trouble a lot."

"We all make mistakes," Edytha said with a wry smile. "None of us is perfect. Only God."

The mention of God seemed strange coming from someone who wasn't one of her Christian cousins, but at the same time, it also made her relax and feel comfortable, to speak about God with someone who might understand her. "My cousins tell me that all the time, that only God is perfect. But I still want to be a better version of myself than I used to be."

"You can be, with God's help. Nothing says you can't have a Do-Over."

"I have a lot to Do Over." She pressed her lips together. "I wasn't all that nice a person in my twenties, even though I believed I was trying to follow my convictions and do what I thought was right. But often I was just being flirtatious and thoughtless. And now that I'm older, sometimes I feel like I'm drowning in regret."

"Like I said—" Edytha smiled with both teasing and tenderness. "—Do-Over."

"Even if I have to Do-Over over and over?"

Edytha gave her an exasperated look. "Now you're just being facetious."

"No, I'm serious. I feel like I'm always trying to escape who I was in order to become a better person, but I keep making mistakes and reverting." She'd alienated Tosh because she'd been disingenuous and vampy, and what did she do as soon as she saw him again? She unbuttoned her blouse and used her girls to charm a complete stranger. "Jenn told me to memorize First John 1:9. 'If we confess our sins, he is faithful and just and will forgive us our sins and purify us from all unrighteousness.' I confess my sins in my prayers, but I don't feel *purified*."

Edytha said in a gentle voice, "No matter what we've done, no matter what mistakes we've made, God always forgives us when we confess our sins. And being forgiven by God is incredibly freeing, in ways we don't always understand."

Edytha brought her hands up to cup either side of Mimi's face so she couldn't look away. "So those mistakes you've made are not forever. Stop thinking you are doomed to always make them. Instead, rely on God to be making you into someone new."

Her words seemed to uplift her and make something in her chest loosen. "I ... I'll try."

"You will find your answers if you start *hunting God*."

What? What did that mean?

But before she could ask, Edytha beamed and released Mimi's face. "I have a great idea. When's your next day off?"

"Tomorrow."

"Why don't you come to my spa?"

"Um ... I'm not really into massages." She still had some scarring from the auto accident the summer after she graduated high school, and it made massages more painful than relaxing for her.

"I think my chef is making lilikoi chiffon pie tomorrow."

"Beam me up, Scottie!"

12

The Warubozu Spa was ten times more beautiful in daylight as opposed to when Mimi had last come here at night. The hibiscus bushes were a riot of color, and the walls of the antique plantation manor house shone with a fresh coat of paint. Mimi regretted that she didn't enjoy massages very much because this was a soothing and delightful background for some self-care.

She had come ostensibly for lilikoi chiffon pie, but she also hoped to have a moment to ask Edytha about what she meant yesterday about hunting God. Edytha's words to her had run through her mind as she lay in bed, but as usual, while she prayed for forgiveness, she didn't feel any different, and the regret didn't feel any less burdensome.

She didn't expect this talk with Edytha to suddenly solve all her problems, but she somehow felt that fully understanding what Edytha had meant would be important for her.

Edytha had told her to arrive anytime, so it was around ten o'clock in the morning when she parked in front and headed in through the front doors.

Mimi was immediately greeted by the sight of a man and woman facing off against each other in the open waiting area, shooting glares so fierce they were almost like laser beams flying in the air between them.

The woman was tall and slender, with dark hair in a pixie cut that suited the shape of her face very well, even if it did make her look more androgynous. The man was at least ten years older and several inches shorter, with light brown hair a bit bleached by the sun. Standing to the side and wringing her hands nervously was a girl almost as short as Mimi—maybe a couple of inches taller, but still below five feet—with chestnut-colored hair pulled up on the sides with two ribbon bows made of exquisite Japanese print fabric.

"It needs to go in that corner!" the young woman bellowed, pointing to the far left corner of the room.

"It's easier to clean up the needles in that corner!" the man bellowed back, pointing to the corner of the room directly to Mimi's right.

"Who cares about cleanup? Guests need to see the tree as soon as they walk inside!"

"You don't care about cleanup because you're not the one doing it! Last year, I was sweeping up needles all the way in the northern wing!"

"Guys …" The tiny girl tried to break into the argument, but the two combatants ignored her.

"People need to see the tree when they arrive!" the woman argued. "If it's in that corner, they'll only see it when they're leaving!"

"People don't come to the spa to look at trees!"

"It shouldn't be hidden away! Sakura spent a lot of time planning the decorations! It's going to look like it should be in the windows of a high-end department store!"

"People come here to relax, not to train for Black Friday sales!"

"I think it would look better in the far corner," Mimi interjected.

All three of them gaped at Mimi. The man recovered fastest. "Welcome to the spa. I apologize for the unsightly actions of my staff—"

"Hey!" the woman objected. "You were the one who picked a fight with me!"

Mimi thrust both palms out at them and said firmly, "All I want is lilikoi chiffon pie."

"Ooh, there's lilikoi chiffon pie?" The woman suddenly grinned delightedly and clapped her hands. "Goodie! Let's go, Sakura!"

"Hey!" The man pointed at Mimi. "There's a guest right there, dingbat!"

"She said she wanted pie, not a massage." The woman turned to Mimi. "Do you want pie or a massage?"

"Definitely pie."

"Thought so. Let's go!" The woman gestured for Mimi to follow her as she headed behind the reception desk to a large atrium at the back of the house. "I'm Lila, by the way."

"Mimi."

"I'm Sakura," said the tiny girl (Mimi needed to stop referring to her as that when Sakura was clearly taller than she was).

"That's Fred," Lila said.

"Um … what about the tree?"

"Oh, Fred'll put it up later," Lila said blithely, then called back to him, "In the far corner."

"Yeah, yeah," he grumbled to her.

"Thank you, honey."

"Isn't he your boss?" Mimi asked. Hadn't he mentioned "his staff"?

"Spa general manager." Lila grinned. "He's also my boyfriend."

She suddenly remembered what Edytha had told her. John Hackett had threatened Lila, but her boyfriend had saved her.

Mimi had a feeling Fred tended to save Lila from lots of other things, too.

When she glanced back to look at him, the long-suffering Fred pressed his fingers to his temples like he had a headache (which he probably did), but he wasn't too slow to follow them.

After all, *pie.*

As Mimi passed the reception desk, she noticed some gift baskets laid out on top with prices. But the ice blue and sage colors of a lotion tube caught her eye. "You're selling lotions from Miwaku." The basket didn't have only Miwaku products, but each of the four baskets on the counter had at least one of a variety of her aunt's lotions in them.

"We have a hard time keeping them in stock," Sakura told her. "When Miwaku suddenly had a large supply last week, Edytha bought up a bunch to sell in our Christmas gift baskets."

"Uh ... actually, I'm the one making the majority of those lotions in my aunt's stillroom," Mimi confessed.

"You are?" Sakura asked.

"She's your aunt?" Lila asked.

"Can you get us more?" Fred asked in all seriousness.

"Fred, don't be rude! Tone down your mercenary side," Lila scolded him.

"Fine." He turned to Mimi again. "*Please*, can you get us more?"

"I can ask," Mimi said. She thought they might have enough ingredients to make an extra batch or two.

The work in the stillroom every morning reminded her of how much she enjoyed making cosmetics and tinkering with formulas. She couldn't do too much of that when making lotions for her cousins, especially because Venus's skin was sensitive.

She thought maybe she could experiment when she got back to California and come up with some new products of her own, but then she nixed the idea. How would she sell them? They had the bare minimum of preservatives and short shelf lives. She hadn't sold them online specifically because of that fact.

Despite her practical thoughts, she found herself asking, "What kinds of lotions do you want?"

"I'd love it if Miwaku had a scar-reduction lotion that's a little more oily for massages," Lila immediately replied. "And with a lighter scent."

"Do you use a lot of the scar-reduction lotion?" Mimi asked.

"Tons," Lila said.

"We have several clients with scarring," Fred added.

The two-story high atrium was filled with light streaming in through the long glass windows, and several tables were set up so clients could relax and drink tea while looking out through the glass at the rear hibiscus garden. There was also a veranda out back where a few more clients were relaxing in chairs.

Lila led them past the tables in the atrium to a short hallway alongside the staircase to the second floor. The door at the end opened into the kitchen.

And what a kitchen it was. Not quite as extensive as Jenn's kitchen at her restaurant, but renovated with modern appliances and gleaming counters as well as high ceilings with skylights to brighten the space in addition to powerful lights.

However, Edytha was frowning as she spoke to a woman who looked like the cook. "Did she say why she quit?" Edytha asked.

The cook shook her head. "That was the first thing I asked, but she skirted around the issue. It was all so sudden and I was so shocked, I forgot to press her for an answer."

Edytha looked more perplexed than upset at the problem, but then she noticed the group in the doorway. Her expression brightened. "Lila, my favorite cousin—"

Lila had started to back away like a rabbit trying to escape a wolf. "We're only second cousins—" Lila began.

Edytha only smiled more brightly and desperately. "You'll help me out, right?"

"Help you out with what?"

"My sous chef suddenly called to say she quit and won't come in for her shift today."

"What?" Mimi yelped. Since she worked at Jenn's restaurant, she knew how catastrophic this situation could be.

"I'm a massage therapist, not a cook," Lila said.

"No one would even want you to cook," Fred told her. "You've ruined peanut butter sandwiches before."

"I meant for you to sweet-talk your dad into letting me borrow one of his kitchen staff," Edytha clarified.

Mimi was completely lost until Sakura leaned over to whisper, "Lila's dad owns a Japanese inn in Haleiwa."

"Wait, you mean Yoshizaki Ryokan?" Even though she normally only came to Haleiwa once in a while to go to the beach, Mimi had heard about it but had never been inside. It had been built about ten or fifteen years ago and had grown to enormous popularity.

"That's the one," Sakura said.

But Lila was shaking her head. "Dad's short-staffed all this week."

Edytha groaned and collapsed into a chair next to a table, grabbing at her head. "I guess I'll have to try a temp agency, but I don't know if anyone can come today."

"I'll do it," Mimi said.

Everyone turned to look at her blankly.

"Did Tosh not tell you what I do?" Mimi asked Edytha.

"He said you worked at your aunt's cosmetics store."

"I'm only helping her for the winter holidays. My normal job is working for my cousin Jenn's restaurant."

In a flash, Edytha was suddenly directly in front of her, grabbing her shoulders. She was so tall and Mimi was so short, she felt like she was being mauled by an overly friendly bear.

"What position in the kitchen?" Edytha asked.

"Pretty much everything. Jenn has a dedicated sous chef and three station chefs, so I mostly work as a pass chef, but I do whatever they need me to do, including prep work and assisting the station chefs. After I got my culinary degree, I started filling in as station chef or sous chef on their days off."

Edytha's head chef looked like she was going to cry in relief.

"Would you really do this?" Edytha looked like she was close to tears, too.

"Wait, wait, wait," Fred said. "You can't just hire her like this. She's going to need to fill out a ton of paperwork."

Mimi knew exactly how much paperwork needed to be filled out, and all for just a few hours of work. But she remembered when she had first met Edytha—she mentioned she often traded her PI work for barter. "Why don't I work for barter instead?"

Edytha looked thrilled while Fred looked like his head was going to explode.

"It's only for today," Mimi said, "so I don't want to fill out all those tax forms. Maybe some massage vouchers?" She could give them to her aunt or cousins if she didn't want to use them herself.

"Done." Edytha's eyes were whirling a bit in manic excitement, but Mimi knew she had saved her from a world of stress.

Lila suddenly put up her hand like a kindergartener. "Does this mean no pie?"

Mimi did not have pie until that afternoon.

The Warubozu Day Spa offered a full relaxation service, much like a resort. After a massage, manicure, or pedicure, clients could relax with tea and snacks either in the atrium or on a lounge chair on the veranda that wrapped around the entire backside of the house and a portion of the wings.

The menu changed often, utilizing fresh local produce, but in general, it comprised of finger foods like what Jenn served for afternoon English High Tea on weekdays at her restaurant. These were the type of snacky bites that Mimi loved making, so she enjoyed herself like a chocoholic in Ghirardelli Square.

Mimi helped the head chef, Geri, to prepare various foods for the guests, but since it was only the two of them, she was kept extraordinarily busy.

Luckily, this wasn't like a restaurant where food was made as customers ordered. Instead, she and Geri prepared all the items ahead of time and simply left them in the large refrigerator unit. When clients ordered, the chef would heat up any food requiring it, which she could do by herself.

"Um … would you be open to a suggestion?" Mimi asked. Geri wasn't unfriendly, but she also didn't smile very much. Mimi was used to Jenn welcoming all input, no matter how nitpicky, so her brain naturally zeroed in on productivity.

But she needn't have worried. "Sure. What is it?" Geri turned to her with eyebrows raised, waiting.

"Right now, customers order what they want a la carte, right? So you have to spend time checking the order and getting the right items before preparing them. But I noticed that you always make sure that all the items on the menu complement each other no matter what someone orders."

Geri nodded.

"If instead you had, say, two size plates—one small and one large—with a certain number of set items on each plate, you could save time. The large plate would be the same as the small plate but with a few more items."

"I see," Geri said. "I wouldn't need to check the order to make sure I got the right items that the customer wanted, I just need to prepare however many small plates and large plates."

"Also, you have more creative control of the overall tasting experience. Everything on the plate will complement each other, without needing to worry about what each customer will order or not order."

"That might make things a little easier when deciding the menu," Geri agreed. "And it'll streamline when some things need to be reheated and others don't."

"About that, I think if you use these types of cups, the mini-quiche will reheat more evenly …"

After discussing reheating and serving options, Geri turned to her and put a hand on her shoulder. Mimi thought she finally might crack a small smile, but instead, she simply nodded and patted her shoulder. "Thanks. That's real helpful."

Mimi was glad she liked her ideas. Geri was a good chef, who was more considerate of her customers' tastes as opposed to trying anything too strange and daring. Instead, she put all her effort into making her food taste the absolute best it could.

Mimi ended up tasting a lot of items (oh what a hardship) so she could know exactly what the chef wanted, and Geri ended up tasting a lot of what Mimi made to make sure they turned out right, so both of them skipped lunch. Mimi only had to help make food for today, but since she didn't know if Edytha would be able to find help tomorrow, she stayed a couple extra hours to make enough for tomorrow, too.

They were just finishing up when Edytha poked her head into the kitchen and announced, "I have come for pie!"

Without looking up from icing the mini cupcakes, Geri remarked, "That's nice."

Edytha blinked at her, nonplussed.

"Didn't you have a late lunch?" Geri chided her.

"There is always room for pie," Edytha replied in all seriousness.

Geri finally looked up from the cupcakes. "I suppose you're right. Top shelf of the small fridge," she said, referring to the commercial refrigerator that stood next to the large refrigeration unit.

"Mimi, you look like you're done. Want some pie?" Edytha's words were a bit muffled since she was shoulder-deep in the fridge with her bottom sticking out.

Mimi, understanding who was the true ruler of this domain, looked to Geri first.

The chef nodded assent, then cast a look of both affection and amusement as she took in the sight of Edytha's wiggling bottom. However, she only scolded, "Don't leave the door open too long."

"I can't find—oh! There it is." Edytha emerged with a tin that only had three slices left of a creamy mousse pie.

Mimi put two slices on plates while Edytha brewed some passion fruit tea, one of several blends that Geri and Edytha had come up with which were exclusive to the spa.

Edytha carried the tray and led the way through the atrium, which was tinted rose gold from the sun just starting to set behind the mountains directly behind the manor house.

In the northern wing of the building, at the very end of a second-floor hallway, Edytha nudged open a door and entered her office. The spacious room had two desks—one with two computer monitors on top and a computer tower tucked away underneath, and a smaller one covered with papers, but they were in neat stacks and paper clipped or stapled together. There was also a round table with a few padded chairs where Edytha set the tray.

Mimi tried the tea first—slightly astringent from the black tea leaves, but with a faint melon aroma and a delicate tartness from passion fruit mellowed by pineapple. "Wow, that's good."

"Now try it with the lilikoi chiffon pie." Edytha had already shoved a bite into her mouth.

It would make sense that the passion fruit (also known as lilikoi) tea would pair well with the pie, but Mimi was amazed. The crisp crust contrasted with the mousse's airy texture and balance of sweet and tart. "I'm in love," she mumbled through a full mouth.

"Geri's recipe," Edytha said, taking another bite. "She makes tartlets for the guests, but only the staff gets full slices of the pie."

Mimi had seen the tartlets in the fridge, which Geri had made yesterday, so there hadn't been a need for her to taste any of it (rats!). "She's a great chef," Mimi said. "She's methodical, efficient, and careful."

"Did you have any issues working with her?"

"Oh, no. We got along pretty well." In fact, despite Geri's aversion to smiling, she was surprisingly chatty while they worked. "She mentioned you wanted to expand into a restaurant in the evenings and catering so you can offer the house for weddings."

"I would like to do that eventually, but lately I've had too many people suddenly quit."

She had mentioned that earlier. "They've all gone to work for the Pleiades Resort?"

"Yes, *all* of them."

"That's kind of suspicious, don't you think?"

Edytha sighed. "Well, the resort probably pays much better, but yes, it's a bit coincidental that they all jump ship to work for Pleiades. I'll have to go about hiring a new sous chef. The problem is that it's only a part-time position for now since Geri usually only needs help making food in the mornings."

"Hopefully, you won't have problems finding a new sous chef. Sakura and Lila stopped by for a snack, and they said that everyone here likes working for you." Mimi had been making tea sandwiches, which the two women pilfered while chatting.

"They weren't saying that just to get more lilikoi chiffon pie, were they?"

"No, because Geri wouldn't let them."

"I can always count on Geri to protect my afternoon snack."

"Geri said she likes working for you because you're understanding about when she has to take off work for medical or family matters. My cousin Jenn is the same way."

"Tell me about your job in California."

It was so easy to talk to Edytha, the woman should have been an interrogator. Mimi probably overshared about her family, including the infamous Oldest Single Female Cousin (unofficial) title that had been the bane of many a young woman's life until Mimi took up the crown for the last several years.

"Are you married?" Mimi asked.

"No, I never found anyone to fall in love with. Then my sister went missing, and I became a single mom to my nephew."

"She's missing? I'm sorry."

A fierce light blazed from Edytha's green-brown eyes. "I'll find her. I won't stop pursuing this."

It reminded Mimi of what Edytha had said yesterday and the main reason she'd come to the spa today (lilikoi chiffon pie notwithstanding). "What did you mean when you said I should start hunting God?"

Edytha laughed a bit self-consciously. "That just kind of came out. It sounds silly when I hear someone else say it. It's a reference to Philippians chapter three, verses twelve to fourteen: 'Not that I have already obtained this or am already perfect, but I press on to make it my own, because Christ Jesus has made me his own. Brothers, I do not consider that I have made it my own. But one thing I do: forgetting what lies behind and straining forward to what lies ahead, I press on toward the goal for the prize of the upward call of God in Christ Jesus.'"

Mimi had read the verse a few times since becoming a Christian a few years ago but hadn't memorized it like Edytha. She had to admit she often skimmed over it because she found some of the phrases excessively complex, and after a lifetime of reading trashy gossip mags, more intellectual reading gave her hives.

Edytha continued, "In contrast to most people who are discontent with their lives, Paul was discontented with his *spiritual* state. He felt his relationship with Christ and how well he knew Christ was too shallow. He was driven to learn more about God."

"To hunt God?"

"Yes. The words 'press on' mean to pursue or chase, which are hunting terms."

"But why did you think that referred to me?"

"Paul was considered a pillar of the church, and yet he still felt too far away from God. He wasn't happy with *who he was*."

Now she was starting to get it. "Like how I'm still regretting my past."

"When I heard you talk about that, it made me think you're exactly like Paul—you're discontented with your spiritual state."

"I … suppose that's true, although I wouldn't have described it like that. I just want to be better than what I once was."

"So, like Paul, you need to strive toward knowing God more and forgetting about your past. Paul said it: 'forgetting what lies behind and straining forward to what lies ahead.'"

But rather than comforting her, the words only made the guilt feel heavier on her shoulders. "But I can't forget about my past when it keeps following me into the present, like how I fell back on old habits and ended up leading Ivan on."

"It's like I told you in the parking garage—we're not perfect, and we'll make mistakes. But we can trust God to forgive us. And if God forgives us, then we don't have an excuse not to forgive ourselves."

"Maybe that's it, that I can't forgive myself. But I somehow feel that's just an excuse I'm telling myself. I worry that I'll always be alone because I'm not lovable enough for someone to want to marry me. At first, I wondered if my standards were simply too high or maybe I just have too much pride. But lately, I feel like I'm searching for something that's not even there, that doesn't exist."

Edytha reached out to clasp her hand. "I can say this to you because I'm in the same boat—I'm getting older and haven't found anyone, either. But we both need to stop worrying about our futures and instead just focus on doing what God wants us to do. We have to trust in God to guide us."

She was right—the words coming from a woman older than herself did pack more punch than if it had come from her cousins, who had married at a much younger age than Mimi was now. She thought about conversations she'd had with Jenn. "I've been trying to learn how to depend on God. It seemed so much harder for me than for Jenn because I've always been independent. My parents favor my brothers over me, and so I became used to doing things myself and depending only on myself."

"You feel like depending on someone else is like asking to be disappointed, right?"

Edytha seemed to understand what Mimi was feeling, and the words kept pouring out of her. "Asking God for guidance and trusting in God is just too frightening and uncomfortable. Even with my ex-boyfriends doing things for me and taking care of me, I never truly trusted them. I only ever trusted in myself and took care of myself."

"God controls everything around you. He is taking care of you, even now. You have the burden of always trying to be in control of everything weighing you down, but don't you think it might even feel a little freeing to have that taken off your shoulders?"

To trust God to take care of her and help her to change. To trust Him to forgive her when she screwed up and help her back on her feet. To trust God to be guiding her path to the right place to be, no matter how crazy and twisty her journey.

To be free of regret, knowing God was all she needed.

"You can trust that God will never fail you," Edytha said, squeezing her hand.

For a moment, Mimi felt a Presence in her chest and all around her. Suddenly she felt completely … filled. With Someone's love for her.

She was not alone.

She had never been alone.

And God loved her still.

It was a moment of awe, like the first sight of a grand and beautiful monument—the peak of a mountain, the endless horizon of the ocean, the deep mysteriousness of ancient woods.

It was only a moment, fleeting. And then the feeling was gone. But Mimi still felt its echoes inside her. She felt like she was grasping at whispers of smoke, trying to hold on to something that had already disappeared.

What did it mean? Had what she felt been real?

Was God really that magnificent?

Had God really been that close to her all this time?

She realized she'd been silent for long minutes, but Edytha didn't seem to mind. She still held Mimi's hand in a gentle clasp, studying her face with a tender smile.

Finally, Edytha said, "I think it was God's will that we met."

"I would never have met you if I hadn't gone to see Tosh."

"And if Waite and Ivan hadn't walked into the restaurant right at that moment."

When she put it like that, it was pretty coincidental. Mimi hadn't noticed before.

"From what you said, you're the oldest among your cousins here in Hawaii, right? But me and Tosh are your age. It's good to have peers who understand you. It's probably why you get along so well with your older cousins in California like Jenn."

"We didn't always get along," Mimi said ruefully. "When I was in my twenties, we were all worried for a while that Trish or I would be arrested for attempted murder. Or at least slashing a car tire or two."

Edytha smiled. "You two get along now?"

"Motherhood mellowed her. Before that, Trish was nuttier than Rocky Road ice cream … aaaaand I admit I enjoyed baiting her to get her to blow a gasket."

"I was like that with my sister." But then Edytha's smile faltered. "What I wouldn't give to be able to prod her off the deep end again." She gestured around the room. "The spa was hers, originally. I was co-owner when she disappeared, so I moved my PI business here and let Fred do the heavy lifting of running the place."

So losing all her employees to Pleiades Resort must feel like she was failing her sister. "What are you going to do about your sous chef?"

"I already contacted a local temp agency, and they said they'll send someone tomorrow morning." But then she tugged at Mimi's hand, pulling her upper body close as if sharing a secret. With a mischievous twinkle in her eyes, Edytha asked, "How would you like to work for me?"

"Huh?" The idea was so sudden that Mimi couldn't quite formulate actual words in response.

"To see if you like it, you can register with the temp agency, and I'll hire you through them for a few weeks."

"But it's only part-time."

"For you, we can extend your responsibilities toward maybe making your auntie's lotions for the spa? We would pay her since it's her formula, but she'd be paying you for your labor, right?"

Mimi grimaced. "Auntie Noriko's idea of payment is an extra serving of dessert."

"You could also develop your own lotions for us to use. Didn't you mention you made some for your cousins?"

She *had* wanted to make lotions to sell online but couldn't because she didn't like putting potent preservatives in the formula, so the products only lasted a few weeks. But if they were used quickly by, say, massage therapists …

Mimi found herself a little short of breath. Was she really considering this? She could imagine herself enjoying working for Edytha and being a sous chef here at the spa.

And as for moving to Hawaii, it wasn't as if she didn't know anyone here. She flew over often enough that it didn't feel like a tropical vacation so much as a visit to relatives.

"The idea has some appeal …" she said vaguely. "But it's a big decision to leave California. I'll need to pray about it and maybe talk with Jenn."

Whoa, had she just said she'd pray about something? Without Jenn prompting her to? Was she asking for God's guidance on a decision rather than just kicking off her shoes and jumping in?

"Take all the time you need," Edytha said.

Like most old houses, the floors creaked like an old man complaining about every aching joint, so they were able to hear someone approaching Edytha's office long before the knock came at the door.

"Come in," Edytha called.

Tosh opened the door and stopped at the sight of Mimi. Was that dismay on his face?

Irritated, she was about to get up to leave when she realized the dismay wasn't for her. "Is that the last of the lilikoi chiffon pie?" he asked.

"There's one more slice left, but that's Geri's," Edytha said.

Tosh looked like a kid who'd been told they were canceling Christmas.

Mimi sighed, propping her chin in her hand, and pushed the plate in his direction. "You can have the rest of mine."

His face immediately turned radiant.

"No, Mimi, that's yours," Edytha said sternly. "Let the bottomless strawberry-cake thief go hungry for a change."

Tosh affected an expression of soul-crushing injury. "Lila *gave* those slices to me, I did not *steal* them."

"She gave you her share of culinary treasure. Your nefarious acts of larceny will not go unpunished. Begone, evil-doer!" Edytha jumped to her feet and pointed dramatically to the doorway.

Tosh looked at the doorway, at Edytha's pointing finger, then at the plate of half-eaten pie. He promptly sat down and pulled the plate toward him. "Thanks, Mimi."

Still standing with her finger pointing toward the door, Edytha glared down at Tosh. "Why does it seem like all the women in your life spoil you rotten? What's your secret?"

Tosh quite obviously did not answer her question. "Is there any tea left?"

Edytha sighed and sat back down. "At least earn your pie. What happened today?"

"Waite left early and went straight home."

"We're all going to be working longer hours because of Black

Friday coming up, so Trinda gave him a short shift today," Mimi said.

"You didn't see Ivan hanging around the shop, did you?" Edytha asked with a more concerned tone.

"No." Tosh glanced at Mimi, and there was a growly quality to his voice that surprised her. Then he said, "I'm … I'm sorry I wasn't able to stop Ivan from following you yesterday."

He had seemed angry, but was he angry on her behalf because of what Ivan did?

"Everything turned out okay," she said.

"You haven't seen anyone outside your auntie's house, have you?" he asked. "No unfamiliar cars on the road?"

Alarm spiked through her. "No, nothing like that."

"Tosh, don't frighten her," Edytha chided him.

"Sorry," he mumbled. "Force of habit."

He must need to evaluate the safety of a lot of different clients, but she thought he might have not been telling the entire truth when he said that. She got the distinct impression that he was worried about her safety. Mimi hadn't expected that kind of concern from him—not for her, at least—but then again, Tosh was always a nice guy. He'd probably be worried about any young woman who'd been approached in an isolated place by a man she had rejected.

"Do you think he'll try to talk to me again?" Mimi asked. "In my experience, when a man has been rejected, he doesn't usually come back for seconds of humiliation."

"He shouldn't have come back at all," Tosh shot back at her. "You weren't disagreeable enough the first time."

"That's because I lavished that all on you," she retorted. "Gimmie my pie back."

He grabbed his plate and held it out of her much shorter reach. "No backsies."

"You're so immature."

"Look who's talking."

"I am going to give *both* of you a spanking," Edytha interjected, rubbing her temples.

"Look," Mimi said, "I never saw Ivan do anything illegal, so it's not like he'll be worried I'll say something about anything on the date. I'm no threat to him even if he's neck deep in drug deals— which I didn't see any proof of."

"He's a pretty big spender considering what his salary must be as a security guard at the resort," Tosh said.

"A man can be a big spender with money he doesn't have, not because he's got an illegal influx of cash," Mimi said.

Tosh grunted in reluctant agreement.

"We're just worried because none of us expected him to come find you," Edytha said.

"It's fine since you were there," Mimi said. "And I still believe that I needed to stand up to him myself rather than hiding behind a protector, otherwise Ivan wouldn't listen to me."

"I agree with you on that," Edytha said.

"But I'm glad I wasn't alone when that happened," Mimi said. "Thanks again for being there, Edytha."

At that moment, there was another knock on the door, but Edytha barely called out before Fred entered, not looking up from some papers in his hands. "Edytha, I have the budget ..." He stopped when he looked up and saw all of them. "Sorry, I'll come back."

"No, I'll let you get back to work." Mimi stood and gathered the plates and cups on the tray. "I'll take this back down to the kitchen."

"No, I'll carry it," Tosh said, adding Mimi's empty plate after eating the last bite of pie.

As they walked down the hallway and out of the north wing of the house, Tosh cleared his throat. "I, um ... I have the last five volumes of *Bunny Foo Foo* in my car if you want to borrow them."

"That would be great," she replied automatically, just like she would when they were teenagers, before remembering that there was a gulf between them that had been carved out by her own hands. "Um ... why do you have them in your car?"

"I was cleaning up yesterday and saw them, and uh ... just in case I happened to see you."

"But you didn't know I was going to be here at the spa when you came to talk to Edytha."

He gusted out a sigh, and his neck turned red, the color creeping up his jaw and cheeks. "I was going to drop by your house after I got off work at the restaurant since I'm not working a full shift today."

Mimi hadn't known that delight could be flowery and effervescent, like those Japanese *ramune* sodas. But Tosh was excruciatingly embarrassed, and she decided not to tease him. "I'd like that," she said coolly. "I'll take them now, and if you give me a few days, I can return them to you at your uncle's restaurant."

"It won't take long to read them," he said in a halting tone. "Why don't I meet you at Judy's Diner tonight after my shift? You can read the books right away and I'll take them back with me."

She was confused as to why he'd go through the trouble, but then she considered how careful he had been with his Japanese books. He probably didn't want to risk something happening to them if they left his line of sight.

"Are you going to be okay driving all the way to Honolulu?"

"Yeah, it's fine. Edytha's got the early shift of watching Waite tomorrow. Around nine?"

"Sure. Text me when you get there."

When she drove out of the spa parking lot, she was so jittery that she hit the gas too hard and almost ran into the mailbox.

13

Two weeks later

Mimi tilted her head and looked up at the 21-foot-tall "Shaka Santa" seated on the outdoor fountain of Honolulu Hale as he merrily waved "shaka" to all the cars passing him on South King Street.

"His nose is kinda crooked," she said.

Tosh smacked her upside the back of the head. "His nose is not crooked! Now you're criticizing Shaka Santa?!"

She rubbed the back of her head even though it hadn't hurt. "I'm just saying ..."

"Why did you even want to come see the Honolulu City Lights if you're just going to insult a Hawaii icon?"

Because if she didn't, she might think this was a date. Which it wasn't. Even if it kind of felt like it.

It seemed like a lot had happened in the two weeks since she met with Tosh at Judy's Diner to read *The Sword of Bunny Foo Foo*, but if she stopped to think about it, practically nothing had happened.

That night, Tosh had brought the entire series, and they had sat re-reading the old volumes before starting on the new ones, stopping to talk and laugh like they used to. Mimi had felt sixteen again, at a time when everything between them was all right.

But then the night ended, and their goodbyes in the parking lot were a little awkward. Still, she'd been glad to read the series and talk with someone about it.

The next day at work, as she was heading to the employee parking garage, he'd appeared out of nowhere beside her.

Mimi jumped so hard she stumbled, her heart jolting hard in her chest. She had to lean against the wall of a building to get her bearings again. "What are you doing? Say hello like a normal person!"

"Oh, sorry."

He didn't look all that sorry, though, which made her want to sock him.

He handed her an envelope. "Massage vouchers for the spa. Edytha forgot to give them to you before you left yesterday."

"Thanks."

He then walked her to her car. She had to admit it made her feel better, after Ivan had accosted her the day before, but she wasn't about to tell Tosh that. They even managed a few minutes of not-too-stilted conversation about a new manga series Mimi had recently read about online before she got in her car to leave.

But then for the next week, if she was alone, Tosh would walk her from her car when she arrived in the morning and to her car after work ended. Sometimes he'd come up beside her on her way to the parking garage, while other times he'd be waiting at the entrance to the garage.

She probably would have been as twitchy as a squirrel if she'd been by herself, and it set her at ease to know Tosh made sure Ivan wasn't trying to talk to her again. They even talked a bit before she left to go home and he went back to watching Waite.

She half-expected to see him in disguise in the store again, but he never did, and Waite never received any strange customers. One day while at her car, she remarked, "You know, except for the thrill of fooling me that first time, your job of watching Waite is super boring."

"You're only now figuring that out?!"

Mimi told Tosh that he didn't need to worry about her the following week, which was Thanksgiving, since she'd be working late with Trinda. But when she and Trinda went to their cars in the evening, she caught sight of him in the parking garage, usually in some disguise so that he never looked like the same person.

One night when she'd left the store before Trinda, Tosh met up with her and she talked about untangling the Christmas lights so they could decorate the store. "I think I'll go see the Honolulu City Lights decorations on my day off after the Black Friday weekend," she mused.

Tosh didn't say anything about it at the time, but a couple of days later, he called her and asked if she wanted to go with him since he also wanted to see the annual Honolulu Christmas decorations. It ended up being easy to match their work schedules.

So this morning, they had met up at Ala Moana before getting a rideshare into downtown Honolulu so they wouldn't have to find parking.

And that's when Mimi had insulted Shaka Santa.

As they headed toward the massive Christmas tree on the front lawn, the sight of a runner passing them on the sidewalk reminded her of the email reminder she got from her cousin last week. "My cousin's husband, Aiden, decided to run the Honolulu Marathon," she said. "Some of my other cousins will be coming with them. I think you met Lex, Trish, and Jenn, right?"

"Yeah. They came one year for Thanksgiving with their families. One cousin was missing—I think her name was Venus?"

"So you didn't meet her?"

Tosh shook his head.

"Hey, speaking of Thanksgiving, how was yours?" Mimi asked.

"My uncle's restaurant is open for Thanksgiving dinner, and he has to start cooking for that early in the morning, so we just had a small family Thanksgiving brunch."

"I bet the food was good, though." Mimi's mouth watered just from remembering the fried wonton appetizers she'd had at the Molokai Red Restaurant.

"This year he only made huli-huli chicken instead of turkey and garlic mashed potatoes with truffle sauce. Mom made the rest."

Mimi stared at him in awe.

"What?" he asked.

"I was pretty happy with my own Thanksgiving meal with my auntie, but at the words 'huli-huli chicken' and 'truffle sauce,' suddenly our dinner seems mediocre."

"Oh, don't be like that." Tosh laughed.

Still, huli-huli chicken required an outdoor rotisserie over an open fire, where the chicken was partially smoked as it cooked. And she could only imagine how decadent his uncle's truffle sauce must have been. "What'd your mom make?"

"Salad. And she heated up the cranberry sauce Uncle made the day before for the Thanksgiving dinner meal. I'll have you know, I cooked more than she did."

"You cooked?"

He puffed out his chest. "Green bean casserole with crushed taro chips and sweet potato chips on top instead of the traditional fried onion strings."

She gave him a narrowed look. "You forgot to buy the onion strings ahead of time, didn't you?"

"Yup, got it in one. But it still tasted good. All Tomoko did was buy Chinese egg custard pie, but she did claim she stood in line for an hour."

"Ooh, from that bakery in Chinatown? I heard it's really good."

"What did you guys have?"

"Auntie made turkey with Asian stuffing, which I'd never had before. It had minced gizzards, shiitake mushrooms, celery, and white bread. Auntie also made her famous twice-baked potatoes."

"Did you cook at all?"

"Of course! I made Chinese chicken salad, but it was Auntie Noriko's recipe. Trinda and her family brought sweet and sour spareribs—because Trinda's husband doesn't like turkey—and mac salad. Uncle Milton bought the ahi and hamachi sashimi—although I sliced it—and we had make-your-own California roll sushi with shrimp, imitation crab, cucumbers, and radish shoots."

"No dessert?"

"I made pumpkin and apple pies the day before."

Tosh considered her list. "Sounds like a pretty normal Thanksgiving."

"Maybe for Hawaii! I usually go to Jenn's house for Thanksgiving, and it's this massive spread of Spanish food that I can't even pronounce."

Tosh looked at her in confusion. "You don't eat Thanksgiving with your folks?"

She tried not to grimace, she really did, but just the thought of her parents' Thanksgiving made bile rise in her throat. "They eat Japanese food every day, so for Thanksgiving, they make traditional dishes. I tried bringing dishes a few times, especially after I got my culinary degree—I was rather proud of my mango-Asian pear chutney cranberry sauce and my matcha cake with strawberry sauce. But Mom just …"

Each year, her mother had sneered at Mimi's offering, no matter what it was, criticizing it as too strange—which was ironic considering they were Asian fusion dishes, which Mimi thought might appeal to her. "Jenn invited me to join her family one year, and it was more enjoyable. I felt more welcomed there."

Tosh gave her a look that was tinted with pity, but she didn't want that from him. She caught sight of an enterprising vendor cart selling chilled bottled water. "Are you thirsty? I'm going to get one."

"I'll get it," he said.

Mimi found space to sit on a low cement wall while she waited for Tosh to return. When he did, the water helped wash away the bitterness that seemed to linger in her throat at the memories.

Mimi didn't want comfort at the moment—her complicated relationship with her mother made her feel like shards of glass all bundled together.

Tosh's knee bumped hers. He seemed to understand her mood because instead of offering platitudes or comforting emotional support, he said to her, "It doesn't matter what you eat, does it? Thanksgiving is fun because you get to eat food that usually requires a lot of prep work, so you can't eat it very often."

"Yeah! Like Auntie's twice-baked potatoes and Chinese chicken salad. And everything tastes good when you're with family—whether they're related to you by blood or not."

"When we were kids, it seemed like you used to make your behavior even more outrageous just to get your mom to notice you. Was that what you were doing with the matcha strawberry cake?"

"That cake was tasty! But … you're not wrong." She wasn't surprised that he had noticed, even at a young age, because he tended to be perceptive. She licked her lips. "I did a lot of stupid things because I was trying to get her attention."

There was a crease between his brows, and she was going to ask why he was upset until she realized that he was upset *for her.* "I'm sure there are lots of other people who value you more," he said in a low voice.

She wanted to convey to him that she was doing okay now—that she wasn't the girl he had known who was so quick to anger or depression at her mother's every word. "These days, I've stopped caring how my mom treats me."

"But I can tell you still do care," he argued.

She wanted to refute him, but she couldn't. "You're right, I do still care a little. But after becoming a Christian, I began to see my worth based on how God sees me and not how my mom sees me. It's made me feel better no matter what she does or says these days."

"You're—?"

When he didn't say anything more, she looked at him in curiosity.

He hastily drank some of his bottled water. After a few sips, he mumbled, "If you want, you can come to my church on Sundays when you don't have to work."

What? His church?

"Or do you already have a church you go to in Hawaii?" he asked.

"Um … When I've visited in other years, I've gone to a church near Auntie's house, but I've been working on Sundays this year and I haven't gone. I'm not as comfortable there because it's larger than my church in California, so most people don't even realize I'm a visitor." She'd been missing Valley Bible Church, where she went with Lex, Trish, Jenn, and their spouses and kids. "I can ask Trinda about adjusting my work schedule so I can make it to service at your church."

"Sure, just text me."

She licked her lips. "I didn't know you were Christian." Although she wouldn't have asked about his church even if she had known, since their relationship had started off so rocky.

"One of my coworkers, Ashwin, got me to go to church with him," Tosh said.

He was silent for a long time, but he had a conflicted, contemplative expression on his face, and Mimi didn't know what to say to him. Finally, he said, "I was angry at God for a long time for allowing the accident to happen and kill both my dad and my girlfriend. When I started working at Mahina Securities with Ashwin, he helped me a lot by listening to me and talking about his faith. After I became a Christian, I eventually was able to accept that God allowed everything to happen for reasons that I just don't understand."

"I'm sorry about your dad," Mimi said. "That should have been the first thing I said to you when I saw you again."

"To be honest, I might have just assumed you were being trite and blown you off, which would have made you deck me."

Mimi laughed, not because he was all that funny, but because she recognized that he was trying to lighten the situation. She was impressed at how he could even do that with her because back when his dad died, Mimi might have added to his overall stress levels with how their friendship blew up just before the accident.

"Was your girlfriend Rae Kahawai?" she asked.

He looked at her with eyebrows raised. "You remember Rae?"

"She was in the drama club with you. I'm sorry about her, too."

The uglier truth was that she remembered Rae because just before their fight, they had been hanging out with a few of his friends, and one of them teased Tosh about how Rae was interested in him, but Tosh was too chicken to do anything about it.

Up until that point, Mimi hadn't considered Tosh a potential boyfriend. But suddenly hearing that another girl was interested in him made her insanely jealous. She started flirting with him more and getting upset when he brushed her off. But after years of them being only friends, of course he wouldn't believe she was serious.

Except that she *was* serious. She hadn't realized she'd started liking him until suddenly faced with a potential rival. She wasn't particularly proud of that fact.

When she finally confessed that she liked him, she was embarrassed about her feelings simply because they were so sincere. So to hide it, she acted in a teasing way, as if she was partly joking, which was why he blew her off. The two of them got into a huge argument and she stalked off.

If she'd been more mature at the time, she wouldn't have given in to her petty jealousy. She wouldn't have disrespected Tosh when she confessed to him.

But had she even changed as she'd gotten older? Look at how she led Ivan on, despite not intending to do so.

Oblivious to the waves of regret washing over Mimi once again, Tosh said, "Maybe because it was so sudden and because Dad was involved, Rae's death hit me pretty hard. I went to counseling in college to help process everything I was feeling, but I didn't feel like I was finally able to let it all go until I started working."

Was he able to get over her loss because he had a crush on Minnie? It was a bit tragic that he might have fallen for someone but couldn't do anything about it because she was already taken.

Tosh didn't still like Minnie, did he? But he was still single at his age, which was the same as Mimi's. He must have had a reason not to want to date other women.

Tosh got to his feet. "Come on, there's still a few more decorations to see."

The Honolulu City Lights were beautiful this year, and Mimi enjoyed walking around to see them. Afterward, Tosh asked, "Want to go to lunch?"

"Sure. Where?"

Tentatively he asked, "Are you okay with going to a Japanese restaurant? There's a good one nearby."

She was touched that he remembered how she'd loathed going to other Japanese restaurants as a teenager since she'd had to eat it so often at her mom's *okazuya*. "That sounds good."

They got another rideshare. Once they were seated and had ordered, Tosh pulled out his phone. He showed her a photo of Mimi, Waite, and another man, and they were standing outside the Wanderlust Pathways travel agency kiosk in Ala Moana.

"That's from yesterday," she said.

"Edytha wanted to know about the man so she could look into him," Tosh said. "She knew I'd be meeting you today, so she asked me to ask you."

Tosh couldn't have shown her the picture while they were walking around in public. That's why he had suggested lunch. Now she felt rather stupid—she'd been thrilled when he asked her to eat with him, but it was simply because of this.

She hid her disappointment and replied, "Yesterday, I was walking to go buy lunch when I saw Waite leaving the travel agency kiosk. He was chatting with this man." She pointed to the photo. "I recognized him immediately—that's Albert, one of the men I met with Ivan at the nightclub."

Tosh's brow furrowed. "We checked him against the screenshots Edytha took that night but didn't recognize him. She must have gotten a blurry photo. Did he recognize you, too?"

"Oh, yeah. He said hi, then he looked at my uniform and asked if I worked at Miwaku, too. I said yes and asked how he knew Waite. Apparently, they went to school together and go to lunch sometimes, since he works at the travel agency and it's so close to my aunt's store." She gave him an apologetic look. "We were busy at the store that day and only had a short lunch break, so we said goodbye quickly and I got something to eat."

Tosh nodded. "I'll tell Edytha. She was thinking of giving all the information she has so far to her friend in the police department." He showed her a few other photos of people who had come into contact with Waite, but she didn't recognize any of them.

Mimi was starving by the time their meals came. She had been surprised when she and Tosh both ordered the *yosenabe*—a hot pot dish filled with chicken, pork, various shellfish, vegetables, tofu, and mushrooms in a *dashi* stock. It was served in the metal pot it was cooked in, presented on a wooden platter, steaming and still simmering a little.

"I don't care if it is Hawaii and eighty degrees out—*this* is proper Japanese winter food." Mimi began fishing out her clams to shell them.

"This restaurant's *yosenabe* is pretty good," Tosh said, sprinkling spicy *shichimi* powder on his soup. "It's why I suggested it."

Had he remembered how she loved *yosenabe*? She rarely ate it when she came during the summer, so they hadn't eaten it together.

Then she almost laughed at herself. Of course he'd remember. She only mentioned it as one of her favorite dishes like *twenty* times.

Mimi reached into her purse and removed a Japanese light novel. "Thanks for lending this to me. It took longer for me to read than I expected—my kanji is rusty. I'm really glad for the *furigana*—I had to look up a ton of words."

They discussed the novel and the tricky translation of a few passages until they were slurping up the noodles at the bottom of their pots that had soaked up all the flavor from the broth. They not only discussed the book but also other Japanese books and authors. Mimi didn't have to hide her light novel and manga interests—with him, she didn't feel ashamed to be a nerd.

Like Ivan, he tried to pay for the meal, but Mimi insisted, and Tosh backed down.

Yeah, definitely not a date.

After another rideshare to Ala Moana, she paused before getting into her car. "Thanks for taking me to see the Honolulu City Lights display."

"Sure," he said breezily. "I didn't want you to go by yourself. I wanted to make sure you stayed safe."

The disappointment didn't crush her, but she felt a little bit smooshed. Or maybe it wasn't disappointment she felt, but guilt for taking up his time. After all, he'd been watching out for her after work, and he probably felt obligated to protect her since he was the one who brought her into this mess in the first place.

He hadn't been at all lover-like during the day. And except for that one moment when he shared about his dad and girlfriend, he had treated her a little more formally than he had his guy friends back when they were kids. There weren't awkward silences, and he seemed to enjoy talking about Japanese media with her, but that might have been because he himself confessed he didn't know anyone else who read that stuff in the original Japanese.

He was likely not interested in rekindling their friendship. He could be simply making the best of the situation he was in. Mimi didn't blame him—after all, she hurt him rather cruelly in the past.

They had been getting along better lately, but they probably would never get back to how close they used to be.

That realization made her sad, but she wasn't about to let it get her down. She had a new focus, drawing closer to God. She could stop thinking about Tosh.

Besides, after they figured out what Waite was up to, he would likely fade out of her life.

14

"It's Jenn's fault!" Trish complained as they hoofed it down Kapahulu Avenue.

"You wanted to see the farmer's market just as much as I did!" Jenn snapped back.

"Guys, hurry up," Lex said, jogging backward (backward!) in front of their group. The woman was over forty and still played co-ed in the prestigious Wassamattayu Volleyball Club. Mimi would hate her if it weren't so impressive.

Mimi and her cousins had *not* come with Lex to drop Aiden off at the marathon starting line, because he'd had to be there by four-thirty (yes, four-while-the-morning-was-still-black-as-night-thirty). They'd instead arrived a few minutes ago and went to the Honolulu Zoo, which was right across the street from the marathon finish line in Kapiolani Park.

Only to stand and read the sign that the zoo didn't open until ten o'clock.

So instead, they walked further up Kapahulu Avenue toward the farmer's market. They were only at the market for a few minutes before Lex remembered to look at her phone and squawked that Aiden was almost done.

The marathon had an app that tracked Aiden's location through a tag they gave him to put on his shoe, and she only then noticed that he was nearing the finish line.

So they had to hustle out of the farmer's market, dodging strollers and toddlers who looked like they were making a break for freedom from oppressive jailers (i.e., their parents). Now they were running down Kapahulu Avenue, aiming to cut the corner and turn onto Monsarrat Avenue, trying to beat Aiden to the finish line.

"Too bad we couldn't bring the kids and take them to the zoo," Jenn said.

"Nuh-uh!" Trish declared. "This is my first vacation *ever* without my children in *fifteen years!*"

"Besides, the older kids wouldn't have been all that impressed with a zoo," Venus said. "We'd be hearing nothing but complaints the entire time."

"Less talk-y, more run-y," Spenser said, jogging with Lex. "Aiden will kill us if we're late."

"You go ahead," Mimi said, gasping. "My legs are not going to magically grow another six inches."

In response, the Efficiency Team, Venus and Drake, each grabbed one of her armpits and hauled her up, speed-walking with her dangling between them.

"Hey! This is humiliating!" She glared at Trish as she was carried past her. "Are you taking pictures?!" she shrieked.

"I'm texting Aiden," Trish said innocently.

"He doesn't even have his phone!"

"What are we going to do after this?" Jenn, the pacifier, changed the subject before Trish and Mimi got into (yet another) catfight.

"Aiden's going to be tired," Lex said.

"If you put me down, I have massage vouchers!" Mimi roared.

She was promptly set back on her feet, although the sudden stop made her stumble a little. She pinned Venus and Drake with a hard look. "Do that again, and I will go to your desks at work and move everything out of place."

Both of them turned pale. Drake put up his hands. "Sorry, it was Venus's idea."

She socked him in the arm. "You would suck as a secret agent if you were captured."

"Come on!" Lex called, and they ran to catch up.

Mimi had to keep running since a brisk walk at her cousins' pace was practically a full-on sprint for her. As a result, by the time they reached Kapiolani Park, she was dripping with sweat as if someone had dunked a bucket full of warm water on her.

"Did we make it?" Edward asked.

Lex checked her phone. "Think so."

"Where are the massage vouchers for?" Venus asked Mimi.

However, Mimi had put her hands on her knees and was sucking in lungfuls of air and couldn't answer right away. Finally, she wheezed, "North Shore."

"Ooh, let's go to the beach!" Trish said.

"I want to go to Kua'Aina," Venus declared.

Everyone stared at her in shock.

"What?!" she demanded.

"You want hamburgers and fries? You, who avoid fat and carbs like they're radioactive waste?" Trish asked.

"Venus does not avoid fat and carbs," Jenn said. "She just picked up a six-pack of peanut butter cups from me last week."

"Peanut butter cups are a separate food group," Venus replied.

"I'm down for Kua'Aina, if only for the fact that since she suggested it, that means Venus isn't going to complain the entire time about the calories," Jenn said.

"I do not complain about calories all the time."

Trish, Lex, Jenn, and Mimi all gave her flat looks.

Venus jabbed a finger at each of them. "None of you gain weight just by *looking* at a fudge sundae."

"Let's get closer to the finish line so we can see Aiden," Edward said, breaking up a potential free-for-all.

"Before we go to the North Shore," Jenn said, "I want to see the Honolulu City Lights. Did you see them yet, Mimi?"

Mimi choked a little but managed to reply in a normal tone, "I saw them last week."

Mimi had managed to spend an entire day not thinking about Tosh until this moment.

It had been hard to stick to her resolve this past week because, although she had the excuse of work to not go to church with him on Sunday, he kept walking her from her car before work and to her car afterward. Or sometimes he met her at the parking garage. But they always spent a few minutes chatting. As a result, she had now borrowed three more manga or light novel series from him. Every time she returned one, he gave her another.

Whenever he started getting more animated in discussing some Japanese media, whether books, music, television, or movies, he'd apologize and confess that he didn't know anyone else who consumed those formats in Japanese. He'd done that twice now, making it obvious he was grateful to her for conversing with him about his favorite topics.

Mimi liked those topics too, so it wasn't a hardship. But it also solidified her suspicion that he was only being so friendly with her because she'd talk to him about things that didn't appeal to his other friends.

But their moments of chatting began to lengthen. Yesterday they'd stood in the parking garage for an entire hour arguing about the socialist and communist themes in a particular anime that had just been released in Japan. When they finally parted and she realized how late it was, she had to rush home to help Auntie Noriko make lotions.

Rather than treating her like the plague or like a duty, he was actively seeking out her company. She'd begun to hope that maybe they could recapture their friendship again, even after all this time.

Mimi should have been happy about that possibility, but instead, she felt a hollow dissatisfaction in her chest every time they finished talking.

Kapiolani Park was bustling with people, both spectators and runners who had already finished. Mimi was getting more impressed with Aiden because all the runners she saw looked younger than he was, but she didn't see many who looked to be about his age. "Is Aiden going to be first in his age group?" Mimi asked Lex.

She tilted her head as she thought. "I think he's in the 45-49 age group, and he's almost 49, so he's at a disadvantage. Maybe? But it's almost nine now, and I think the winners of that age group would have better times than four hours."

As they headed toward the finish line, Mimi heard the very faint sound of taiko drums. She turned toward the noise and realized it was coming from the race course, but it must be about a mile away. The deep bass rhythm—at this distance all she could hear were the larger drums—seemed to energize the air. It would have been pretty amazing to be running past the full ensemble of drummers on the way to the finish line.

Lex glanced at her phone, then yelped. "He's almost there!" All of them broke into a run, except for Mimi, who began an all-out dash on her short legs like she was running away from a wild boar.

They saw the banners of the finish line and the long final stretch down Kalakaua Avenue. It was a testament to the huge size of the marathon that there were so many runners, they couldn't see Aiden immediately.

And by "immediately," Mimi meant a few seconds before he appeared next to them. "Hey, guys," he greeted them.

They all whirled to stare at him. He was munching on a deep-fried, sugary malasada that made Mimi's stomach growl, with his finisher medal and a seashell lei hung around his neck and his finisher shirt tossed over a sweaty shoulder.

"When did you finish?!" Lex wailed. "We wanted to be there to see it!"

"A few minutes ago," he said, unperturbed as usual.

Mimi would probably have cried if she had finished all alone, but then again, Aiden tended to be pretty inexpressive, and he wasn't the type to need lots of social affirmation when he accomplished something. He found satisfaction in meeting his personal goals. It often drove Lex crazy, and she kept nagging him to *let* people celebrate for him.

Mimi gave him a disgruntled look. "You don't look like you were straining for the past four hours." Aside from the fact he was still dripping in sweat, there was hardly any weariness on his face—maybe only a bit of tiredness around his eyes.

He grinned. "Three hours and some change. I didn't place in my age group, but that's a personal best."

Trish placed her fists on her hips and glared at him. "You are so disappointing! You're supposed to run panting through the finish line, too exhausted and winded to talk as you break some Honolulu Marathon record—"

"I'm not that fast a runner," Aiden protested.

Trish ignored him. "—and when we see you, we're supposed to run and embrace you and congratulate you—"

"Yeah, I didn't hear any congratulations," Aiden said.

"—and you'd say something moving and cheesy like, 'Thank you for being here for me,' and we'd hug you and tell you, 'Of course we'd be here at the finish line for you, because that's what family is for.'"

"Except you weren't at the finish line," Aiden said.

"Exactly! You ruined it!"

"Congratulations!" Mimi tried to inject a super-sized sugar-frosting sweetness into her voice.

Everyone else echoed her but with more sincerity. Aiden looked a bit embarrassed by the praise.

Lex went up to her husband to get a look at his finisher medal, nudging Mimi aside, so she stepped back. It was at that moment that she turned to look around her, and she saw Tosh.

He had on a dark T-shirt and board shorts with rubber *zori* slippers rather than running clothes and shoes, but the lean muscles in his legs made her think he might be a runner himself, even if he didn't compete in the marathon. He was with the other spectators along the sidelines of the finish line.

Tosh hadn't told her he knew someone running today, even though she'd mentioned Aiden running. Maybe he simply didn't consider them close enough to naturally volunteer information like that. Maybe he hadn't wanted her to know for some reason.

At that moment, his face lit up and he began cheering. He

wasn't that far away and she heard his yells, but people passed across her vision so she lost sight of him often.

Then he was jogging alongside the sidelines to where the finishers spilled out, some heading for the water misters to cool down, others moving to get their finisher medals and congratulatory malasadas. He made a beeline for a slender young woman in a pink running top, pink cap, and black shorts, sporting long, slender legs.

Tosh caught the woman up in his arms, laughing and shouting. She giggled and returned the embrace, and the two of them stood there hugging tightly.

All the muscles along Mimi's shoulders and chest pulled taut. She swallowed, but it was hard to breathe. She couldn't take her eyes away from the couple.

He was ecstatic to see her, to congratulate her. His smile was wider than any he'd given to Mimi since she saw him again. He was truly happy.

Mimi had been deluding herself into thinking Tosh enjoyed her company. His beaming face was how he looked when he was truly pleased and excited. With Mimi, he'd just been … lukewarm.

She needed to turn away from them. She didn't want to be caught staring at him …

Too late.

Tosh released the woman, who hurried away to get her finisher medal, and he happened to look up and see Mimi.

Who was, of course, gaping at him with glassy, wide eyes like a dead fish on display at the fish market.

His lips parted. She thought he might be about to say something to her, maybe to call out to her.

She never got the chance to find out.

"Hey, Mimi!" Lex called.

Unfortunately, Lex was a mere few feet away from her, so her cousin's voice was the volume of a firecracker going off next to her ear. "What?! What?!" Mimi exclaimed, recoiling.

"Let's go get something to eat," Lex said, ignoring Mimi's reaction. "Where around here is good?"

"You realize I don't actually live in Hawaii, right?" Mimi whipped out her phone to consult Oh Great Google.

They decided on a restaurant, and Mimi replaced her phone in her pocket. When she looked up again where she'd seen Tosh, he and the girl were gone.

15

Trinda stared at Mimi in shock. "You look terrible. Who died?"

"No one died! And I look fabulous!"

"Yeah, like a zombie bride looks fabulous. Are you not getting enough sleep?"

"Maybe," Mimi mumbled. She hadn't gotten much sleep at all last night. Even though she tried not to think about it, she kept replaying the scene in her head of Tosh hugging that unbearably cute girl in the minuscule running shorts.

Why was she upset? It wasn't as if Tosh was cheating on her. Hadn't she been convincing herself he was only hanging out with her either to protect her or to be nice?

This was just like high school again! Had she not moved on from high school?!

Worse, it was affecting her work. She realized she'd just added sales tax twice to a customer's order and had to start all over again.

It was close to twelve-thirty, and Mimi was standing near her station but staring off into space. She was wondering if she had low blood sugar when suddenly a face popped up in front of her. "Hi, Mimi!"

She blinked. She hadn't even noticed the door opening. She pasted on a smile. "Welcome to …"

Wait a minute! It was the cute marathon girl!

Mimi glanced around, but Tosh was not with her. What was going on?

The girl giggled. "Do you not remember me? It's Tomoko, Tosh's sister."

Sister. She was his sister. "Tomoko! Wow, it's been a long time."

Her heart beat sluggishly. Her insides were burned like acid reflux by the shame that she'd been so upset at seeing Tosh with another woman, but she was even more ashamed at her relief that it was only his sister.

Tomoko had a darling pixie haircut which showed off her high cheekbones and sweet round face. She was eight years younger than Tosh and Mimi, so she hadn't often hung out with them. Mimi could only barely see the trace of the elementary school girl she'd been.

"Tosh told me you recently reconnected," Tomoko said. "I needed cosmetics anyway, so I came here to shop and say hi."

Mimi immediately went into customer service mode. "I can totally set you up. What kind of cosmetics were you looking for?"

Tomoko's skin was so smooth (and youthful, Mimi noticed enviously) that she didn't think the girl really needed cosmetics. But remembering the marathon, she suggested some facial lotion, foundation, and powder that all had UV protection.

As Tomoko tried various shades of lipstick against the skin of her hand, Mimi asked how she was doing lately. Tomoko complained about her workload now that she had gone back to school to get her MBA and gushed about her boyfriend Hideo, who was a mechanic at an auto body shop in Mililani. Tomoko eventually chose a cherry blossom pink lipstick that made her look five years younger.

As Mimi was ringing her up (and giving her a slight discount with Trinda's blessing), Tomoko gave Mimi a mischievous smile. "I talked all about my boyfriend, but are you seeing anyone?"

Well, that was like handing her a live stink bomb. Mimi hoped her smile didn't look too pained. "No, not at the moment."

Tomoko's dark eyes glittered like faceted onyx as her smile widened. "Oh, I'm so glad!"

Was she going to try to set Mimi up or something? Mimi steeled herself to gently refuse.

Tomoko continued, "It must be fate that you and Tosh reunited after all these years."

Except they hadn't *reunited*. Maybe began hostilities? Took offensive action?

Tomoko leaned closer to Mimi and lowered her voice. "You may not know this, but when he was still working at Kahiko Gemstones, he had a huge crush on you."

What?

"And after he got laid off, he didn't date anymore," Tomoko continued. "I was so worried about him, but now I think it was because he still had feelings for you."

The only person Tosh might have had a crush on while at Kahiko Gemstones was … Minnie. Which, now that she thought about it, sounded an awful lot like her own name.

Tomoko gave Mimi a wink. "Maybe something will happen now that you're both single?" She picked up her bag with the cosmetics. "Thanks so much, Mimi! Bye!" She practically skipped out of the shop, followed by flowers and singing birds and rainbows.

Tomoko had mistaken Mimi for Minnie, Raymond's fiancée. Was she right and Tosh was still in love with Minnie? She was inclined to think Tosh's sister would know better than anyone else.

Mimi fought the urge to bury her face in her hands and groan long and loud from her gut.

Did Mimi remind Tosh of Minnie, maybe? Was that why he'd been friendly with her for the past several weeks? (Well, not exactly *friendly*. More like civil with occasional bursts of anime-induced excitement.)

In one hour, she'd gone from the depths of broken-hearted depression to soaring heights of relief to crushing insecurity. The rest of her day was pretty much shot.

When she messed up a customer's order and the nice old lady very gently corrected her, Trinda sent her home. "Get some sleep, and tell my mom to stop keeping you up so late making lotions."

Today, Tosh wasn't there to walk her to her car, which was a relief. Until Edytha jogged up to her, Mimi had been hoping she could sneak away unnoticed.

"I'm leaving a little early today," she told Edytha. "I'm tired and making too many mistakes."

That was probably too much information and Edytha couldn't care less, but she smiled anyway and said, "Okay. Drive safely."

As she drove home, Mimi wondered if it was even worse for her to be alone with nothing to keep her mind from going over what she'd learned today again and again, like a goldfish swimming around a bowl. Too soon, she was pulling into her aunt's carport.

She expected Uncle Milton's truck to be gone since he was at work, but Auntie Noriko's car was also missing. Mimi said a fervent prayer for the safety of the drivers out on the roads today.

As soon as Mimi unlocked the door from the carport, she stopped in confusion. There was a breeze blowing through the house, and it was colder than it should be.

She found the culprit quickly—the door to the backyard was wide open. Had Auntie Noriko forgotten to close and lock it before leaving? But she'd remembered to close and lock the door to the carport, so why would she forget the backdoor?

Mimi locked the door and headed to the kitchen to root through the refrigerator. But she hadn't yet reached it when from deeper inside the house, she heard a loud *thump*.

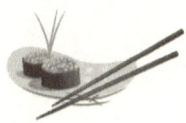

Mimi froze. She should have been alone in the house. So what was that noise?

She stood there like a statue for several minutes, her racing heart making her breastbone pulse with each beat, but there were no other sounds.

She had to go check it out. She forced her feet to move.

But instead of going directly toward the back of the house, she skirted to the other side of the kitchen, then to the front door. She grabbed the old wooden baseball bat that Uncle Milton kept behind the door, wrapping her fingers around the smooth handle. The tip shook a little with her trembling hands, but she gripped it tightly.

Mimi softly made her way down the hallway to the back bedrooms. She used the barrel of the bat to ease open the first door on the right, which creaked as it revealed her aunt's empty office. The desk was covered in papers, but there wasn't anything that might have fallen and made that loud noise.

The next door was her bedroom, and she immediately saw that the lamp had fallen to the floor. Why was it there? It had been tucked away near the back of the bedside table this morning.

She moved to check the other rooms—the guest bathroom, the master bedroom and attached bathroom, then down another short hallway to the stillroom extension. But there was nothing amiss.

Mimi returned to her bedroom, looking around more carefully. Was she hallucinating, or was there a faint musky smell in the air?

She shivered and wriggled all over like a dog. That seriously creeped her out!

But other than that (which may or may not have been her overactive imagination), she couldn't tell if anything had been moved or was missing.

Within moments, her phone was in her hand. Her finger hovered over Tosh's name, but was she able to talk to him after what she'd just learned? She took a moment to regain her sanity, then dialed Edytha instead.

But as soon as she answered, Mimi chickened out.

"Hi, Mimi. What's up?"

"Uh …" She considered lying and saying she accidentally butt-dialed her, but decided instead to downplay what had happened. "No, it's nothing. The lamp on my bedside table fell, and I freaked out. I'm sorry to bother you."

After all, Edytha was watching Waite. Mimi couldn't ask her to drop everything to come stare at her fallen lamp. Or worse, she'd send Tosh to check out the house, and Mimi couldn't bear to see him just yet. "I'll talk to you later. Bye!" She hung up and set down her phone.

Mimi felt a bit ridiculous, but she decided to change the sheets on her bed and vacuum the carpet.

It was fortuitous that she vacuumed because she found an envelope that had fallen under the bedside table. It was the massage vouchers Mimi earned from working in the spa's kitchen, which Edytha had given to her through Tosh. Only Mimi's name was scrawled on the front in Edytha's long, slopey handwriting, just under the logo of the spa. As Mimi sat on the bed, she again took out the personal note from Edytha that had been tucked inside and re-read it:

> *Mimi,*
> *It was truly a joy to get to know you better. Please know I'm praying*
> *for you. I also hope that you're praying about my job offer.*
> *Edytha*

At the top of the note was printed, "Edytha Guerrero, Private Investigator" and her phone number, right under another logo that she realized looked similar to the spa logo.

Mimi sighed as she replaced the note in the envelope. She was still thinking and praying about the job offer. She wasn't about to say no simply because Tosh lived in the same town as the spa, but she also both hoped and feared that she wouldn't see him often if she did take the job.

As she slipped the envelope back on top of the bedside table, her phone vibrated and the screen flashed "Tosh."

Mimi hesitated, then rejected the call.

The next moment, an insistent rapping sound at the window made her shriek and leap off the bed.

Tosh's face was looking in at her from between the open slats of the glass jalousie windows. "Did you just ghost me?" he demanded.

"I could have been changing clothes, you know!" Mimi shouted at him, trying to calm her racing heart.

"But you're not. And you totally ghosted me."

She ignored that. "What are you doing here?"

"Edytha said you sounded strange and asked me to stop by to make sure you're okay."

Naturally, he wouldn't be stopping by because he wanted to talk to her.

"I didn't sleep well," she muttered. Then, because he might be able to tell that she wasn't telling the complete truth, she said, "I met your sister today."

He groaned. "I told her to leave you alone."

"Why? I haven't seen her in years. It was nice to see how she's grown up. She doesn't seem as geeky as you."

"Speaking of geeky, do you have free time right now?"

"Well, I'm having dinner with my cousins tonight, but I don't have anything right now. Why?"

"I'm going to a Japanese bookstore in Honolulu. Want to come?"

She shouldn't go with him. She should try to avoid him, because seeing him with a girl, who turned out to be his sister, and then learning he might still be pining for Minnie all in the space of twenty-four hours had been like a stomach-churning emotional rollercoaster.

But of course she didn't do the wise thing. "Sure."

16

Trinda stared at Mimi in shock. "You still look terrible. Did *you* die? Are you a zombie?"

"I am not a zombie! I look fabulous!"

Trinda crossed her arms while shaking her head. "I thought sending you home early would make you get more sleep."

"I did get enough sleep! I'm having a bad hair and makeup day, okay? And thank you for pointing out the obvious and crippling my self-esteem!"

Trinda sighed. "Come here, I'll do your makeup."

Mimi would have sniffed and walked away, but she truly had been having problems with her makeup this morning. She pouted but dropped her butt into the padded stool near Trinda's station.

When Trinda was done, Mimi looked less like a corpse and more like an "interestingly pale" Japanese tourist.

From the time the doors opened, the store was very busy, so Mimi didn't have much time to think about yesterday. But as soon as there was the inevitable lull in customers, she found herself brooding.

She'd had a great time with Tosh yesterday. They went to a Japanese bookstore in Honolulu that had a large manga and light novel selection, and they had coffee and dessert at the attached cafe. They argued about the best character in a popular series, *The Demon Lord Has Returned and Wants to Open a Knitting Shop*. He treated her like one of his guy friends.

And that fact alone made her depressed because she realized she didn't want to be one of his guy friends.

The entire time she spent with him made her even more convinced that Tosh was still in love with Minnie. She couldn't think of any other reason he still hadn't married.

In high school, he had probably been grieving over his girlfriend, and Tosh had told Raymond that he was harassed by gossip in college. Then he met Minnie and suffered from unrequited love.

It perfectly explained why he was almost forty years old and had never married. Minnie was bright and cheerful rather than old and cynical and gloomy like Mimi. But she pitied Tosh since Minnie was going to be married soon.

For the next few hours of her shift, the revelation didn't hit her smack between the eyes, but instead grew upon her mind like mold overtaking her brain.

She had fallen in love with Tosh.

But he would never want to be with her.

And she realized that truth made it too painful for her to even spend time with him.

She wasn't a teenager anymore, wanting the experience of drowning in her melancholy emotions so she could feel the absolute depths of her exquisite pain. (She cringed at the thought of how much of a drama queen she'd been.)

After all, she'd done the adult thing and taken courses on reducing her stress levels. Why would she deliberately put herself in a situation that would give her acid reflux?

By closing time, she had decided to tell Tosh that he no longer needed to walk her to her car and watch over her in general. After all, it had been weeks and Ivan was unlikely to be a threat to her anymore, if he ever was one in the first place.

She left the store before Trinda, and as she headed to the

parking garage, she both looked for him and dreaded seeing him. But all her anxiety was for nothing because it was Edytha who appeared to walk her to her car.

"No Tosh?" Mimi asked. She tried to keep a light, disinterested tone but failed miserably.

Edytha eyed her with both concern and an expression of *yuck*. "Why do you sound like the caretaker of a graveyard named Bodies R Us?"

Mimi stopped trying to pretend and slouched against her car. "I had been hoping to talk to Tosh."

"He had to go to work early at his uncle's restaurant tonight because a bartender called in sick."

Mimi gave a gloomy sigh worthy of a certain blue-gray donkey. "He'll probably be too busy to talk to me." After all, he'd been yelled at by his boss the two times Mimi had interrupted him at work.

"But it seems like you need to talk to him about something important," Edytha said. "I'm sure he can take some time for you."

"I'm starting to think that cowardice isn't so bad."

"No, no." Edytha put her hands on Mimi's shoulders. "Just get it over with, like ripping off a scab."

"Ew!" Mimi recoiled. "Isn't it supposed to be a bandage?"

"Not if it's going to make you bleed." Edytha eyed her with worry.

Yes, it was definitely going to make her bleed, if only metaphorically. "Fine, fine." She got into her truck and waved at Edytha as she drove away.

At the reception desk of the Molokai Red Restaurant was the same young woman as the last two times she'd been here, so this was number three. She probably thought Mimi was a sad old lady who came here to drink alone. She probably wasn't far off the mark.

As Mimi walked through the open archway into the bar lounge, she searched for Tosh behind the counter … and froze.

Tosh was entering the storeroom behind the bar, but he wasn't alone. Minnie was clinging to his arm and grinning up at him.

And Tosh was smiling right back at her. There was a light in his eyes that reminded Mimi of how he'd looked when he had embraced Tomoko at the finish line of the marathon—happy and proud.

But why would he look like that at Minnie?

And why would Minnie be visiting Tosh alone? She couldn't see Raymond agreeing to that very easily. Or did Minnie perhaps break up with Raymond? Was that too wild a possibility?

Tosh looked delighted to see her, which only reinforced Mimi's belief that he still hadn't gotten over his crush on Minnie.

Or was Mimi reading more into the situation than was actually there?!

Her brain felt like a particularly manic ferret.

Either way, she didn't want to interrupt them. She'd go wait in her truck for half an hour, then come back inside.

She walked out of the restaurant, trying not to jump to conclusions … but her mind was leaping off buildings anyway. She barely paid attention as she headed down the walkway lined with those Molokai Red hibiscus bushes, then wove through the lanes of the parking lot. With each step, a hollowness echoed inside her, as if her torso had turned into an empty wooden barrel.

She was jarred out of her thoughts by a strong hand suddenly grabbing her arm in a painful grip. She started and jerked, but couldn't pull away. A shadow loomed over her.

It was Ivan, dressed stylishly but all in black. With an equally black thundercloud expression on his face.

He sneered down at her. "You're coming with me."

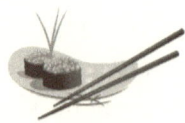

Mimi tried again to pull away from him, this time planting her feet firmly and yanking with all her strength. But then a sharp, sharp jab in her side made her cry out.

He had a knife.

"What do you want?" she asked. Her voice trembled.

"You're going to come with me without any fuss."

Sure, and monkeys might fly out of her butt!

But Mimi's brain began flipping through possibilities. She needed to stall him here, in the parking lot, because surely someone would drive in to eat at the restaurant, right? If she made a big enough fuss, someone would come to her aid and Ivan would have to leave.

So she began to whimper and shout. "No! Where are you taking me?"

He ignored her and dragged her further into the darkness at the back of the parking lot, away from the street lamps.

Mimi needed to stop him before she was out of view of any cars. "Stop it! Let me go!" she howled.

He hit her across the face.

She had been half-expecting it—she'd had some terrible ex-boyfriends, she had to confess, but they gave her experience in how to roll with a punch.

Although the blow wasn't that hard, she broke down crying hysterically. His grip on her arm had slackened when he hit her—another reason she'd been trying to provoke him—so she was able to pretend her knees gave out. She sank to the ground, curled up in a ball around her handbag.

Instead of acting like a victim, she wanted to tell him, *Hit me again and my foot will jeopardize your ability to sire progeny*, but she restrained herself.

"Get up!" Ivan tried to haul her to her feet, but she had taken self-defense lessons. She knew how to relax all her muscles and drop her center of gravity, making it difficult for him to move her even though he outweighed her. He finally gave up.

As soon as he let go of her, she began wailing again. "Why are you doing this to me? What have I ever done to you?"

"You can't pretend anymore with me."

"I don't know what you're talking about."

Ivan dropped down to balance on the balls of his feet as he glowered at her. "Were you investigating me the whole time? You and your PI friend."

"What PI friend?" Mimi sniffled.

"Don't play games with me. When I saw she had offered you a job, I looked her up and recognized her from the parking garage."

He knew about the job offer? Which meant *he had been inside her house.* She hadn't been imagining things.

She almost told him that it was his BO that gave him away, but she swallowed her retort. Now wasn't the time for her smart mouth to get her in trouble.

"The job offer is something unrelated," Mimi protested. "I'm not a private investigator. I sell makeup."

"Did you get the makeup job so you could keep an eye on Waite?" Ivan's voice was becoming sharper. "Were you the one who arranged for someone to watch Albert?"

"Albert?"

"You think I didn't know it was you? He thought someone was following him only after he and Waite ran into you at Ala Moana."

That day they'd been going to lunch. She told Tosh, who had mentioned that Edytha might pass the information on to the police. Had they taken her seriously and started watching Albert?

That must have been the reason why Ivan decided to search her house. Bile rose in her mouth at the thought of him invading her bedroom.

And once he did some internet research on Edytha, he'd see a photo and recognize her from the time he approached Mimi in the parking garage and Edytha had come up to them.

Why was she always getting in trouble in parking lots?

And why weren't there any cars entering the lot?

The gravel bit into her stockinged knees and she smelled the warm, slightly metallic tang of the Haleiwa red dirt.

"Now get up!" Ivan tried to pull at her again.

She tucked her arms in closer to her body. "No! You're going to kill me!" Wasn't she shouting enough to bring someone to help her?

Then she felt the knife blade just under her ear. His deep, guttural voice had a bite to it as he said, "I will kill you right now unless you shut your mouth and get up."

She had been hoping for a car to come, but it looked like she needed to just do her best with what she had.

Please, God. Please save me.

Her heart beat wildly, and she was finding it hard to breathe, but she somehow did seem to feel a Presence near her. She wasn't alone.

Ivan grabbed her arm and yanked her up, and this time she didn't resist him. Her handbag dropped to the ground.

She didn't need it anymore anyway.

As soon as she was on her feet, she held her breath, closed her eyes, and hit him square in the face with a shot of pepper spray.

She'd taken the pepper spray out of her bag when she was huddled on the ground with it. She'd also shoved her cell phone into her cleavage, which she was abnormally grateful was large enough to hold it. Lastly, she'd managed to slip three of the rings in the bag onto the fingers of her right hand (she couldn't find the fourth ring for some reason) and wrapped her fist around a pen for support.

Ivan screamed, but his grip on her tightened instead of releasing her, so she jabbed him in the throat with her (lightly armored) bling-infested fist. He gagged and she was finally free.

She ran, but Ivan recovered faster than she expected. Or maybe he simply pursued her half-blind. Suddenly his weight was on her back, slamming her onto the ground. She lost her grip on both the pepper spray and the pen in her fist, and a ring flew off somewhere.

Mimi tried to scramble to her feet, but he was too heavy. She reached for the spray, but his clawed hand pressed her arm to the ground, keeping her from moving. She tried aiming her other elbow at his head but wasn't in a good position to give more than a few muted blows.

"I might have let you live," his voice grunted in her ear, "but now I'm just going to kill you."

She screamed and thrashed about, managing to hit him sharply somewhere on his face with her head, although it sent a sharp pain and momentary stars through her vision. But then his forearm was at the base of her skull, shoving her face into the gravel, cutting her skin.

Please, God. Need a miracle here.

Then she heard it. A car entering the parking lot.

Mimi tried to scream, but her jaw was held shut by the pressure on the back of her head keeping her face down. She tried to struggle again, but she was getting tired and he was too heavy, too strong.

The lot had several empty spaces closer to the front door restaurant, but the car moved down one of the other aisles and then parked.

This was her chance. *God, give me strength!* She braced her feet and knees and twisted sideways.

But she wasn't strong enough or she didn't have enough leverage to throw Ivan off of her. The car door shut, and footsteps walked away.

Mimi felt tears sting her eyes, or maybe that was simply sweat since she'd been using all her strength to fight Ivan. The person had walked away, but she wasn't giving up. She grunted as she continued to try to wiggle free.

But the more time it took her, the more time Ivan had to recover from the pepper spray.

She realized that he must have lost his knife or he surely would have simply slit her throat to silence her (or had she watched too many slasher movies?). She supposed it was lucky she'd managed to disarm him.

The weight on her back lifted suddenly, but only for a brief moment. Then a thick wad of cloth was shoved into her mouth, which smelled of dirt and sweat. *Ew!* He'd taken off his shirt and put it in her mouth. She gagged, but it only made it harder for her to breathe.

She tried to reach up and pull it out, but he grabbed both her arms and hauled her body up, the strain causing pain to shoot up her shoulders. He was going to dislocate both of her shoulders or give her a muscle sprain.

But then she realized that she'd have to worry about something worse than a muscle sprain if he found his knife.

At that moment, footsteps came running out of the restaurant, and a voice shouted, "Mimi!"

Her heart leaped. It was Tosh! How had he known?

She pulled against the grip on her arms, enough to get some leverage for her feet, and then stomped hard on Ivan's instep.

For once, she was heartily glad for the pumps required for her work uniform. The heel was more solid than a ballet flat and sharper than a sneaker.

His grip didn't quite release her, although it did loosen.

She didn't stop there. She lashed out again with her heel, this time slamming into his shinbone.

He finally released one of her arms enough for her to pull free, and she dragged the shirt out of her mouth and screamed. "Help!"

"Mimi!" That was Edytha's voice.

She tried to scream again, but Ivan clamped a hand over her mouth.

She bit his finger.

He cursed and loosened his hold enough for her to scream again, but this time, her breath was coming in shorter gasps and she couldn't call as loudly.

She didn't hear anyone approach, but abruptly Ivan was tackled to the ground. His grip on Mimi's other arm yanked her down with him, but then he released her and she rolled away.

Tosh was on Ivan's back and wrestling with him, but it was clear who was the better fighter. In moments, he'd put Ivan in some kind of weird contorted hold that placed Ivan's neck in the crook of Tosh's elbow while his other arm seemed to tighten the choke. Ivan couldn't fight him because Tosh had also wrapped his legs around Ivan's waist and seemed to be pulling his torso taut.

Then Edytha was next to Mimi and tugging at her shoulders to drag her away from the two struggling men. "Are you all right?"

"Why are you here? Aren't you supposed to be watching Waite?"

"He was arrested tonight not long after you left," Edytha said as she helped Mimi to sit up.

"What?"

"Both he and Albert, who was working at the travel agency kiosk. The police tried to be discreet about it, but I'm afraid people were gawking at your aunt's store for a while. I was worried that maybe Ivan would have made the connection between you and them, since the police hadn't known about Albert until I told them what you had seen the night of your date and at Ala Moana."

And Edytha hadn't had to watch Waite anymore, so she had come to the restaurant, knowing Mimi planned to talk to Tosh. "But how did you know I was out here in the parking lot?"

"At first I saw your truck and thought you were inside."

It had been Edytha who drove into the lot, and she'd skipped the earlier empty stalls to park next to Mimi's dilapidated truck. She'd never been so grateful for a rust bucket that was imminently identifiable.

"When I saw you weren't with Tosh, I knew something was wrong," Edytha said.

"Thank You, God," Mimi croaked. She had asked for a miracle, and He delivered.

They became aware that the sounds of scuffling had stopped. Tosh was breathing hard, his arms and legs still wrapped around Ivan's limp body.

"Is he dead?" Mimi tried not to screech, but she might have impersonated an owl.

"No, he's not dead!" Tosh glared at her (or she thought he glared—it was hard to see in the darkness of the parking lot). "He's unconscious."

"Can you stand up?" Edytha asked her.

Mimi got to her feet, although her legs quivered like gelatin.

"I'm going to call the Waialua police," Edytha said, pulling out her phone.

Mimi stood there, staring at her, so she didn't see Tosh when he approached her.

The next thing she knew, his arms were around her, pulling her close to him. She would have thought that human contact would have freaked her out after what had just happened, but she suddenly smelled green kiawe wood, and beach grasses, and lime, and everything inside her relaxed. She remembered this smell, even though it had been twenty years. She reached her arms around his waist and hugged him back.

"Mimi, you're going to give me more gray hair," he said, his voice muffled.

"Hey, don't blame that on me." She lightly thumped a knuckle into the bones of his lower spine.

"Ow! Hey, watch it, I'm getting old."

"Yeah, well, we're both not getting any younger."

There was a pause, then Tosh said, "No, we're not."

He pulled away from her slightly, even though she was certainly not ready yet to let go of him. Then his hand was on her cheek, and he was kissing her.

Wait, he was kissing her! This was Tosh! He knew this was Mimi he was kissing, right?

He broke the kiss and sighed against her mouth. "Mimi, I can practically hear your brain running around like a headless chicken."

"I am not a headless chicken! You know this is me you're kissing, right?"

His eyebrows knit as he looked down at her. "What does that mean?"

"Aren't you still in love with Minnie?"

Now he looked like he'd been hit in the head with a two-by-four. "What?"

"That's what your sister said."

His mouth turned into a flat line. "I'm going to kill her."

"Not in front of the police, please," Edytha chimed in.

Mimi became aware of flashing lights and saw that a squad car had pulled into the parking lot, shining a spotlight at them as Edytha waved. Mimi pulled out of Tosh's embrace, and the evening air felt cold against her skin.

A man exited the car, and Edytha walked up to him. "Hey, Gavin, I didn't know you'd come yourself." She tilted her head toward Ivan's inert form. "All yours."

Gavin—or rather, since he was in plainclothes, maybe he was Detective Gavin—was of medium height, with light-colored hair that practically glowed in the police car's spotlight. He heaved a sigh that seemed to come up from the bottom of his stomach.

"Edytha, you're going to give me more gray hair."

17

It took remarkably little time for Detective Gavin Oshiro to arrest Ivan for assault. Mimi noticed that while Edytha was casual and friendly with him, the detective's eyes lingered on Edytha's face a bit longer than Mimi would expect of a mere friend.

Hadn't Edytha said she hadn't found anyone? Maybe she simply wasn't looking in the right direction.

Edytha walked with Mimi to the women's restroom inside the restaurant, and soon Minnie came in to join them.

"Tosh told me what happened!" Her eyes were wider than Chinese *dan-tat* egg tarts. "Are you okay?"

Mimi had smoothed her hair before limping into the restaurant so that she wouldn't make the customers come unglued at the sight of her, but she still looked like she'd been thrown off a roller coaster and then run through a burning building.

"You'll be sore tomorrow," Edytha said, "but for now, let's wash you up."

Minnie helped get some of the stains out of Mimi's skirt and vest while Edytha cleaned her face and disinfected some of her cuts. She mostly had bruises and sore muscles rather than anything bleeding heavily.

Mimi gave them a truncated version of what happened before trying to very casually ask the Important Question she'd wanted to voice since spotting Minnie in the restaurant. "So Minnie ... did you come here for dinner? Where's Raymond?"

"Raymond's at home. I told him that he had to let me come alone to show he has faith in me."

"Faith in you?" Edytha asked.

"He thinks Tosh has a crush on me, but more importantly, even if he did, it's not like I would encourage him. So I told him that to prove he trusts me, he had to let me handle this by myself."

"Handle what?" Mimi was more confused than before she'd asked.

"We finally got a venue for our wedding!" Minnie gave a cute little squeal (which was exactly why men like Tosh would fall for her even when she was clearly in love with her boyfriend). "It's on the North Shore, and I came to talk to Tosh's uncle to cater it. Buster sent me to talk to Tosh about the wines. Then Edytha found us and asked where you were. They left me in the storeroom and raced out."

So her excited expression while clinging to Tosh was because she was excited about the wedding? That was very like Minnie, she supposed.

Mimi's stomach gurgled rather loudly. "Ugh, I'm starving." She looked down at her stained (although slightly less than before) skirt. "I can't eat here. I better go home."

But Tosh found her trying to sneak out of the restaurant and steered her back into the storeroom behind the bar, sitting her at the table in the breakroom section at the back. "I'll get you something to eat. Edytha, Minnie, you want something too?"

"No, I have to go home and feed my teenager," Edytha said.

"I have to feed my fiancé," Minnie said with a giggle. (Oh my goodness, she was so *cute*! Mimi didn't know how she always managed to make the room seem a little brighter and more cheerful.)

And soon it was just Mimi eating the most amazing loco moco she'd ever had in her life. "What the heck!" she practically shouted at Tosh. "What did your uncle put in this?! There aren't illegal substances in it, are there? Or did he marinate it in MSG?"

"He made the hamburger patty with local beef, sweet Maui onions, and a mix of Hawaiian sweet bread and house-made sourdough bread," Tosh said, not even trying to hide his pride in his uncle's cooking. "The eggs are fresh from that farm in Wahiawa, and his gravy is a secret recipe."

Mimi was shoveling food in her mouth. "If this is how you eat all the time, I want your Uncle Buster to adopt me."

Tosh, sitting across from her at the staff table, propped his chin in his hand and stared at her. "If he did, then I couldn't date you."

Mimi choked. After coughing and drinking some water, she pounded a fist on the table. "Don't lay that on me when I'm eating! I wasted that heavenly bite of loco moco!"

"So you care more about the loco moco than the fact I just kissed you and confessed to you?"

The kiss was rather nice but unfortunately, she didn't remember most of it because her brain had been whirling like a hamster wheel.

He still had his chin in his hand. "You don't remember the kiss because your brain was combusting, right?"

"It wasn't combusting!" Although that might have been close. "This is just so sudden. I mean, your girlfriend died so tragically and then you had that crush on Minnie—"

"I didn't ... well, okay maybe for a little while when I first met her, but I got over her pretty fast since she was already dating Raymond."

"Your sister said you were still pining for her!"

He rolled his eyes. "Tomoko is delusional."

"She said you didn't date at all."

"I did date!" He sounded rather offended. "I wasn't a monk, okay? But there was a lot of gossip at college once people found out about my dad, so I didn't want to date anyone. I did get involved with a few women when I was out of college, but the relationships ended so fast, Tomoko never knew about them."

"Oh." Now she felt awkward. "I guess all this time, I was thinking you were in love with anyone other than me."

"Mimi … I've been in love with you since high school."

She was so shocked she dropped her fork. "What? But you rejected me!"

"I thought you were pranking me!" he retorted.

She was going to demand why he thought she'd be pranking him, but just in time, she remembered exactly how she'd come across. "I'm sorry," she mumbled. "I was embarrassed because … well, I actually did like you. But I acted like … *that* instead of telling you my true feelings because I was simply a coward."

Tosh's mouth had dropped open. "Really?"

Mimi's face flamed. "Yes, really," she said with irritation.

"I'm sorry," he said, his dark eyes sober. "At that time, I was embarrassed, too. I mean, you were pretty and popular and I was awkward and short. I got angry because I thought you were just teasing me and that you weren't serious, so I reacted harshly."

She looked down at her food, slowly growing cold (although to be honest, she'd already scarfed down most of it because it was so delicious). "I didn't see you that way. You knew me when I was still a tiny, scrawny kid. You were friends with me not because of my looks or popularity—which only came later—but because of my personality. I haven't dated anyone like that."

He reached across the table. "Mimi, when I realized you were rooted inside me like a weed—"

"Hey!" She tried to yank her hand away.

But he merely held fast, grinning at her so that the dimple at the corner of his mouth appeared. "I was going to try to move slowly. After everything that happened between us, I thought it would be better to take my time so that we could be friends again. But after seeing him hurt you tonight …"

There was pain in his eyes as he lightly stroked her cheek, where there was some swelling from when Ivan had hit her and scrapes from when she'd been on the ground.

"… I realized I couldn't wait any longer," he said.

"I came here tonight to tell you I'm in love with you, expecting to be rejected again," Mimi confessed. "I was going to tell you that you didn't need to watch over me anymore."

"Look at all the trouble you got into in only a few weeks!" he said. "You need a babysitter!"

"You jerk!" She pulled ineffectively to free her hand, but he held on tighter.

"How about a boyfriend instead?" he asked.

She stopped fighting.

"I know you're going back after New Year's," he said. "I'm willing to try a long-distance relationship. At least until you accept Edytha's job offer." He grinned at her.

She tried to glare at him, but it was very difficult when her mouth insisted on smiling. "I'm not moving to Hawaii just because of you."

"I'm at least seventy percent of the reason, right?"

She made a disgusted noise, but she didn't try to take her hand out of his again. "You're so conceited."

"It's part of my charm."

"Are you two done yet?!" demanded a voice from the other end of the storeroom.

Mimi and Tosh separated like magnets with matching poles.

Tosh's manager had opened the door and was peering inside at them. "Come on, Tosh, we just got a large order. I need you at the bar." She shut the door.

He sighed and rose to his feet. "We'll slay dragons tomorrow?" he asked, quoting an oft-repeated line from *Bunny Foo Foo*.

"You're such a geek." She smiled at him. "Sure."

EPILOGUE

Mimi frowned at the little pillows of cone sushi as if the uneven sizes would magically fix themselves if she glared hard enough.

Jenn had made this *inarizushi* recipe often enough for the family, and Mimi had helped her—but she'd never made it by herself before. It was becoming obvious she was not as good at this as she had thought.

"Why don't I help?" a gentle voice sounded at her side.

Tosh's mother took one of the cone sushi and added just a little more sushi rice so that it wouldn't look like a runt next to its fellows. She licked some rice off her finger. "Mmm. That turned out well."

"It's my cousin's recipe," Mimi said. But she admitted she was rather proud of how it turned out. Sushi rice usually needed tasting and tweaking during the mixing, so it took a little bit of skill to get the balance of sweet and sour just right.

They were in the kitchen of the Molokai Red Restaurant, which looked cavernously empty with just Tosh's family plus Mimi and Tomoko's boyfriend, Hideo. Everyone was helping to cook, but Tosh's Uncle Buster shouldered the majority of the work. Mimi had been doing her best to help.

"Are you all right not having Christmas dinner with your aunt and uncle?" Tosh's mother, Yoshiko, asked. Ever since Mimi was small, she'd called her Auntie Yoshiko despite not having any blood relation to her.

"We had a big Christmas brunch with Trinda's family this morning," Mimi said.

"What will your uncle and aunt do for dinner?" Auntie Yoshiko asked as she scooped rice into another seasoned deep-fried tofu pocket.

"Probably go to Trinda's house. Auntie Noriko will take any excuse to play with her grandkids and not have to cook."

Auntie Yoshiko laughed. "That's just like Hideo—he has Christmas brunch with his family, and he joins us for dinner."

"No way am I giving up a chance to eat Uncle Buster's cooking," Hideo called from where he was washing lettuce for the salad.

"What did you do for brunch?" Mimi asked Auntie Yoshiko.

"Well, last night we were up late serving our special Christmas Eve prix fixe menu," Auntie Yoshiko said. "Our reservations always fill up fast and we were busy from opening until late at night. We all got up late this morning and had a simple lunch."

"Which was just sandwiches," Tosh grumbled. He was washing dishes at the sink.

"Hey, don't complain," Auntie Yoshiko chided him. "You didn't even have to make your own sandwich."

Mimi gave Tosh a withering look.

"Which was the best sandwich *ever* made," Tosh amended in a raised voice.

"Okay, Happy Hour is on!" Uncle Buster brought a platter of his famous pork-filled deep-fried wontons to a small table in the kitchen, and everyone sat. In addition to the wontons, they had sashimi and cone sushi for pupus.

Christmas this year had been so much better than the slightly tense dinners Mimi had with her family in California. Jenn and her other cousins always invited her to their houses, but Mimi had felt obligated to have Christmas with her parents, even if they didn't act like they cared whether she was there or not.

Like Christmas brunch with Mimi's aunt, uncle, and cousin, dinner with Tosh's family was casual and relaxing. They joked with each other and even included Mimi and Hideo as if they were already family.

The conversations layering on top of each other at the table made her feel like a glass of champagne running over with bubbles. Tosh's family reminded her of Jenn's in-laws, who always warmly accepted Mimi, although they weren't related to her.

Even though they were eating appetizers and drinking a very nice bottle of wine, Uncle Buster and Mimi were still cooking. He checked the prime rib at the same time Mimi checked the baking crab legs. Then she went ahead and made her auntie's Chinese chicken salad, since Uncle Buster had expressed an interest in tasting the recipe. While she did that, he whipped up his special macaroni salad recipe.

When the prime rib was done and set in the center of the table, steaming and dripping with juices, Tosh asked, "Is it all right if I bless the food?"

Tosh's family was not Christian, but Auntie Yoshiko nodded. "Of course." Everyone bowed their heads.

Mimi had never been brave enough to ask to pray for her own family dinners. Maybe, just maybe, she could do it when she went back to California.

The food was delicious and the conversation lively. Mimi was reminded how everyone in Tosh's family liked to tell stories. It was no wonder that he enjoyed theater.

There was a lull after dinner while people digested their food, and the family moved to the main dining room of the restaurant, pulling up a table and chairs next to the huge Christmas tree in the corner. Rather than artful decorations in coordinated colors and matching ornaments, the tree had an eclectic assortment of ornaments that peeked through the heavily scented boughs draped with lights.

Tosh sat next to Mimi. "Every year, each member of the family gets a new ornament," he said. "All the ones on the tree are ours."

Mimi realized the true beauty in the gesture when she saw that the design of each ornament held personal significance for the recipient. Tosh's ornament was a circular frame with a photo of an original painting of *The Ritual Metallurgist* main character.

"This is a copy of a drawing that only had 200 copies made back when the series ended," Tosh marveled. "Where did you get this?"

Tomoko made a superhero pose with hands on hips and chest puffed out. Then she gestured toward the tree with a flourish.

Her obedient servant—er, Hideo pulled out a wrapped present and gave it to Tosh. It was one of those 200 copies in a wooden frame.

Tosh was speechless.

Mimi gaped, but she recovered her voice faster. "How did you get this?"

"The original owner sold it on an online auction site," Tomoko said. "And don't worry, it's real. The whole family chipped in to buy it for you. Then I took a photo of the drawing to make that ornament for you."

"I can't believe I get to own one of the 200 copies!" Tosh said.

"I can't believe I get to see one of the 200 copies!" Mimi said.

Tomoko gave them both an exasperated look. "You two are so perfectly made for each other, it's kind of disgusting."

"Be quiet, brat," Tosh said, but then he gave her a huge hug.

"Mimi," Auntie Yoshiko said and handed her a small square box.

"You didn't have to get one for me …"

Ignoring her, Auntie Yoshiko gestured to the box. "Open it."

Inside was a delicate glass ball ornament with the most exquisite painting of a phoenix upon it, with red, gold, and orange streaks in the magnificent outstretched wings. It took Mimi's breath away.

"The phoenix symbolizes new beginnings," Auntie Yoshiko said. "I hope you'll have a fresh start with a new job in Hawaii."

Mimi had accepted Edytha's job offer as a part-time sous chef at the spa, but it might become full-time in the future if Edytha opened the spa up into a restaurant and a wedding venue. Mimi also arranged with her aunt to make her aunt's lotions at the spa. Since the building had once been an old plantation manor house, there happened to be an old-fashioned stillroom attached to the kitchen. It had been used as a pantry, but the chef, Geri, was clearing the worktable for Mimi to do her work.

The majority of the lotions would be used by Edytha's staff, although when her aunt needed more stock, Mimi could make some for her. The spa would pay Mimi a discounted rate for the lotions, but she would pay a royalty to her aunt for the formula. Mimi hoped to eventually create original lotion formulas to be used exclusively by the spa.

"Thank you," Mimi told Auntie Yoshiko, her throat tight. The phoenix ornament touched her on a deeper level because in addition to new beginnings, it also symbolized rebirth. She had been meeting with Edytha for a one-on-one discipleship group and learning how to forgive herself for her past mistakes and accept God's forgiveness. She was too much of a control freak to depend upon God very easily, but Edytha could relate since she was the same way, and their time together was helping Mimi to learn to trust God more.

After that, the family exchanged Christmas gifts, which had been placed under the tree earlier today.

As Tomoko passed out the presents, Tosh explained to Mimi, "Usually everyone chips in to get one expensive gift for each person. That way, everyone gets something both personal and also a little extravagant, something they wouldn't have bought for themselves."

"Here, Mimi," Tomoko handed her a small box about the same size as her phoenix ornament box.

"Hey, you told me not to bring any gifts for the family," Mimi said.

"And you completely ignored me," Auntie Yoshiko chided her.

"Not completely …" Mimi had brought the crab legs for dinner as well as several bottles of wine.

"Open it."

Inside was a little anime figure of Bunny Foo Foo, rendered in exquisite detail. "Wow! Thanks!" Some of these types of figurines could cost hundreds of dollars, so she hoped they hadn't spent too much on her.

Uncle Buster received some expensive bottles of sake, Japanese whiskey, and Japanese shochu, while Auntie Yoshiko received tickets to a show in Honolulu.

When Tomoko unwrapped her new electronic tablet, she cried out in delight and hugged it tightly to her. "I didn't know what I was going to do when my other one broke." The relief was practically dripping from her face.

"Don't break this one," Tosh said.

"It wasn't entirely my fault," Tomoko shot back. "It fell out of my bag in my MBA class which, I might add, I'm taking for the collective good of the family—"

"And which you never forget to mention two or three times a week," Tosh interrupted.

"My turn," Hideo said, probably to forestall another sibling squabble. His face lit up as he unwrapped the gift. "Oh, yeah!"

Mimi blinked at the bunch of little metal pieces and the one large metal piece that looked faintly like a miniature torture rack. "What is that, exactly?"

"Cylinder heads and valves for my Datsun 240Z, a car I'm restoring," Hideo said. "These can be hard to find."

The gifts were all thoughtful rather than simply expensive. She compared it to her own family—her parents usually gave her cash, which was nice, but she also knew they gave a little more to each of her brothers. It still enflamed her sense of righteous indignation and made her want to rail against an out-of-date patriarchal mindset, but that had never done anything for her except expend brain cells and raise her blood pressure.

In contrast, here, she felt cherished. For her gift, they'd taken into account her interests, and they had given her an ornament that symbolized their kind hopes for her.

Thank You, God, for giving me this special Christmas with this family. I hadn't known I needed this.

Uncle Buster had drunk a little too much and was yawning, so everyone helped clean up the kitchen. They all headed home, but Tosh asked Mimi to stay behind.

They sat out on the back deck of the restaurant, pulling up chairs next to the fire pit. It wasn't as cold in Hawaii as in California at this time, but she was glad for the warmth of the fire pit and the coconut hot chocolate that Tosh made for her.

For a long time, they sat in a comfortable silence. Tosh brought out an old ukulele and idly played Christmas carols.

Finally, in a low voice, Tosh said, "Edytha told me what happened to Ivan. Did you want to know?"

"Of course." Mimi sat up straighter.

"He was receiving cocaine shipments from an overseas source at drops along different North Shore beaches. Since he was the only one picking up the drops, the police couldn't catch him."

"So he really was dealing drugs?" Well, she could pick 'em, couldn't she?

"He was selling drugs at the Pleiades Resort to hotel guests and also using Waite as a courier to transport drugs to Albert at that travel agency. Albert delivered it to other customers."

"No wonder he suspected me. I met every link on his distribution chain."

"It was because you identified Albert when he met with Waite that the police started watching him. When they questioned him, he gave away everything he knew. Ivan's been charged not only for attacking you but also for the drugs."

"I'm glad I don't have to worry about him anymore."

An especially cold breeze suddenly blew past them, making the flames leap around wildly. "Here, might as well use your Christmas present." She gave him a gift bag.

Now that they were officially dating, they'd agreed to only make their Christmas gifts for each other, although Tosh had been reluctant since he wasn't a crafty person.

Tosh took out a skinny blue tube scarf and instantly recognized it. "This is Binkiebutt's scarf!" The Ritual Metallurgist's friend (somehow) used his trademark blue scarf as a weapon. "You knit this?"

"Of course I knit it. Why, does it look bad?"

He poked a finger through a gigantic hole she hadn't noticed and wiggled it at her.

"Oh, man! Give it back, I'll fix it."

"No, I like it." He wiggled his finger at her some more.

"It's terrible! Give it back!" She finally managed to wrest it away from him. Their struggle stretched it out a bit, but it didn't matter since she'd just be unraveling part of it and then re-blocking it.

"This is for you." He handed her a large envelope. "Don't laugh, okay?"

She didn't laugh. The warmth that had spread in her chest from the lively family dinner, the carefully chosen gifts, and Tosh's hot chocolate began to spread all through her body, and she felt … radiant. "Tosh, these are so nice!"

"Don't exaggerate," he scolded.

"I'm not. You put so much thought into this." He'd made bookmarks for her out of cardstock, stickers, and a laminator machine. He had managed to find stickers of characters from her favorite manga and light novels, as well as stickers with a kitchen theme. As kids, they'd gone to the Star Wars movies all in costume, and Tosh had printed the photos of them posing, cutting them out and arranging them on the bookmark with other Star Wars-themed stickers.

He had also printed Philippians 3:12-14 on one bookmark, decorating it with pretty flower stickers. The embarrassment of buying those feminine stickers must have caused him physical pain, and yet he had done it anyway.

With Tosh, she felt appreciated not only for their past together, but also for who she was now, and how she was trying to focus on the future. He'd known her as an awkward kid, then a selfish teenager, and he still saw worth in her as an adult. He saw that her worth was determined by more than her outside appearance or even her past mistakes.

"I want to go back to California with you," Tosh said. "I want to meet your family and Grandma." After Ivan had been arrested, he'd only briefly spent time with her cousins before they had to go back home.

"I don't mind, but are you sure?"

"Yes. Are you afraid your family won't like me?"

"I don't care," she declared boldly. "I like you, and that's all that matters."

He smiled and reached out to take her hand.

"Also, I loved having Christmas with your family," she said. "It was so different from the Christmases with my own family."

"My family likes you too."

"They eased some of my self-esteem issues," Mimi said. "Sometimes I felt that my cousins *had* to accept me because we're blood-related. And then I was single for so long and all my younger cousins were getting married before me. I felt like the lone rice ball left on the plate that no one wanted to take."

"Good thing I like rice balls."

She smacked him in the arm. "That's so cheesy!"

"But it made you feel good, right?"

She settled deeper in her chair. "I guess."

Tosh got to his feet and took her cup of chocolate from her, placing both mugs and his ukulele on the table nearby. Then he put his hands on the armrests of her chair and leaned down toward her.

"You're not a lone rice ball anymore," he said.

Then he kissed her.

CONNECT WITH CAMY

Thank you for joining me on Mimi's trip to Hawaii! I grew up in Hawaii and based a lot of her experiences on my own, including Thanksgiving and Christmas in Hawaii. Family gatherings in the islands usually center pretty heavily around food, so while it seems like all Mimi's and Tosh's families do is sit around and eat, that's kind of true!

The next Mahina Security hero is Lennox, who stars in *Sushi and Suspicions*. I'm also bringing to the islands Liv Whelan, who was a minor character from my romantic suspense novella, *Unshakeable Pursuit*.

Edytha's story continues in the Warubozu Spa Chronicles, my Christian Romantic Comedy Suspense series that will be releasing next year. You'll hear when book 1 is published if you're on my email newsletter. I only send 1 or 2 emails a month with a new release, a sale, or a freebie.

Right now, you can get a free novella eBook, *The Wedding Kimono*, when you sign up for my newsletter. *The Wedding Kimono* is Lila and Fred's story, and it's a prequel to the Warubozu Spa Chronicles, set the year following *The Lone Rice Ball*, in August. I hope you enjoy it!

You can also read chapters of my books ahead of publication

and get access to Easter Eggs, behind-the-scenes tidbits, research notes, and random author commentary when you join my Patreon (https://patreon.com/CamilleElliot).

Camy

Get *The Wedding Kimono* free when you join Camy's Newsletter

Join Camy's Patreon